THE WINTER OF WINTERS

◆• THE HISTORIES OF SPHAX SERIES •◆

BOOK TWO

ROBERT M. KIDD

Copyright © Robert M. Kidd, March, 2021

While some of the events and character are based on historical events and figures, this novel is entirely a work of fiction.

978-1-8382720-3-6 Kindle/e-book
978-1-8382720-4-3 Hardback edition
978-1-8382720-5-0 Paperback

All rights reserved. No part of this publication may be reproduced, stored in a retrieval system, or transmitted, in any form of by any means, electronic, mechanical, photocopying, recording or otherwise, without the prior permission of the author.

The Histories of Sphax series
~ book two ~

for Max & Kitty,
Mischa & Ceri

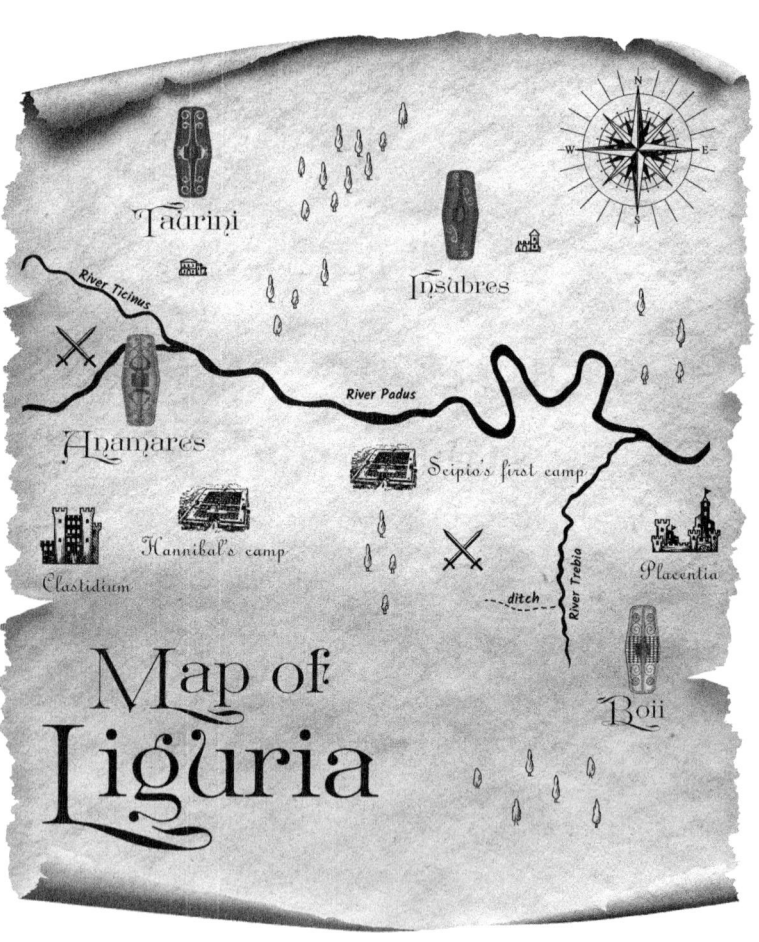

LIST OF PRINCIPAL
⸻· CHARACTERS ⸻

characters marked with an asterisk are real historical figures. The rest might well have been.

Adherbal	veteran Numidian eshrin captain and Maharbal's second in command
Aribal	Numidian eshrin captain
Artula	daughter of the Anamares elder, Garos. Wife of Meilyr, Anamares chieftain
Astegal	Numidian eshrin captain
Corinna	daughter of Queen Teuta of Illyria* and a hostage of Rome
Dasius	Brundisium garrison commander of Clastidium
Gala	veteran Numidian eshrin captain
Garos	elder of the Anamares tribe, Liguria
Hannibal Barca*	born 247 BC, Carthage. Renowned Carthaginian general who invades Italia in 218 BC
Hannon	Numidian veteran in Sphax's eshrin
Hasdrubal	noble Carthaginian commanding Hannibal's Iberian cavalry
Himilco	Numidian eshrin captain

Idwal son of Lord Cenno, chief of the Cavari Gauls. Idwal is the leader of the Cavari contingent in Hannibal's army and Sphax's closest friend

Jubal Numidian. The youngest member of Sphax's eshrin

Jugurtha Numidian veteran and chief scout in Sphax's eshrin

Mago Barca* younger brother of Hannibal

Maharbal* Numidian, and the son of Himilco. Hannibal's second in command in charge of his cavalry

Manissa veteran Numidian eshrin captain

Orison chief of the Oretani tribe in Iberia and general in Hannibal's army

Silenos* Hannibal's secretary and tutor from Kale Akte, Sicily, who accompanied Hannibal during the second Punic War and wrote an eyewitness record of Hannibal's campaigns, but no copies of his work survive

Sosylus of Lacedaemon* Greek historian in the 3rd century BC. Campaigned alongside Hannibal throughout the Second Punic War, recording the events of his campaign

Sphax born in Numidia, January, 235 BC. Son of Prince Navaras of Numidia* and Similce Barca,* sister of Hannibal Barca

Zwalia Corinna's Nubian servant

PART ONE

THE WOUNDED CONSUL

ONE

Sphax stared at the Roman cavalry forming up half a mile away. In their crimson cloaks, dyed horsehair plumes and saddlecloths, they looked like some blood-red plague about to ravage the land. He was spread comfortably over his mare, Dido, who'd obligingly laid on the ground for him, a trick he'd learned from the older man lying next to him. Scouring the river banks over the last three days they'd used this trick many times as they'd followed Consul Publius Scipio's legions westwards over the wide plain beside the Padus river. Lying flat, no more than knee-high, ensured that even the keenest Roman eyes would never spot them from half a mile away.

'Just cavalry now,' growled Jugurtha, his best scout, lying beside him. 'They've left their infantry to guard that bridge of boats we saw yesterday. Looks like the spawn of two legions, but I can see contingents from every ally of theirs south of the Tiber ... dog's twat!' he suddenly cried. 'They've brought along their javelin throwers. That's what's been holding them up ... they're waiting for their wretched footsloggers!'

The Winter of Winters

'Velites,' observed Sphax, brushing his long dark curls from his face to get a better look. 'They're Lucanians. I can piss further than they can throw a javelin.' He'd seen enough. The Roman cavalry were coming their way without their legionary infantry. And even better, they were doing it at a snail's pace. 'Let's go,' he said, and they both began crawling back from their prone horses to the cover of a copse of willows. He'd left his men breakfasting around campfires five miles back, and Maharbal, Hannibal's general of cavalry, was hard miles beyond them. The sun would be high before they reached him with the news. Suddenly there was no time, even though their enemies seemed to have all the time in the world. If they were to make the most of this opportunity their scattered cavalry would need to concentrate, and fast. A low whistle and both mares were up on their hooves and trotting towards their masters. Both men leapt onto their horses' backs without them having to break stride.

His eshrin of Numidian cavalry had been the first to catch sight of the consul's straggling columns marching beside the northern bank of the Padus, so the honour had fallen to him to report the news to his uncle, general of Carthage's armies, Hannibal Barca. But at first his uncle had been dismissive. 'Scipio! Not possible. We left him behind at the Rhodanus five months ago. By now he's probably making acquaintance with my brother Hasdrubal, somewhere in the Pyrenees.' More scouts were sent out. All confirmed Sphax's initial

PART ONE: The Wounded Consul

sighting. Hannibal changed his tune. 'There may be an opportunity here, nephew. Follow them.'

That was three days ago. Three days of leaden skies and filthy weather. Three days of riding until every muscle in his body screamed out for rest. Three days with little sleep or food, where the incessant cold seemed to enter his very bones. Not much of an *honour*, his men had begun bellyaching. They were right. So this morning he'd left twenty-eight men sitting on their arses around campfires, and set out at dawn with his scout, Jugurtha.

This was the land of the Insubres, who along with their neighbours, the Boii, were one of the Gaulish tribes that had rebelled against Rome and sent leaders to the great council held beside the river Rhodanus in the summer. There they had pleaded their cause and begged the great army of Hannibal to come to their aid. It was the Boii and Insubres who'd provided guides to lead them over the mountain passes and down to their homelands on the great plains of the Padus. Carthage had kept her part of the bargain. But where were the Insubres? Where were the Boii? Where were the tens of thousands of warriors promised by solemn oath?

Every day a trickle arrived in their camps, but his uncle needed a river, not a trickle, and to march on Rome they would need a torrent. Scipio's legions had driven a wedge through Boii territory. They were now cut off and isolated somewhere to the south. This flat watery land in winter's grip seemed to be waiting, watching, holding its breath. Who was the stronger: Rome or Carthage?

Sphax knew that the Insubres, like so many of the Ligurian Gauls, were hedging their bets. Who was the stronger? He knew that one great victory would bring the tribes flocking to their standards. But that victory had to come soon.

They'd staggered down from that last ice-bound pass over the mountains like a rabble of half-starved savages, the remnants of a once magnificent army that had set out from the Rhodanus with such hope. They no longer looked like Carthaginians. To stay alive in the blizzards and freezing cold they had stripped their enemies and their own fallen comrades of any garment that might keep them warm. Keep them alive. Men had killed Gauls for beaver-skin cloaks or fur-lined boots. Now they themselves looked like a ragged warband, clad in the garments of every Gaulish tribe from the Allobroges to the Taurini. If it wasn't for his men's olive skin and braided hair, it would be hard to distinguish Numidian from Gaul.

Carthage had indeed kept her part of the bargain, but she had paid for it in blood. More than half their number had been slain or had taken the coward's way out and melted into the night. Scattered over the high places and bleak valleys of those accursed mountains were the shallow graves of their fallen. Amongst them his beloved Fionn lay still and cold, beneath her cairn of stones. Hannibal had called them the bravest of

PART ONE: The Wounded Consul

the brave ... the strongest of the strong! But in truth, Sphax knew they were just the survivors, the lucky few.

Rome or Carthage. Who was the stronger? Sphax touched the ivory image of Artemis he kept beneath his tunic. The flames licking through his belly told him he would find out today. One way or another.

* * *

'Ave, dux bellorum. Quid agis?'

'My dear Sphax, I swear by Ba 'al Hamūn that if you ever use that accursed language in my presence again, I'll have you castrated and feed your roasted bollocks to my dogs! Do I make myself plain?'

Even in sunnier times Maharbal had the temperament of an irascible bear. But after he'd broken a leg on that last snowbound pass over the Alps, what sun was left lay hidden behind a cloud of pain and immobility. Still wearing a leather-strapped wooden brace, he'd suffered the humiliation of having to ride with a saddle and be carried around on a litter, which had done little for his dignity and even less for his temper. Now he was like a wounded bear that had been cornered. Not a happy combination.

'Perfectly.' Sphax was careful to reply in ancient Tassynt, the purest form of Numidian. 'But we have more pressing concerns, Sir. The consul is heading our way with all his cavalry. He's left his legionary infantry behind to guard those bridges over the Ticinus and Padus. There's more, Sir, something to make your

The Winter of Winters

mouth water: he's decided to encumber himself with three hundred Lucanian javelinmen. Their pace is now slower than oxen at plough!' For the first time in weeks, Sphax watched as a smile began to play out at the corners of his general's lips.

'Scouts?'

'None, Sir. They're Roman, they don't believe in reconnaissance!'

'Then today we teach them a lesson in this art. We'll strike them hard, and we'll strike them fast. This is the opportunity we've been praying for. There's no time to be lost. Your jennet is the swiftest, Sphax. Ride back to Gárgoris and Hasdrubal. They are to ride forward and join us in this position with all speed. I will fall back if necessary, but I would prefer to fight here,' gesticulating with a sweeping hand over the flat and featureless plain in front of them. 'The Iberians must form up in the formation we've practiced all week. I'll divide my forces and put a thousand Numidians on each flank. Go, lad, before we waste the day!'

Maharbal's final words were almost lost as he nudged Dido into a furious trot before urging her to the canter. Even amongst African jennets Dido was a race apart, and only Maharbal's Egyptian mare could match her stride for stride. She cantered with such effortless grace, barely raising her hooves as they floated over the ground in their easy lope. Over shorter distances the Iberians' big stallions were faster, but none could canter all day like Dido. Besides, his Numidians were

PART ONE: The Wounded Consul

contemptuous of the Iberians' horsemanship, as they were of any rider who needed reins, bridle and saddle to master a horse. Behind their backs they called them *h'mar zobi*, an uncouth phrase referring to the penis of a donkey. But that morning, as the miles raced by and the sun climbed higher, he began to curse them with less flattering terms. Where were they? They had been told to keep pace with Maharbal and the Numidians.

When Sphax finally caught site of the Iberians he was sweating copiously beneath his beaverskin cloak and was not in the sweetest of tempers. The sight of six thousand horsemen casually watering their stallions in the river whilst their generals stood around idly passing the time of day did little to improve his humour. Deliberately he drove Dido directly at a party of officers gathered around Hasdrubal and Gárgoris. Only at the last possible moment did Sphax ease Dido to a trot and in one sinuous movement slide from her rump, three paces from Hasdrubal.

'The tricks of Numidians,' Hasdrubal greeted him dismissively. But Sphax was pleased to have noted a moment of alarm in those jackal-grey eyes. 'To what honour do we owe this lightning bolt, Master Sphax?' Hasdrubal was a high-born Carthaginian, foisted on Iberians, so Sphax directed his gaze at the savage, battle-scarred face of Gárgoris, a true Iberian Keltoi.

'Consul Scipio is blundering towards us with all his cavalry and a body of Lucanian skirmishers. Maharbal asks that you ride with all possible speed to join him in the formation you've practised together. He's divided the Numidians and they will cover your flanks. Sir, he thinks this a golden opportunity!' As Sphax had spoken the Iberian's face slowly lit up as if scenting blood.

'So do I, Numidian,' he growled, already beckoning his chiefs to join him.

'It's bound to be a trick, boy,' sneered Hasdrubal. 'He knows we are stronger in cavalry, so why would he risk battle?' Sphax watched as a malicious grin spread over that arrogant face. 'The consul is no fool. He's trying to draw out the Numidians just as he did at the Rhodanus. I seem to remember the Numidians were worsted on that occasion.'

Sphax flushed to the gills, his knuckles instantly tightening on the clutch of javelins he carried. But Hasdrubal had come close to a painful truth; they had indeed blundered into Roman cavalry that day, and in the deadly tangle that ensued lost many good men. It was only when Maharbal skilfully led the Romans into an ambush had they managed to turn the tables and inflict an even greater slaughter on their enemies. In this, his first battle, Sphax had been lucky to escape with his life.

He was spared a confrontation with the Carthaginian by the timely arrival of Hannibal surrounded by his standard bearer and bodyguards, all magnificently arrayed on horseback. Sphax bowed low to his uncle then gazed up into that austere, mirthless face.

'Do you bring news, nephew?'

PART ONE: The Wounded Consul

'I do indeed, Sir,' and Sphax relayed the message he'd ridden so hard to deliver, praying his uncle grasped the urgency of the situation.

'Was it you and your eshrin that observed the equites' movements and informed Maharbal?'

'It was, Sir, and the general urged me to ride with all speed to bring up the Iberians. I believe speed is now vital—'

'No, Sphax, you should know me better by now,' and his uncle bequeathed that rarest of gifts: a smile. 'Information and detail are *more* important. Speed comes later. Start at the beginning of your observations this morning.' Sphax groaned inwardly, cursing this further waste of precious time, before recalling in his mind's eye the sight of that red plague crossing the Ticinus on their bridge of boats. His uncle was particularly interested in the siting of this bridge, along with the greater construction they'd used to cross to the north bank of the Padus some days before. When Sphax had finished his description of the morning's events his uncle closed his eyes briefly, lost in thought.

'And now, nephew,' another smile — he was being showered with gifts today! 'Speed is indeed of the essence. Maharbal's plan is sound.' Raising his voice he now addressed the dozens of officers that had gathered around him. 'Roman cavalry have dared to ride out and challenge us! Let us strike our enemies hard. Today Romans will taste Iberian iron. Today we drive them like cattle back to Rome!'

Cheering broke out as Iberians leapt into their saddles. Soon the ground shook with the thunder of six thousand hoof-beats as the great host rode east to meet their enemies in battle for the first time.

Sphax was disappointed the pace was not raised above a steady trot, but he soon discovered the reason for this. From the chaotic mass of stallions that had set out, order was gradually being restored as divisions and squadrons formed into lines, galloped into position on the wings, or slowed to form up as reserves in the centre. And all this was accomplished on the hoof, as it were, without having to marshal squadrons waiting idly in line astride their stallions. Within four miles, Maharbal's new formation was revealed in all its complexity. Or rather, its simplicity. For it was just a crescent moon, with depth in the centre thinning out at each crescent tip. Although the strength was in the centre, the positioning of the reserves provided flexibility, for each wing had been allotted generous reserves. He realised the entire formation had been designed with one thing in mind; to outflank, envelop and eventually surround an enemy confronting it. When they eventually joined forces with Maharbal's Numidians, adding over a thousand horsemen to each wing, this irresistible host would not only outnumber the Roman cavalry by ten to one, it would also stand a fair chance of surrounding and annihilating it. Maharbal's plan was more than sound, and with growing excitement Sphax felt certain it would succeed.

PART ONE: The Wounded Consul

But his immediate problem was Dido. With every stride he sensed his mare's impatience. Trotting was just a drain on her natural rhythm, like a man in a hurry trying to stride along a crowded street. But if she was to retain enough stamina to reach the battlefield and fight, he knew he must garner her reserves and restrain her inclinations. His own frustrations were of a different nature; riding directly behind his uncle's guards he could see no further ahead than the crescent atop the Carthaginian standard. His remedy was to give her the freedom to canter every mile or so, taking them out to a wing where he could gaze into the distance in the hope of sighting Maharbal and his Numidians.

On his sixth foray onto the northern wing he was rewarded by such a sight. His heart leapt. There they were. Two thousand horsemen gathered in two distinct groups, with a small party of ten riders now thundering towards them. Sphax dug his knees into Dido's shoulders and she almost unhorsed him in her eagerness for speed. A glance over his shoulder told him that Hannibal had also seen the Numidians and was galloping out to meet them. Sphax arrived first and halted before Maharbal.

'Where have you been, boy?' the general thundered. 'I asked you to bring up the Iberians, not sit around playing knucklebones!'

'But I—' he began.

'I don't want to hear your excuses!' When Maharbal was in this mood there was no arguing with him. 'Here's your uncle. You will answer to him.'

'Well, Maharbal, where is this golden opportunity you promised me? Is our enemy ripe for plucking?' Hannibal was staring into the distance, but his eyesight had always been poor and made worse by the milky cast in his left eye.

'Ripe enough, general. Four miles east of us on perfect ground for our cavalry. Not only do we heavily outnumber them, but they have shackled themselves with Lucanian velites. This will prove to be their undoing, for they've placed them in front of the legionary cavalry, right in the centre of their line.'

Hannibal raised a questioning eyebrow. 'How will this prove advantageous?'

'If we charge them boldly at speed, the Lucanians will turn tail and flee, and their only passage to safety is through the Roman ranks, thereby hampering their ability to deploy and meet our charge.'

Without shifting his gaze from the distant horizon, Hannibal said, 'I do hope you're listening carefully to this wise council, nephew? You will learn much at such times from my general of cavalry.' He turned to face Maharbal. 'I will lead this charge myself. Let no man overtake Arion. My sword alone will be the first to slay a Roman this day!' Sphax had never seen his uncle in this mood. Nor had he ever seen that distant, other-worldly glint in his mismatched eyes. 'We will do ourselves a great favour if we can take that bridge of boats, Maharbal. Think on whilst you're slaughtering Romans. And show mercy to their *alae* and the Lucanians. If they

PART ONE: The Wounded Consul

are ever to throw off the yoke of Rome we must spare them.' With a last glance in Sphax's direction he added, 'My nephew's not to blame for our tardiness, Maharbal. Hasdrubal has been slow today,' and with that he was off. His uncle's eyesight might be poor, but there was nothing wrong with his ears.

Even though his fellow captains were grinning at him, Maharbal still glared. The general was short on apologies at the best of times. Instead, he began barking orders.

'Adherbal and his captains will lead their men and form up behind the Iberian left. I will do the same on the right. Be sure to let their stallions take the impact of the charge before you work our ladies around their flanks. Remember what our general said about that bridge of boats; that would be a fine prize! I have a dozen jars of sweet Malacca for the eshrin that captures it.'

Sphax was nudging Dido to follow Adherbal when a restraining hand gripped his shoulder. 'Not you, lad. I want you to lead your eshrin and form up directly behind your uncle in the centre of the Iberian line. You and your men will protect his life. Even at the cost of your own.'

Sphax's shoulders slumped. He was desperate to lead his men in battle. To fight as Numidians fight, thundering forward, letting javelins fly, using their incomparable horsemanship to taunt their enemies in what he knew would be a great victory. Playing nursemaid to his uncle was not part of this glorious vision.

'But he's surrounded by his sacred band, Sir!'

'He's surrounded by young fools from good families in Carthage, Sphax, not warriors.' Maharbal had stopped glaring and was staring desperately at him. 'You saw your uncle's expression. When this mood takes him he becomes reckless and courts death. Have you heard the expression *Tannith pene ba 'al hamūn?*' Sphax nodded, 'Then you will know our flaming goddess with the face of Baal is the moment you face your death. I saw this in his eyes just now.'

Sphax had also seen something. He lowered his eyes, resigned. 'My eshrin will defend him to the death, Sir.'

'May your uncle's protector, Melqart, give you the strength to do so.'

Trapped in a gorge surrounded by screaming Allobroges warriors, Sphax had once gazed into the goddess's blood-soaked eyes, but by whim or destiny, he'd been spared by the gods. Touching the ivory image beneath his cloak he silently prayed to Artemis that his uncle receive the same grace on this day of battle.

He was taken aback when his men thought it a great honour to guard the life of their leader, especially after he'd told them that Maharbal considered Carthaginian noblemen and six thousand *h'mar zobi* not up to the task. So here they were, all thirty of them, grinning at their seventeen year old captain, spread out in a thin line behind the most sumptuously equipped cavalry in the entire Carthaginian army, whilst they were

PART ONE: The Wounded Consul

unarmoured, unhelmeted, dressed in rags and riding horses that were considered ponies in comparison to the proud stallions in front of them.

But all Sphax could see ahead of him were stallions' backsides. Dog's twat! He may as well have been condemned to the depths of Tartarus! And so they waited. And waited. The one thing he was utterly incapable of doing was sitting still and doing nothing. He was on the verge of nudging Dido sideways to search out Maharbal when shouting and animated conversation broke out in the ranks in front of him. Had they at last sighted the enemy? The answer came soon enough.

All along the line a score of trumpets blazed out their silvered tones the signal to advance. As one, eight thousand horses strode forward. Within twenty strides came the more strident call to advance to the trot. Flames of thrill and fear in equal measure shot through Sphax's belly and rose to his throat.

'At last! Today we kill Romans!' he yelled along his little line. 'Death to Rome!' He more than most, had cause to hate Rome. Today he would avenge ten years of miserable slavery.

'Death to Rome!' came the resounding reply along the line. And then his ragged little line found themselves galloping headlong at an enemy that still remained infuriatingly unseen. Within three strides, Sphax and his Numidians ground to a halt behind a seething mass of horsemen involved in a life and death struggle with an invisible enemy. If it wasn't for the clang of iron on iron and the battle screams of Iberians as they hurled spears, his Numidians would not have known that the armies of Carthage and Rome had met on the field of battle. It was only later that Maharbal told him that his plan had worked to perfection. Once the Lucanians realised that nothing would halt that ferocious charge they'd turned and fled for their lives through the Roman ranks, throwing that line into utter confusion and checking its momentum. Like a great wave crashing on a beach, what happened next was inevitable.

'We're as much use here as a eunuch in a whorehouse, Sir.' It was Hannon, the old veteran with grizzled beard and flecks of grey in his plaited hair. Further down the line Jugurtha raised a javelin and yelled, 'We should dismount!'

They were right! He was a slackhead, not thinking straight. He'd never fought on foot before, but his eshrin had, many times.

'Dismount,' he yelled, 'find gaps.' Slithering from Dido's rump he removed the leather throwing thong from his pouch and selected a javelin. Ahead of him all he could see was a writhing wall of horsemen. But then he did notice gaps. In that instant he understood what his men had been urging him to do. Now it was every man for himself. All he had to do was search out prey and stalk it. But within a few paces it became treacherous underfoot; he stumbled and almost fell on a tasselled Roman helmet, every step met a discarded

PART ONE: The Wounded Consul

shield or a spent spear. Three more strides and he was slithering amongst the dead and dying, sandals oozing with blood, or worse.

At last he was standing in the battle line. Three paces either side of him men were locked together in fevered butchery, hacking away at one another or thrusting with spear amidst a cacophony of screams and curses. Horses reared or screamed in their death throes as forelegs buckled and they crashed to the ground. It became impossible to judge who was winning or losing. Impossible to distinguish between victor and vanquished. Only death seemed to have the upper hand here. But there in front of him was a gap in the equites' ranks, created by the space left between two adjacent squadrons.

Sphax sensed someone beside him and turned to see a Numidian launch a javelin at an unhorsed Roman staggering to his feet. Its aim was straight and true, sinking deep into the man's throat as he staggered backwards.

It was Agbal, wide-eyed and savage, a year younger than Sphax and the butt of the eshrin's jokes for the puppy-fluff sprouting from his chin. 'Look for Hannibal or his standard, Agbal,' he yelled above the din of war.

But there was no time for this. They'd been spotted by two equites who'd decided Numidians on foot were easier meat than falcata-wielding Iberians on horseback. Sphax already had his throwing thong coiled. He let fly and caught the man a gouging blow to his cheek before the barb lodged in the scalloping of his boetian helmet.

Agbal's next javelin was truer, burrowing its way into the Roman's chest so that he slumped forward and slid from his mount, dead before he hit the ground.

Now both of them frantically scanned the battle line for Hannibal and his standard. 'There,' yelled Agbal, pointing to his left. Helmeted, swathed in armour and protected by a great shield embossed with the crescent insignia of Carthage, Sphax might not have recognised his uncle immediately, but there was no mistaking Arion, his mount, a lion's head and mane draped over his noble neck. The sleek grey stallion had been the swiftest and most celebrated chariot horse in Rome. Sphax had trained him himself, and presented him as a gift to his uncle.

Hannibal seemed well defended, flanked on either side by spear-wielding guards, and what's more, the equites facing him appeared to be frantically trying to back away and retreat. It was obvious they'd had enough. But it was a different story to their right. Here, the hacking and stabbing looked to be in the balance, with no side prepared to give way. This is where they might tip the scales, Sphax decided.

Hannon joined them. Pointing to the struggle on their right, Sphax bawled above the racket, 'Let's empty a few saddles.' A decurion, struggling to bring his men forward to fill the gap between the squadrons was the first to fall, pierced through the shoulder by Hannon's javelin. Next, Agbal sprinted forward, releasing his throwing thong and sending the javelin into its deadly spin. That too found its mark. Sphax was next, and this time he made no mistake, emptying yet another saddle. It only took two heartbeats to wind a throwing thong around a javelin, but by taking turns, it allowed them time to catch their breath and select a fresh target. This couldn't go on for long though, and soon the three of them were down to their last javelin, or in Sphax's case, his precious saunion.

But at least they'd torn into the open flank of the equites, bringing at least eleven down, and the tide was beginning to turn. Hastily retreating back to the safety of their own lines they were almost thrown to the ground as six Iberians barged their stallions into the gap they'd left and began hacking their way into the Roman ranks. Sphax saw for himself the terror etched on Roman faces. Fear could be hidden behind helmets and cheek-guards, but eyes never lied. In the space of a javelin's flight it was all over.

Equites tried desperately to back away, or frantically yanked on reins in an attempt to turn their mounts around. Crushed together as they were, there was no room for this manoeuvre, and the attempt to do so often proved fatal as shields were lowered or shoulders exposed to thrusting blades or spears. There was no escape. Horses instinctively reared or kicked out in a frenzy of terror, ready to bolt at the earliest opportunity. When some in the equites' second rank managed to turn their stallions and flee, enough pockets of space were created for their comrades to join them.

What followed was not so much a rout as a half-crazed stampede.

Fear is transmitted faster than a trumpet call. Everywhere he looked, he now saw Roman cavalry in headlong flight with Iberians hot on their heels, whooping and jeering in triumph. *Fight as one or flee as many*, goes the old adage. For all his youth, Sphax had seen it all before. He knew the enemy would have reserves that would try to stem and rally the fugitives, but these were the legionary cavalry, the rich elite of Rome. If they would not stand, why should Campanians, Samnites or Lucanians?

Once the Iberian reserves had thundered past them, Sphax and twenty-nine Numidians suddenly found themselves alone on an empty field of victory. Whilst Hannon, Agbal and several others were recovering javelins and searching for trophies, everyone else gathered around their captain and began whistling for their mares. Hannon was sporting a decurion's tasselled helmet as he handed Sphax four bloodied javelins.

'Our duty is fulfilled. We don't need to defend our general from an enemy that is routed and fleeing for its life,' he cried. Leaping on to Dido's back a thought occurred. 'Maharbal offered a prize of Malacca to the eshrin that captures that bridge of boats. What say you, lads?' This met with universal approval.

After riding for three days through these watery flatlands, Sphax knew this ground better than a lover's face. The shortest path lay north-east, so that's where

PART ONE: The Wounded Consul

he led them at the canter. Within a mile they'd caught up with the running battles at the rear of the fleeing cavalry. He could see a squadron of Campanians frantically trying to extricate themselves from hordes of Iberians swarming around them like hyenas on a kill. Their magnificent winged helmets and bronze greaves would soon become the spoils of war and sold to the highest bidder around campfires that night. In the bloodlust of battle it seemed his uncle's plea to spare the Roman *alae* was not being heeded. Sphax gave them a wide berth and continued.

He guessed the bridge was still about six miles away. Could they reach it before the fleeing Romans? Even if they got there first and managed to capture it, could thirty lightly armed Numidians hold off hundreds of fleeing Roman cavalry?

Within another mile or so he saw Numidians for the first time. Welcome though this was, the sight that met his eyes was confusing. Half a mile ahead, an eshrin appeared to have given up the fight and was galloping in the same direction as him. Were they heading for that bridge of boats and Maharbal's prize? They were Numidians, so there wasn't a hope in Hades of catching them. Sphax cursed his bad luck. His eshrin would not be the first to the prize after all.

Then something strange happened. Someone must have spotted his eshrin, for a rider peeled off from the front and began galloping at breakneck speed towards them. It was Astegal.

'Adherbal has sent messengers. He's cornered the consul's squadron,' he said between gasps for air, 'but if we're to capture him he needs more men. Are you with me, Sphax?' Publius Cornelius Scipio, the Roman consul, was a far greater prize than all the bridges in Rome!

'My eshrin's right behind you, Astegal. Lead on!'

By keeping up Astegal's furious pace, they slowly managed to overhaul the captain's eshrin, and only then did he ease up as the two joined forces. Sphax worried that by the time they reached Adherbal, their mares would be so winded as to be useless in a fight, but Astegal had the reputation of being Maharbal's most wild and reckless captain, and that afternoon he was determined to prove it.

With every mile he sensed tiredness creeping into Dido's limbs. It was a bone-chilling day, yet she was sweating copiously. Looking around, it was all too obvious that his men's mares were also suffering from the relentless pace. They had to stop!

Half a mile ahead of him he spotted a rare feature in this monotonous landscape: rising ground that almost amounted to a tree-lined hill. By the time their two eshrins had climbed its gentle slopes their horses were panting and in a sorry state. Raising his javelins in the air he hoarsely shouted, 'Halt.' Furious, Astegal impatiently drew in his mare and brought her to a halt.

'What now! In the name of Ba 'al Hamūn, why have you stopped?' But Sphax ignored him and stared at the extraordinary sight laid out on the plain below him. Two distinct battles were taking place. The first, and more distant, was unfolding just north of the Padus and was more in the nature of a horse race. The Romans were winning, but only by a short head. By now both eshrins had gratefully dismounted and were gathering around Sphax, watching the spectacle of the second battle taking place at the bottom of the hill, no more than half a mile away.

'Who's supporting Adherbal?' he asked.

'Looks like Juba's eshrin,' answered Astegal, now as fascinated by the sight as everyone else.

'The consul has three squadrons with him.' It wasn't difficult to work out that Scipio had ninety men. Sphax knew that equites fought in what the Romans call a *turma*, the equivalent of a Numidian eshrin of thirty men.

'Then Adherbal's outnumbered and needs our —'

'And he'll get it, Astegal! Just as soon as our ladies have caught their breath.' Sphax was getting intensely irritated with the hothead, who seemed to have the patience of a rutting stag. What had his uncle said? *Speed comes later.* 'It seems to me that Adherbal and Juba are more than holding their own.' This was perfectly true.

It was like watching a bout of wrestling between two ill-matched opponents; the one nimble, skilful and light on his feet, the other slow, clumsy and brutish. Fighting in a constant state of retreat, groups of Numidians would gallop forward, release a flight of javelins then ride smartly back to their own lines. If the Romans dared to charge, the Numidians would scatter in every direction, many ending up on the exposed flanks of their pursuers where they were perfectly poised to launch yet more deadly barbs. Consul Scipio was making good his escape back to that bridge of boats. But they were hard miles, and Adherbal was making sure he exacted a terrible toll.

Sphax examined the terrain carefully, just as Maharbal had trained him to do, marking every wood, copse and ridge that lay between himself and the enemy, anything that would give them an advantage or the element of surprise. Making up his mind, he shaped a smile and turned to Astegal.

'What did you intend to do? Just charge down the hill at them?'

'Yes ... well, no ... I don't know, Sphax. You're the scholar. What do you think we should do? I only care that we do it soon!'

Sphax shifted his gaze to the enemy and then to his men. 'Instead of following this track down the hill, I think we should head south and use these trees for cover. Once we reach the bottom of the hill we form our line, then walk our mares east to the edge of that wood over there' — he paused to point to where the edge of the woodland abruptly gave way to the flat grasslands that stretched to the Padus. 'With luck and a prayer, there's every chance we'll remain unseen. I judge we'll only have three hundred paces to cover out in the open. The Romans have eyes only to their front, where Adherbal and Juba are taunting them. The consul won't be expecting a javelin up his arse!'

PART ONE: The Wounded Consul

'It's a good plan, Sphax, I'll grant you. But could we do it NOW!' Once again, Sphax ignored Astegal and addressed both eshrins.

'We only have one chance to do real damage, so let's make that first charge count. Under no circumstances do we tangle with them at close quarters. Remember the last time ... by the Rhodanus?' Nobody needed reminding of that slaughter. The only defence Numidians had against thrusting swords and spears was a flimsy hide shield virtually useless in close combat, so he never carried one. Sphax had his sword strapped to his back, but even amongst his fellow captains, few possessed swords. The only way Numidians could take on Roman equites was to charge at speed, launch their javelins and smartly turn around and retreat. This required skill, perfect timing and superb horsemanship. Qualities Numidians possessed in abundance. That is why they were so feared.

Astegal's impatience deepened as they began descending the hill. The undergrowth beneath the trees was so thick and treacherous that progress became painfully slow, but once they reached the bottom the trees thinned out somewhat, and the Numidians began to form a ragged line, leaving wide gaps between each horsemen. So far so good, thought Sphax; at no point during their descent could they be seen by Roman cavalry. As they nudged their mares to walk in the dappled light filtering through the trees, men unslung the hide shields from their backs, threading forearms through straps. Throwing thongs were removed from pouches and twisted carefully around their best javelin, the one Sphax had told them *had* to count.

All he felt at that moment were the twin fires of fear and thrill as they surged through his belly and licked at his parched throat. He both lived for these moments, yet dreaded them. Elysium in Hades, or was it the other way round? Sphax could never decide. He caught sight of Astegal, and the two of them grinned inanely at one another. The edge of the wood was now in sight, and beyond it lay the open grassland, and the enemy.

No order or command was given. Sixty-two horsemen simply strode out from under the trees into the feeble sunshine of a winter's afternoon. Within three strides they were trotting, within three more cantering, saving everything for that last headlong rush at the rear of the Roman lines. By the grace of the gods the Romans did not see them coming until it was too late. Ten strides from that red plague he selected a target and raised his javelin. Two strides later he dug his knees into Dido and she leapt like the wind into a thunderous gallop. Sphax let fly his javelin and watched as it uncoiled and spun towards its target. The rest was pure skill and a lifetime of practice.

Sphax had learned to ride as soon as he could walk. At six he could pick up stones from the ground on the back of a galloping pony. Eleven years later few horsemen were his equal. The trick was to release the javelin at high speed as close to the enemy as possible, but with enough space remaining to be able to turn the mare around and ride out of harm's way to the rear. Get this wrong, or overstep by a single stride, and the mare and rider would career into the enemies' lines and meet certain death from spear or blade. Sphax had trained Dido to do something special. She'd learned to slow from a full-pelt gallop to a dead stop in one stride, then, like an uncoiled spring, use all her momentum to turn around in a half stride and head off at high speed. Skilled horsemen though they were, most Numidians could only manage this feat in two strides. Fewer turning strides meant getting closer. When Dido turned he could almost smell the sweat of his enemies. And so, in that heart-stopping moment, this was the manoeuvre he managed to execute perfectly.

Only when they were safely out of spear-shot did the Numidians draw in their mares and turn to see the damage they'd inflicted on the enemy. It was a terrible sight.

Wherever Sphax looked he saw riderless horses stepping aimlessly amongst a carpet of red, or cavalrymen slumped over the necks of their stallions, barely able to stay in the saddle. In the centre of the Roman line he glimpsed two horsemen sidling alongside a wounded consul of Rome to prop him in the saddle and prevent him joining the dead and dying littering the ground. A decurion leapt from his horse to grasp an eagle from the dying hand of a standard bearer. Their two eshrins had struck at the centre and left of the Roman line. The right hand squadron had got off lightly, and were now beginning to wheel their stallions around to protect the rear of what was left of the consul's squadrons.

In that moment Sphax knew Rome's ill-fated consul was finished. All they had to do now was co-ordinate with Adherbal and Jubal to complete an encirclement that would bring about the surrender of Publius Cornelius Scipio. Capture him, and what was left of his legions would be rendered leaderless and demoralised. He also realised the surrender of a consul of Rome would be a humiliation that would strike at the very core of Rome, its reverberations echoing through the walls of the senate to the very doors of the temple of Janus. But Sphax had not taken into account his hot-headed companion.

'Let's finish them off,' screamed Astegal. 'Charge, Numidians!'

'Stop,' yelled Sphax, 'stop ... STOP!' But it was too late. Astegal's eshrin were already picking up pace, and the command had been given so forcefully that most of his own eshrin had joined the charge. The right hand Roman squadron had almost completed its wheel when Astegal had ordered this second charge. There was a sickening inevitability to what happened next. All it needed was a quick-thinking decurion, and the squadron possessed such an officer. Sphax watched in horror as the Roman squadron seized the opportunity and began a spirited charge aimed to smash their big stallions into the flank of the oncoming Numidians. His only thought now was to save what he could of his own men.

PART ONE: The Wounded Consul

Only six of them had been left behind. 'Follow me,' he roared, leading them off at a furious pace and hoping to circle around the Romans and do whatever damage they could in their rear. Seeing the circuitous route he was taking, his men guessed his intentions, so when they arrived in the rear of the equites they had formed themselves into a line. Ahead of them was a tangle of men and horses. Exactly the lethal, close-quarter fight Sphax had warned them to avoid.

'Javelins,' he screamed, but in the confused fight that was taking place ahead of him he dare not risk launching a javelin himself. He lacked the skill of his men, so instead he reached over his right shoulder and drew his sword. If he was a novice with the javelin, he was a beginner with the blade, but Romans had never met the like of his long Gaulish sword. As he leant back to slow Dido to a trot he saw Agbal desperately trying to fend off a Roman spear with his shield. The man's spear arm was an inviting target. Sphax pressed Dido to rear up, and with the additional height slashed down hard with his blade. There was a scream and the man slid from his horse in the wake of his severed arm, allowing Agbal time to back away to safety.

Two cavalrymen, violently wrenching at their reins to turn their stallions, now turned their attention to the sword-wielding Numidian, who presented more of a threat than hide shields. But they were too slow. Keeping Dido constantly stepping backwards and forwards he slashed out wildly at anything that moved.

Most of the time he missed, but when he did connect with flesh, the sword did the rest. It helped that his blade was half as long again as the equites' weapons. Two more Romans were swiftly accounted for.

Turning Dido around, he saw the six that had charged with him dismount and rush forward, javelins raised and readied. But what he saw beyond them alarmed him more than any sight he'd seen that day. A lone Roman was galloping full-tilt towards them, and no more than sixty paces behind him, a fresh squadron was desperately trying to catch up.

'Mount up, Numidians,' he began yelling as he nudged Dido forwards to join them. The lone cavalryman must have seen what he was about to face, yet he didn't rein in his stallion. If anything, Sphax thought he was urging him to greater speed. All his men were now trotting forward to meet this new threat. Pointing his sword at the lone horseman, he shouted, 'Leave him to me. Slow down the rest with a javelin.'

As he nudged Dido into a canter, at last he saw the Roman begin to rein in his stallion. He sheathed his sword and reached for his iron saunion, and in a couple of strides had it threaded and raised. So this would be decided by single combat, thought Sphax. So be it. The Roman was still reining in his big horse as Sphax dug his knees into Dido's flanks and she responded with a jolt of exhilarating speed. He aimed her javelin-straight at the oncoming Roman, who'd now slowed his stallion to a trot. Dido flashed past the startled Roman, close enough to clasp hands. Sphax got a fleeting impression of burnished bronze and silver as he instantly leant back and eased his mare into a turn. Now was his chance. If he could turn quicker than the Roman he could aim at his unarmoured back. He came close, but not close enough.

Tensing the throwing thong he took aim and let fly. For once his aim was true, and the saunion spun towards the Roman's shoulder blade, but instead of sinking into flesh, it struck the edge of his solid bronze cuirass and glanced off, leaving his enemy merely winded and bruised.

Now there was no alternative but to draw his sword again. After the Roman had easily parried his first wild slash and Sphax had miraculously managed to avoid a lethal thrust, it became clear that this wasn't an equal fight. His enemy had skills with sword and shield that Sphax could only dream of. But he still had his long blade, and the Roman was wary of it. With a combination of skilful horsemanship and scything slashes, he managed to keep the Roman at bay.

But nothing could keep at bay the dozen horseman from the squadron that had caught up with their decurion and now stood to defend him. And that's when Sphax's luck ran out.

He felt a sudden jolt and an excruciating pain in his side, then a shield boss slammed into the side of his head and the world began to spin and dissolve before he sank and slid into the gathering darkness.

TWO

It felt as if Hephaestus himself was using his skull as an anvil. Every heartbeat became a hammer-blow that immersed him in pain, but he feared opening his eyes would make the pain unbearable. It did, almost. But the sight that met his eyes was a pleasant one; that of Maharbal's woman, Ayzabel.

'He's awake,' she spoke to someone unseen in the pavilion. 'I'll get Cesti to bring you some broth, Sphax. You need to build up your strength.'

He tried to sit up on the couch, but collapsed as a new pain seared through his body like molten iron, this time in his side, above his right hip. Soon his servant women, Cesti and Lulin appeared carrying bread and a bowl. Cesti knelt down and proffered the bowl to his lips. He managed to swallow some of the hot liquid. When he'd finally drained the bowl and managed a few mouthfuls of bread he did feel slightly better. He recognised his surroundings as Maharbal's pavilion, always sparsely furnished, except for the clutter of shields and weapons.

PART ONE: The Wounded Consul

'Your goddess must be fond of you lad, she's spared you yet again.' Maharbal hobbled over to him from the back of the pavilion carrying his favourite three-legged stool. He was walking with the aid of a stick. Placing the stool beside the couch, he sat down heavily, elbows resting on his knees whilst both hands gripped the stick. Despite the pounding in his head, Sphax managed a thin smile.

'You're walking, Sir, and the brace has gone.'

'Indeed it has, lad, thank Ba 'al Hamūn. Last night, after my Greek physician stitched that wound of yours he freed me from my wooden prison to hobble around in these old bones of mine.'

It was then that Sphax remembered. Images and memories suddenly flooded into his head, along with a stream of questions.

'Did we capture the consul? What of my eshrin? And Astegal … Adherbal and Jubal? Is Dido safe? How was I rescued? Please, Sir, tell me what happened?' Sphax clutched the bearskin that was covering him and tried to raise himself again, but the pain was too much.

'Easy, lad. All in good time,' Maharbal answered soothingly. 'Your mare's unhurt. As for your eshrin, they were luckier than you. They all got away with a few scratches … no harm done. I've questioned Jugurtha at length. It was him that bound your wound and saved you, otherwise you would've bled to death. I've also questioned Adherbal, Jubal and Astegal. Especially Astegal.' Whilst the general was speaking, Sphax ran a hand down his right side and felt the wound that had been closed and stitched. He got the sinking feeling that it had all been in vain, and closed his eyes.

'Consul Scipio got away, didn't he, Sir?' He didn't see Maharbal's twisted smile.

'He did, Sphax. But only because his son valiantly came to his rescue. When his turma saw him galloping off alone to save his father, they were shamed into following him. You were fighting Publius Cornelius Scipio, son of a consul of Rome, a lad of your own age, I'm told. One of his men speared you whilst another gave you that headache.'

Sphax opened his eyes in recollection. 'He was better with a sword than me.' Maharbal burst out laughing. '*Everyone* is better with a sword than you! I've told you before, lad, you'd do more damage with your prick! I don't know why you carry it.'

'My prick or the sword, Sir?' His general laughed briefly before continuing.

'Despite your best efforts, and those of Adherbal and Jubal, the lad managed to rescue his father and get him to safety. But he lost many men doing so, and all reports suggest that the consul is very seriously wounded ... perhaps even dying.' The general sighed, adding coldly, 'Not that Astegal covered himself in glory.' Sphax said nothing.

'Nevertheless, yesterday was a great victory. Cavalry from two legions were utterly routed and fled. Amongst our prisoners are Lucanians, Campanians and Samnites. Today alone we captured six hundred left behind to defend their bridge over the Ticinus.'

'You captured the bridge?' Sphax was impressed.

'The men, not the bridge. They managed to burn that before we arrived. But it's a clear measure of their desperation. Scipio's legions are finished. My guess is that he'll retreat to the safety of Placentia and await reinforcements. We need to cross the Padus and harry him, give him no respite and drive home our advantage.' Maharbal had ceased to look at him and was gazing intently at some distant horizon, in the future, in the unknown. Finally his vision returned to the present, and his eyes rested on Sphax. 'Sleep now. Regain your strength. I'll need you soon enough,' and with that he quietly left the pavilion. Sphax was asleep before he'd reached the vestibule.

An hour after first light he was beset by a stream of visitors. He would have given anything to have been left alone to sleep and doze late into the morning. First his servants Cesti and Lulin arrived with breakfast and a change of clothing, then the most grim-faced physician he'd ever encountered pronounced his wound was healing, and he might, if Asclepius favoured him, see out the rest of the day. Sphax reminded himself that the unlucky god of healing was himself struck down by a thunderbolt from Zeus. Not the best of omens. At least the toga-clad Greek was followed by someone he was delighted to see. Idwal was the son of a Gaulish chieftain, and his dearest friend.

'One of these days, my friend, your luck's going to run out.'

'I thought it had!'

Idwal was grinning down at him. Even in the half-light of the pavilion, his winter-blue eyes were sparkling with good humour this morning. Sitting astride Maharbal's stool as if he was mounted on a stallion, he flattened his generous mustachios against his cheeks and wagged a mocking finger.

'Next time you choose a sparring partner for sword practice, don't choose the son of a Roman consul ...'

'O how the righteous and the just envy the lucky fool.'

'Menander?' Sphax shook his head. 'Then it must be Epicurus?' Another shake of the head. 'Surely not Aristotle?'

'Wrong on all counts, my learned scholar. None other than Sphax, son of Navaras, that repository of Numidian philosophy who almost got the better of a pampered Roman brat, almost captured his illustrious father, and singlehandedly, almost brought down the Roman republic with a stroke of his mighty Gaulish blade.'

'And *almost* got himself killed into the bargain. Yes, I did hear our cavalry had a minor victory ...'

'Minor victory!' Sphax raised a protesting arm, but instantly regretted it. 'I wouldn't describe the routing of the legion's cavalry as a minor victory.'

Idwal was laughing. 'I'm glad to hear your pride and dignity were unharmed.'

PART ONE: The Wounded Consul

'But what about today, Idwal? Maharbal told me last night we were pressing and harrying. Is this still the case?'

His friend's face dissolved into that all too familiar frown of concentration. 'We are marching westwards whilst our enemies march eastwards, so in truth, we are in retreat. But this retreat will last only until your Numidians find a ford to cross to the southern bank of the Padus. Then we shall press and harry.' Despite the pain that shot up the right side of his body, Sphax sat up on the couch and gathered his cloak against the morning chill.

'Then you are right. Just a minor victory.'

'I wouldn't say that, my friend. Look at the facts. The cavalry from two Roman legions have been routed. Scipio has crossed to the southern bank of the Padus only because the northern bank favours cavalry. And cavalry is what he now fears. He's seeking the safety of the walls of Placentia, which lies on the southern bank of the river. Reinforcements will be directed there.' His frown deepened. 'There are rumours that Sempronius Longus, Scipio's fellow consul, is marching with all speed from Ariminum. Your uncle will know more. Every night his informants and spies steal into camp and make their way to his pavilion in secret.'

Idwal stood and stared out at the view framed by the pavilion's vestibuled entrance. In the distance he could just make out the silver-grey ribbon that marked the course of the Padus. 'All roads, it seems, lead to Placentia.'

After Idwal left, Sphax managed to struggle to his feet. Grimacing, he called out for Cesti and Lulin, and with their support managed to hobble his way over to his own more modest pavilion. After the loss of so much blood the physician had warned him that the worst effects of this would be light-headedness and fatigue, and the only remedy, food and rest, so for the next week all he did was eat and sleep. On the tenth day he felt well enough to ride for an hour. His wound was healing and his strength returning. Tomorrow, he decided, he would be strong enough for duty.

* * *

Maharbal was like a man reborn. He even looked ten years younger than he had a right to. The stick was still in evidence, but he was moving more freely and with less discomfort, and his Egyptian mare was no longer saddled, removing his greatest indignity. Ten of his Numidian captains had been summoned to attend him at dawn. Sphax got wind of it from Jugurtha. Although he'd not been included in the summons, he decided to turn up anyway. Unfortunately, he arrived late, and was soon to discover that the restoration of his general's health had done little to improve his humour. At the sight of him hobbling into the crowded pavilion, Maharbal glared at him.

'Back to your sickbed, boy! Come back when you're fit to ride that mare of yours—'

'But I rode for an hour yesterday,' he bleated.

PART ONE: The Wounded Consul

Maharbal ignored him and carried on with his instructions. 'Adherbal will command the eshrins of Jubal and Astegal and ride west. Hiempsal, Himilco and Aribal will spread out and ride north. The rest of you will follow me. We cross the bridge and follow the southern bank of the Padus. You all know how desperate the situation is, so take carts and wagons. I want them filled with anything you can lay your hands on; wheat, barley, beans … anything that will fill our men's bellies and stave off hunger for another week. And remember, the Insubres are our allies. I don't want any of you arsewits roughing-up their elders or offending their womenfolk. You don't take so much as a flea-ridden goat without paying for it in silver. Bring everything to the new camp that's being constructed south of the great river.' Maharbal cast a stern glance around the assembly. 'Now get out of my sight.' Noticing that Sphax was about to leave with the rest he bawled, 'Not you, slackhead! You stay here.'

Sphax stared down glumly at the wonderful patterns in the Seleucid carpet beneath his sandals and wondered what torment of inactivity the general had planned for him today. 'You say you rode for an hour yesterday.'

'Yes, Sir.'

'Have you made arrangements with your servants to move camp tomorrow?'

'I have, Sir,' he lied, reminding himself to do so.

'Are you fit to command?' Sphax nodded, eagerly. Maharbal sighed. 'Well, I suppose there's no reason for your eshrin to remain idle today.'

The general made up his mind. 'Take them over the river and due south. That's the only region unexplored so far. Treat it as a day of drill. Teach them some of those riding tricks of yours and stay out of trouble!' Maharbal clasped Sphax's shoulders. 'Go, before I think better of it and change my mind.'

Within the hour, twenty-nine grumbling Numidians were following their captain over the bridge of boats Carthaginian engineers had constructed over a narrow section of the Padus river. Despite their empty bellies, his men had been looking forward to a leisurely day of drinking and gambling around warm campfires. Instead, they found themselves brushing showers of hailstones from their cloaks; they tightened the draw-strings of their hoods and resigned themselves to another wintry day in Liguria. At least by mid-morning the showers of hail had drifted off to the east and the skies cleared and brightened. But there could be no respite from the unrelenting cold. From time to time Sphax yelled, 'Line!' and his men half-heartedly obeyed, forming a ragged line either side of him, otherwise they rode on in disgruntled silence.

For weary miles, the country south of the Padus looked much the same as that to the north of the river: flat grasslands broken only by occasional stretches of open woodland and criss-crossed by a myriad of streams that were no better than open ditches. Even their mares drank reluctantly from their sluggish brown waters. The land was desolate; its grasslands should

PART ONE: The Wounded Consul

have supported large herds of everything from cattle to horses, or if cultivated, yield rich harvests, but now it lay empty and abandoned. Sphax was puzzled by this. What had cursed this land and driven away its people?

On the broad horizon to the south and east he could see a low range of hills rising from the grasslands of the plain. The rough track they were following south seemed to be heading for the nearest of these uplands. To the west the horizon seemed endless and featureless as it followed the course of the great river. By mid-day, they came at last upon a settlement.

It was a poor, mean place, just a cluster of Gaulish roundhouses with a fog of wood smoke drifting above the thatch. At the sight of them the villagers fled in alarm, grabbing whatever came to a hand, be it child or chicken. By the time Sphax reached the centre of the settlement at the head of his eshrin, the place had emptied. Or so he thought.

'What do you want with us?' came a voice from within one of the roundhouses. It sounded like the voice of an old man, and he'd spoken in Latin. Two of his men were about to dismount and enter the house where the voice had been heard. Sphax signalled for them to wait.

'We are Numidians from Hannibal's army,' he replied in Latin. 'We have come to free all Gauls from the yoke of Rome. We are friends of the Insubres, and of the Boii. They are our allies and our brothers. We mean you no harm and come in peace and friendship.'

A grey-haired old man shrouded in a long grey cloak suddenly appeared at the threshold. He was tall and had the bearing of a warrior, yet he gripped not a spear, but a stout wooden staff in the shape of a shepherd's crook. He was blind.

Taking a few tentative steps towards Sphax, he said, 'I am neither Insubres nor Boii, though they are our cousins. I am Garos, an elder of the Anamares, or what is left of us after Rome butchered our young men and drove us from our homes. I know nothing of Numidians and little of Hannibal, but those who are enemies of Rome the Anamares welcome as friends and guests.' Garos half turned towards the entrance to the roundhouse and shouted commands in his native tongue, after which a young boy emerged gripping a huge hunting horn. After another command from Garos, the boy took a deep breath and blew on the mouthpiece. The sound was startlingly loud and strident. Not a few of the eshrin's mares stirred skittishly at the blast.

Slowly, at first in twos and threes, the villagers cautiously returned, gathering around their elder and staring suspiciously at the Numidians astride their horses and clutching javelins. Garos spoke to them at length in his Gaulish dialect. Soon, benches and chairs were removed from houses and placed in a broad circle in the centre of the settlement. Women brought bread, bowls of fruit and jugs of mead and wine.

Sphax switched to his native tongue. 'These are poor folk. Yet they offer you what they have stored

PART ONE: The Wounded Consul

against this cruel winter. I beg you as honourable Numidians, be respectful and grateful for such bounty.' At the sight of such a feast his half-starved men needed no encouragement.

The bread and mead were excellent, but Sphax ate and drank little, only what politeness demanded. He was seated beside Garos, and began to question the elder about the history of the Anamares and the extent of their lands. It was a sorry tale.

Five years ago they had sought peace with Rome to bring an end to the strife that had lasted a lifetime. But Rome would have none of it, Rome scented complete victory and sent its legions north again. Once more the Anamares joined with their allies the Insubres and the Boii to fight the invader, and once more they were defeated. Garos told him that a great battle had been fought just south of them, before the walls of the Roman town of Clastidium, where the consul Marcellus had defeated the Insubres chieftain Viridomarus in single combat. A great slaughter had taken place, and what was left of their people crossed the great river and fled north. Within the year the Insubres had surrendered and sued for peace. 'As you see,' said the old man at last, 'some of my kin have returned, but only so that I can live out the last of my days in my birthplace and be buried in our ancestral chambers.'

Sphax's curiosity had been aroused at the mention of this Roman town to the south of them. Garos described it as a walled hill town, with gates at its northern and southern perimeters. 'None of my people trade there now. For us the land thereabouts is cursed with evil spirits and it holds too many painful memories.'

Sphax looked again at the face where eyes had once illuminated a mind undoubtedly endowed with intelligence and wisdom. Garos' blindness had nothing to do with nature. His eyes had been gouged out, unnaturally, leaving behind a scarred and hideous reminder of their absence.

'It must also be painful for you, Sir, to live in your birthplace without being able to see its woods and fields, and recognise your kin.'

'There are other ways of *seeing*, Numidian, which I have had to learn these past seven years. I am grateful to our god Alumnus for teaching me his ways of healing and prophecy. I might be blind to this world, but I'm clear-sighted in others.'

'If you don't mind my impertinence, Sir, what happened seven years ago to cause you to lose your sight?'

Garos lowered what remained of his eyelids, giving a pale impression of a sighted person closing his eyes. 'A great battle. Against Rome. You may have heard of it. We remember it as Telamon, the Romans may call it something else.' Sphax had more than heard of it; as a slave in Rome he'd been granted the honour of standing with the cheering crowds as Lucius Aemilius

PART ONE: The Wounded Consul

Papus paraded in triumph to the Capitoline, dragging behind him prisoners in chains, bound for the misery of slavery. Sphax had not cheered.

'To look on me today you would not believe it, but seven years ago I was a feared warrior, a Gaesatae worthy of hire for my sword. Morrigu had become my shield-maiden through many a battle, and so on that day seven years ago I stood beside Aneroëstes as the severed head of Consul Regulus was tossed at his feet. Victory should have been ours that day. Valour demanded it! But fate and Morrigu decided otherwise. We were defeated and I was captured. That day Consul Papus spared ten prisoners to send news of his victory north into the lands of the Insubres. Along with tidings of defeat, these messengers would also send out a dire warning of retribution and punishment should Gauls ever rise against Rome again. I had the misfortune to be chosen. I begged for death, but was given life, a life of darkness. Such is the cruelty of Rome.'

Sphax knew all about Roman savagery. Like Garos, he was living proof of it. After legionaries had butchered his parents, he'd been taken into slavery and spent the next ten years of his boyhood in misery. He would always carry the *fugitus* sign that had been branded into his right forearm; a punishment for trying to run away when he was fourteen. He'd been lucky: as he was still a boy he was spared being branded on his forehead like most runaways.

'They think themselves civilised,' he said at last, 'yet they're no better than savages. Our army must drive Rome from the face of the earth, so that even the memory of these barbarians is erased from history, and the world forgets that they had ever lived.' Sphax noticed that all the villagers' eyes were upon him. He rose from his seat and raised his cup.

'I thank you all for your friendship and generosity in sharing what little you have with my men. We are indebted and grateful. I will speak of your kindness to my uncle, Hannibal, leader of our army. I'm sure he will wish to reward you. But I will say one last thing. Numidians will always remember the noble Anamares.' Cups were drained and benches rapped in gratitude. Sphax embraced Garos and pressed the small purse of coins Maharbal had given him into the elder's hand. Signalling to his men, he whistled for Dido and strode from the village.

When they were all mounted and clear of the village they gathered around him. He was pleased to see that food and drink had restored their humour.

'Where are we going, Sir? asked Hannon.

'I found out from the old man there's a small Roman town just eight miles south of here. Shall we pay it a visit?' The faces of his men lit up and everyone exchanged grins.

'What are we waiting for?' said Jugurtha.

Sphax quickly urged Dido to the canter, and at this pace they came in sight of the walled town within the hour.

PART ONE: The Wounded Consul

By that time it was as if they'd passed a threshold and entered a new country. Gone were the endless miles of empty grassland, replaced by thickly wooded hills, burbling streams and steep-sided valleys. He halted them in a woodland clearing beside the track, no more than four hundred paces from Clastidium. From where they sat their mares, the northern gate of the town was clearly visible, set deep into the town wall, yet nowhere did they see guards or men carrying weapons, either by the gate or high on the walls. Neither could they hear the everyday sounds of work and activity; everything seemed clothed in eerie silence. If it wasn't for the evidence of smoke rising from a score of fires, Sphax would have sworn that the town had been abandoned. He was about to send out scouts to reconnoitre the walls when a sudden movement caught his eye.

Nudging Dido around to face the way they'd come, he saw a strange sight. Not more than fifty paces behind them were two women on horseback. One was wearing a sky blue stola beneath a crimson riding cloak, sitting motionless astride a huge grey stallion, the other was a Nubian, clad in palla-grey on her piebald mare. For a few heartbeats they just stared at one another. Then crimson-cloak dug her knees into the stallion and veered off at speed into the woodland, whilst the Nubian headed off in the opposite direction.

Without a moment's hesitation Sphax gave chase to the stallion and plunged into the woods to his left. The beech and chestnut trees were spaced widely enough apart to enable both horses to gallop at full stretch, although at breakneck speed Sphax soon discovered he needed all his wits about him to avoid calamity. A low branch and then a false stride as Dido's hoof caught an upturned root almost unhorsed him. The ground was gently falling away downhill, and at a thunderous gallop, a stallion would always have the advantage over a mare, and crimson-cloak was making the most of it, pulling away from him with every stride. Bent low, balanced perfectly over the stallion's neck with cloak billowing in the wind, she was riding as Numidians were taught to ride, without reins, guiding by subtle touches from either knee or the palms of hands on the animal's neck. But crimson-cloak was doing far more than that — weaving skilfully through the trees she was continually feinting a change of direction to left or right, so that Sphax found himself guessing and having to constantly check Dido's stride.

When he saw they were heading for a wide stream in the woodland floor his heart leapt. She might ride well, but few horsemen, let alone a woman, had the skill to jump. Now he would have her! A quick scan ahead told him there was only one place a clear jump might be attempted, and that was to the left. Anticipating her change of direction gained him half a stride, but there was no slackening of the stallion's pace, which could mean only one thing. Crimson-cloak was going to risk the jump.

His heart was in his mouth as he watched. Of course he wanted to catch her. She'd thrown down a challenge. But she was no enemy, just an innocent woman out for a ride who was doing her best to avoid him. Yet a perilous leap across a stream as broad as this could prove fatal for rider or horse.

His concerns were misplaced. Timing her approach perfectly, she sailed high over the stream's bubbling waters, landing so lightly on the far bank that not half a stride of momentum was lost by the leap.

Sphax was mightily impressed. Now he and Dido had to be on their mettle. It needed a big jump. He was relieved when the mare made it across. After he'd landed, rather heavily if he was honest, he caught sight of crimson-cloak turning around to check on her pursuer. He could have sworn he heard her laugh.

The chase continued, but now steeply uphill, and this is where Dido came into her own, being lighter, more agile and with a well of stamina. He sensed the stallion was flagging. Crimson-cloak was having to use her hands and knees more frequently to encourage the stallion onwards, and Sphax was definitely gaining. At one point the stallion stumbled on a bare root and lost a precious stride. Sphax dug his knees into Dido's flanks and she surged forward so that he could almost reach out and touch his quarry's cloak. But with his next breath he was cursing his luck. They suddenly emerged from the trees into open fields, scattering goats as the two horses thundered by.

Everywhere looked downhill from here, and Sphax realised he now stood little chance of catching her. As they entered yet more woodland at the far end of the field, he began easing Dido's pace and considered giving up on what had now become a fruitless chase. But then she made her first and only mistake. Jumping the trunk of a fallen tree that lay across her path she mistimed her approach, leaving it half a stride too late. Clipping a hoof on the way over the stallion landed heavily, tossing the rider from her saddle like a bundle of rags.

He brought Dido to a halt and ran over to where she'd fallen. Kneeling beside her prone body he gently turned her over and pulled back her hood. She was out cold, badly winded, her breathing shallow, but other than that he could see no obvious injury. He found it almost impossible to stop himself examining that face. Her eyes were closed, but even without the hidden promise of those eyes, the woman was the most beautiful creature he'd ever seen.

Sphax had never seen skin so pale and unblemished, lips so full and generous, and all framed by lustrous raven curls that tumbled on to her shoulders. He had an irresistible urge to caress those lovely cheeks and wake her with a kiss. Removing his beaverskin cloak he placed it beneath her head as a pillow, bent over her, and waited. Gazing at such loveliness, Sphax knew he had a ridiculous smile on his face, but there was nothing he could do, he just couldn't help himself. She began to stir. Sphax waited. Then her eyes suddenly opened and she gave out a wordless gasp of fright. The promise of those eyes was more than fulfilled; they were a rich hazel and fathomless, set below thickly arched eyebrows the colour of her hair.

For a few heartbeats they just stared at one another. Tearing himself away from those eyes he sat upright and asked in Latin if she was hurt.

'No … I don't think so,' stretching her limbs a little whilst still resting her head on his cloak. 'Am I your prisoner?' Her voice was low and resonant, and she spoke Latin with a strange accent.

'Maybe … it depends.' I should be so lucky, thought Sphax. 'I mean you no harm, if that's what you're thinking.'

'Pity,' she muttered in Greek under her breath, 'I would gladly surrender to a pretty boy like you.' That's more like it, he thought, grinning at her and switching to the Greek tongue.

'I am Sphax, a Numidian. My general is Hannibal, leader of the Carthaginian army that has come to destroy Rome.' She returned his grin.

'And you speak excellent Greek, I hear.' She raised herself on an elbow and gazed about her. 'Is my horse unharmed? He must have taken a blow to his hoof.' Sphax gestured over his shoulder.

'He's well. Grazing with my mare. A fine stallion, lady. Where did you learn to ride like that?'

'I have always loved horses, and learned to ride at an early age.' With a grunt she sat upright and frowned. 'I also know that only a Numidian could have caught me.'

'Then you should have known it was futile to run away.' Her lovely face came alive with a mischievous smile.

'But I gave you a run for your purse, did I not, Numidian?'

'You certainly did, lady, but you have not told me your name or your business near this Roman town.'

'Neither have you! What business has a troop of Numidian cavalry with a Roman town garrisoned by Greeks from Brundisium?'

'Greeks, you say. Not legionaries,' his curiosity aroused. She fell silent, got to her feet and begun rearranging her tunic and dusting down her crimson cloak with the flat of her hands. Finally she gazed down at him.

'My name is Corinna. I'm the woman of the garrison commander, Dasius the Pig,' she said coldly. 'Other than that, my business is my own.'

Sphax was shivering. He crawled forward to retrieve his beaverskin cloak, but all he felt was a powerful kick to his shoulder that sent him sprawling on to his back. In the next instant Corinna had drawn a dagger hidden beneath her cloak and had it pointed at his throat. 'It seems the tables have been turned, my pretty Numidian.'

He stared at a face transformed. Still beautiful, yet all the softness had vanished from those generous

PART ONE: The Wounded Consul

lips and soft cheeks, and her eyes had darkened and narrowed.

'Move but a finger and I swear I'll slit your throat.' He didn't doubt it! Without taking her eyes off him she whistled shrilly for her stallion. Sphax heard hoof beats approaching, but not those of a stallion. 'Now you're going to stand, very slowly, and one false step on your part and you will feel this knife bite.'

'It's been a tiring day, lady,' he said, feigning a yawn. 'I'm quite content to rest here for a while if you don't mind,' he added, shaping a smile. Sphax's keen hearing had noticed the approaching hoof beats were not those of a big stallion, but of jennets. 'Besides, I don't think you're going anywhere today, my pretty little harpy.' He noted the sudden confusion in her eyes. Behind her two familiar figures were now framed in his field of vision, either side of her raven curls.

'If you care to look behind you, I think you will see two javelins raised and pointed at that lovely neck of yours.' She did look.

Sphax seized his opportunity and viciously wrenched her wrist away from his throat. She cried out in pain. 'You're hurting me!' He squeezed harder and the blade fell from her fingers.

It was Jubal and Jugurtha that had rescued him from his embarrassing predicament. Both were now grinning at him. Grabbing the knife he got to his feet and turned his back on them to hide his acute sense of foolishness. 'Bind the bitch!' he yelled with unnecessary ferocity, 'bind her hands behind her back.'

'Fear not, Sir,' smirked Jugurtha. 'We will truss her as we would a lioness, with ropes and cords. You're not to worry, captain, we'll defend you!'

Jugurtha was a great storyteller. Sphax realised he'd provided the old goat with yet another tale for the campfires, and with that thought he chuckled at last, his anger evaporating. Corinna was grimacing as Jubal tightened the cords. Squatting down on his haunches he faced her, twirling her knife between his fingers.

'Now, lady, you're going to talk. You're going to tell me everything. How you got here, how you became the woman of this Dasius the Pig, how many men he has, their weapons and the numbers that guard the gates and walls. You can start by telling me why this shithole of a Roman town merits a special garrison from Brundisium?'

'Then first you must know that I'm not a common whore!' she said with venom. 'I'm Dasius' woman. He loves me. He can't live without me. But he has a hold over me that means I have to suffer his fat and greasy carcass.'

'Then if I can free you from this greasy carcass and break his hold over you, will you help us?'

'Break his hold over me!' she said with a hollow laugh. 'If only that were possible, Numidian.'

'What if we capture him and hand him over to Hannibal? Surely he could no longer harm you then.'

'I'm not sure …' It took a great deal of argument and reassurance, but eventually a bargain was struck, after which she described the town and its garrison in great detail. By the time she'd finished, the rest of his eshrin had arrived with the Nubian in tow, and like her mistress, bound at the wrists.

'You wouldn't believe the trouble it's taken to run this one down.'

'Believe me I would, Hannon. Has anyone from the town seen you?'

'No, Sir. She galloped off like a gazelle, away from the walls. She answers to the name of Zwalia. She's the servant of that one,' he said, pointing at Corinna.

Gulussa, the giant of the eshrin, unceremoniously lifted Zwalia from her saddle and dumped her beside her mistress. Hannon was frowning and shaking his head.

'Dog's twat, Sir! What in the name of Ba 'al Hamūn are we to do with 'em?'

It was a good question. But one to which he had no answer.

He spent what was left of the afternoon in earnest discussions with Corinna and her servant. Just before dusk he gathered his men together and led them into a steeply wooded valley where Corinna had suggested it would be safe to camp and light fires that could not be seen from the town. He had no other option but to trust her now, but against all her protestations, he refused to untie her hands. For the moment.

Sphax allowed his men just two fires. Once they had shared out what little food they had and settled down around the warmth of the flames, he untied Corinna's hands and the two of them stood at the centre of his eshrin and explained the plan they'd devised.

It was a long night. There were many questions, objections to be ironed out, contingencies to be planned for and details decided on. His wound was burning and he felt weak from hunger and exhaustion. It was very late when he posted guards and lay down beneath his cloak. But the last thing he did was take a single cord and bind his ankle to that of the woman lying near him. Only when this was all over could he afford to trust her completely.

THREE

He woke just before dawn, cold, hungry and miserable, with his wound throbbing. Not the best start to the day, he decided, but there was nothing to be done, and he knew every man in his eshrin would wake up with that same gut-wrenching emptiness in their belly. After untying the cord that bound his ankle to Corinna he yelled, 'Wake up, you arseholes.'

Wandering amongst the snoring, comatose bodies on the ground, he began kicking backsides. 'Breakfast awaits you!' he proclaimed. 'We have freshly baked bread, hot and steaming from the oven, ripe fruit of every description dripping with sweet juices, we have grapes and honey, meat off the bone and the finest wines by the flagon. Get up you lazy bastards … this morning you earn your breakfast!' Agbal sat up and rubbed the sleep from his eyes.

'That's cruel, Sir. You torture us!'

'But it happens to be true, Agbal. This morning we win our breakfast, it will not be handed to us on a plate.'

When the horses had been watered and what was left of the campfire embers doused, he gathered them all around him and went carefully through the plan once more. There were no questions this morning, so when he'd finished, he made a point of untying Zwalia's bonds himself. When she was free he gripped her shoulders and looked fiercely into her nut-brown eyes. 'The lives of all my men and that of your lady are in your hands today, Zwalia. Can I trust you?' She said nothing, but nodded firmly.

Taking no chances, he removed the ivory image from beneath his tunic and put it to his lips, offering up a silent prayer to Artemis.

'Jugurtha, Hannon, are your parties ready?' Both nodded. 'Then go with Zwalia and take up your positions. And may Ba 'al Hamūn be with you.'

Turning to Corinna, he said, 'I'm afraid I have to bind you again.'

'Of course, it's part of the plan. Let me first mount.' Sphax wasn't falling for that! Once in her saddle she could be off like a thunderbolt, and only Dido was capable of catching her.

'Come and hold the stallion's reins, Agbal, whilst I bind the lady's hands.' Corinna glared at him as he lifted her into the saddle

'What will it take for you to trust me?' she demanded. He grinned up at her.

'Your stallion is skittish, lady,' he lied. 'I dare not risk you falling with your hands tied.' When he'd bound

PART ONE: The Wounded Consul

her he asked Jubal to secure the reins to his mare's neck cord. Now she couldn't make a quick getaway.

For the first few miles he rode beside her, guided by Jubal and the stallion's trailing reins. Still resentful, Corinna refused to look at him or speak, so the journey passed in silence. Besides Jubal, he'd chosen nine men to accompany him. The mid-morning sun was high in a leaden sky when they joined the track they had followed from the Anamares settlement yesterday. Soon they entered the clearing where they'd gathered to view the southern gate and the town's walls. Everything looked much as it had then, with no sounds of activity in the town. All they had to do now was wait for the first signal. It wasn't long coming.

High on a cliff overlooking the eastern ramparts of the little town, a curl of smoke began to rise in the wintry sky. 'It's time. Follow me,' he said, nudging Dido forward at the walk.

'Jubal, when we get within a hundred paces of the gate, lead the lady off the track and into the trees. She must remain hidden. I'll hail you if you're needed.' Turning to Corinna he added, 'Only as a last resort will I turn to your desperate measure, lady. Let us pray that we can fool Dasius into surrendering Clastidium with our trickery.'

'He will not be fooled, Sphax. Only my plan will succeed. You're wasting your time.'

Twenty paces from the gate he halted Dido and turned to warn his men. 'Remember what I said this morning, they may try to rush us. You must be on your guard with javelins coiled and levelled. Your lives may depend on it.'

Now he could clearly hear the grinding wheels of oxcarts beyond the gates. This was the shipment of grain bound for Placentia that Corinna had told him about. Looking along the length of the ramparts he couldn't see a single sentry. Even above the gate, guards had not been posted. Corina had told him that they felt so secure in Clastidium, Dasius never bothered with sentries, but he still couldn't believe they could be so stupid.

'Dasius!' Sphax yelled. 'Dasius of Brundisium! Come out from hiding, you weasel. Carthage wishes to speak with you.' The great oak gates opened slightly, but were then slammed shut and he heard the locking bars being hastily replaced. Men began appearing on the battlements above the gate and on the adjacent walls. He counted a score, but none wore helmets or armour, and most were not even armed. Finally, a great hulk of a man appeared above the gate clad head to foot in furs. Even from thirty paces, Sphax could hear his rasping breath from the effort of climbing the tower.

'I am Dasius. Who are you? What is your business here?'

He smiled up at the bearskinned hulk, wheezing and leaning hard on the battlements, 'I am Sphax. General of Hannibal's cavalry. His great army is camped no more than ten miles away. I come with three hundred

PART ONE: The Wounded Consul

Numidians to ask you politely to open the gate and surrender this miserable little town to Carthage.' He heard a ferment of muttering and whispering above him.

'Do you think I can't count, Numidian. I see not three hundred, but ten wretches on horseback.'

'Then look around you. Our signal fires are clear to anyone who has eyes to see.' Sphax pointed to Hannon's beacon that was now burning away gloriously on top of the cliff. From here, Zwalia had told them that the entire town could be viewed, so they'd chosen this as the site for the first signal, warning that the ox carts had been loaded and were rolling towards the northern gate. 'Besides a hundred Numidians, I have Cretan archers up there who will fire this town and burn it to the ground. It is a cold day, Dasius, shall I ask them to warm you against its chill?' Men either side of Dasius were now pointing to Jugurtha's beacon, blazing away not a hundred paces from the southern gate.

'I see your men have saved me the trouble of pointing out yet more of my Numidians. Whilst your garrison have been idle these past days, my men have been busy making ladders. We know every stone and brick of your walls. Every weakness.' He almost chuckled as he faintly heard Hannon's ten men charging around and trying to make a fearful racket, whilst Jugurtha would now be parading his men through the trees in a continuous circuit, creating the appearance of scores of horsemen. It wasn't difficult to create the illusion of numbers! Most of Dasius' men had hurriedly scampered along the walls to take a look at their besiegers, leaving only three beside the now silent Dasius. Men began returning, presumably reporting what they had seen, for Sphax could hear urgent discussion and argument taking place around Dasius.

'And where are your men, Numidian? I still see only ten barring my path.' Sphax groaned inwardly, there was too much defiance in that grating voice. Every instinct told him Dasius was considering making a run for it.

'I only need ten, to fight drunkards and storekeepers!' Now alarmed, he watched as Dasius hurried from the battlements. 'Get ready men,' he said under his breath. 'They're going to rush us and try to escape.' He was right.

The great oaken gates slowly creaked open and horsemen began to emerge. Sphax had already backed Dido into the line his men had formed. As the first men warily edged their horses through the gates it was obvious that none of the men from Brundisium had the stomach for a real fight, a killing fight. Few carried weapons, and none held shields. There were perhaps a score by now at the threshold, and Sphax could clearly see the great bulk of Dasius being helped into a saddle, screaming and cursing for his men to ride forward and kill.

'Now,' Sphax said calmly, and his men trotted forward a few paces and unleashed a volley of javelins.

PART ONE: The Wounded Consul

Its effect was immediate and deadly. Amidst screams and cries of pain, six riderless horses trotted towards them whilst the dead and wounded were being dragged back through gates that were being frantically closed and barred.

Sphax handed his javelins to Gulussa, dismounted and walked back towards the gates. It wasn't long before Dasius again appeared above him on the gatehouse tower. He noted with satisfaction the red face and desperate expression.

'You bastard! Whore's puss! You piece of rat shit!' he screamed, now beside himself with rage and frustration. He knows he can't win, thought Sphax. Now was the time to twist the knife.

'You have sixty-two ... my apologies, Dasius ... fifty-six men left. We captured your last shipment of grain to Placentia some five days ago.' Sphax let this lie sink in for a while before he continued. 'Consul Scipio must be scratching his head by now. Where is my grain from Clastidium? Is Clastidium still loyal? Is Dasius a traitor, perhaps? Has he sold my grain to another bidder? But you can be certain of one thing; when today's shipment doesn't arrive, his fury will know no bounds, Dasius!' Sphax could now see the entire garrison crammed on to the walls above the gate, hanging on his every word. 'He will send out a few men to drag you back to Placentia in chains. Luckily for you, we will lie in wait and slaughter them. He may even send out more parties, but we will kill them just the same. You no longer have friends in Placentia, Dasius, only enemies, a Roman consul who thinks you've betrayed him.' He paused again, and glanced over the faces staring down at him in hushed silence. 'You are all dead men. Enemies of Rome.' As the muttering began, he casually turned his back on them and began to walk slowly towards his men.

'Wait!' It was Dasius. Sphax slowly turned around. 'If we give you the shipment of grain that is ready by the gate, will you leave us alone?' Taking a calculated risk, he remained silent, turned his back once more and continued walking towards his men.

'If what you say is true, Consul Scipio will send us back to Rome in chains.' It was Dasius again, desperate. 'Yet Hannibal will just as surely slit our throats.'

'You could not be more wrong, Dasius. Hannibal's fight is with Rome, not with Greeks from Brundisium. We have come to free the likes of Brundisium from the shackles of Rome, not slit their throats. Besides, our army is starving. If you were to lead your wagons into our camp you would be greeted as saviours and allies. We would shower you with gifts and silver, then provide you all with the means to return safely to your homes and families. Rome is our enemy, not Brundisium. Hannibal is a friend of Brundisium, not its enemy!'

'Yet you have just killed and wounded my men! How can I trust you, or believe a word you say ...'

'You gave me no choice! But think on, Dasius, if nine Numidians can inflict such injury, think what

PART ONE: The Wounded Consul

three hundred might do.' There was much muttering at this. 'But there is no need for further bloodshed. I swear by all the gods, if you leave this place with your wagons, Hannibal will reward you with silver and treat you as free men and allies. This I swear.' There was now uproar on the battlements above. Everyone seemed to be talking or shouting at once. Finally he heard Dasius yelling for silence, and it was his voice that spoke next.

'Then we have agreement, Numidian. Ten of my men will ride out with our ox carts to your camp. If they return to us tomorrow unharmed, with reports of a favourable welcome, we will declare for Hannibal and defend this town against his enemies and supply him with grain. At a price, of course.'

This was not the bargain Sphax intended. He wanted the slippery weasel and his garrison out of there and the town and its stores surrendered. Corinna had told him that a train of supplies from the south was due in two days. Time was running out.

'You will all leave, Dasius, with your ox carts. Clastidium must be surrendered.'

'You heard my terms. Take them or leave them.'

'Then you leave me no choice.' Sphax turned towards his men. 'Bring the woman,' he commanded. Corinna had been right all along. Dasius had not been fooled, and had guessed that he didn't have the numbers to storm the town. All his elaborate plans and deceptions had proved to be a waste of time.

Now it was time for her plan, and the last throw of the dice. Moments later Jubal led forward Corinna astride her grey stallion. At first there were gasps of surprise, then everyone on the battlements above fell into an uneasy silence. He fixed his eyes on Dasius and stared. Gulussa lifted her down from the saddle and pushed her roughly towards him, her wrists still bound behind her back.

Sphax was impressed by Corinna's performance, she was putting on quite a show for her all-male audience. The instant she'd come in sight of the men on the battlements she'd kept up an endless wailing and caterwauling, interspersed with heartrending sobs accompanied by *real* tears. He made a great play of removing his sword from its scabbard strapped to his back. Perfectly on cue, Corinna screamed and her audience gasped. Dasius began raging and cursing him with every oath known to the gods. Sphax put his arm around her and pointed his sword at the Brundisian.

'I believe she is precious to you, Dasius. Unless you and your men do as I ask, now is the time to say your farewells.'

'Save me, my love. Save me!' Corinna wailed, between great guffawing sobs. 'He is cruel and vicious.' Under her breath she hissed, 'Look as if you mean it, imbecile!' Sphax tightened his grip and placed the blade across her throat.

'Stop! Stop!' screamed Dasius. 'I will do as you ask. Do not harm her, I beg you. Please!' Sphax was astonished at his sudden transformation. After a few wailing sobs, the blustering bully had become a snivelling worm. He could only imagine the power Corinna had over this brute. He watched as the battlements emptied and a great commotion began behind the oaken gates.

Slowly, one of the gates creaked open and Dasius himself stumbled towards him before sinking to his knees in supplication. It was a piteous sight. His bearskin cloak was open at the waist, revealing a filthy tunic that could barely contain his great belly; matted hair hung lifeless and unkempt about his shoulders, and his jowly, pock-marked face was almost crimson in colour.

At that moment, the only pity he felt was for the woman who had been forced to give herself to this creature because he held her infant son hostage, five hundred miles away in Brundisium. Now a broken man, Dasius the Pig raised his bloodshot eyes and whimpered, 'I've done as you asked, free her … I beg you.'

'Seize him!' was Sphax's reply. 'Truss him like a butchered pig to the back of a horse, and shove a rag in his mouth. I find his speech more offensive than what comes out of his arse!' Amidst a torrent of curses that suddenly fell silent, two of his men roughly manhandled Dasius to his feet and led him off.

Sphax stared through the half-open gate at the men gathered in the courtyard beyond. They were muttering, looked restless and there were far too many of them for his liking. Once all eyes had been fixed upon the bargaining going on at the gate, his orders to Hannon and Jugurtha had been that they should make their way back to the northern gate unseen, guided by Zwalia. He was sorely in need of them at that moment. Dejected and leaderless as they appeared, what remained of the garrison still outnumbered him by five to one. He turned to one of his men. 'Go back and find Hannon and Jugurtha. Bring them here. Fast!'

Corinna strode over to him, her wrists still bound behind her back. 'Don't worry about that rabble,' she said with a twisted smile, 'without Dasius they are like children, they haven't the courage to try anything.' He began untying her hands.

'Nevertheless, I'd feel safer with twenty men behind me.' He whistled for Dido and turned to his men. 'With me,' he said, and once mounted, rode with his men through the open gate into the courtyard where Clastidium's garrison were assembled.

'I will keep my word,' he said with a confidence he didn't feel, 'my men will escort your wagons to Hannibal's camp, where Hannibal will reward you and set you free to return to Brundisium. Your allegiance to Rome is ended. Gather your possessions together, we leave soon.' Corinna had been right: they looked no more threatening than a flock of sheep, storekeepers rather than soldiers.

As they sullenly sloped off, he slid from Dido and began to examine the three ox carts that were lined

PART ONE: The Wounded Consul

up in the courtyard. Loosening a rope that secured the canvas cover he ploughed his fingers through its precious contents. Hannibal and his starving army would be overjoyed. In these three carts alone was a veritable harvest, for each one was full to the brim with golden wheat.

'There's plenty more where that came from, warehouses full of it, as well as oil, wine and salted meat.' It was Corinna, now astride her stallion, and behind her he was relieved to see Jugurtha and Hannon riding through the gates to join him.

'First, I promised my men breakfast, and that's what they shall have. Lead us to the feast, lady,' he said with a broad grin.

'Zwalia will see to it their bellies are filled. You and I have another matter to attend to, one that cannot wait. Mount your mare.' Soon he was riding beside Corinna's stallion through the deserted streets of Clastidium towards the southern gate. Jubal must have given back her dagger, for it was now visibly on show, hanging from a belt around her waist.

'When news reached Clastidium that Hannibal's armies had descended on Liguria, every Roman citizen fled for the safety of Placentia. Could you blame them? You've seen for yourself our *brave* Brundisians. Some obstinate farmers and landholders in the district remained, but in the town itself you won't find as much as a Roman slave within its walls. That's why it's empty. Brundisium was left to fend for herself, and as long as the grain shipments to Placentia continued, Rome left us alone. But there was one who stayed.'

'And presumably, we are about to pay him a visit.'

'Yes. We are going to the house of Lucanus Flavius: merchant, tax collector, slaver and thief. Chief misery of all who live in these parts and the only Roman left in Clastidium. For the past two years he and Dasius have robbed and cheated every citizen from here to Placentia. Be warned, he has a giant of a man he pays to guard him.'

They were almost too late. As they approached a grand villa, a four-wheeled carriage followed by a lone horseman began pulling away. With a shock Sphax saw that the southern gates of the town had been forced wide open. The horseman must have spotted them, for he took off like a thunderbolt, making for the open gateway. But he was no match for Corinna and her stallion, who were gaining on him with every stride. He'd almost reached the arched gateway when Sphax saw the silvered glint of a dagger spin through the air and the man slump in his saddle.

By now the carriage, pulled by two bays, was also tearing towards the gate. He glimpsed a driver clutching a spear. Digging his knees into Dido he sped after it. Corinna had now caught up with the slumped figure in the gateway.

'Corinna!' he yelled. 'Behind you!' Just in time she managed to nudge her stallion out of the path of the carriage as it thundered through the gateway. He feared

PART ONE: The Wounded Consul

a spear being flung at her, but mercifully the driver had not used his weapon.

As Dido's hooves clattered on the paving beneath the gateway, he reached for his saunion and fingered his leather thong. Sphax had fought a giant of a man before, a brutal Gaul from the Cavari tribe, but he'd never fought a Roman giant and was curious to compare sizes.

With little effort, Dido soon drew level with the carriage and its driver. Riding alongside at a safe distance from a spear-thrust, he examined the man gripping reins and a long-shafted spear in his right hand. Beneath the hood of his tunic, all Sphax could see of him was a great beard, a bulbous nose, and what appeared to be two slits for eyes, sunk amidst the folds of flesh on his face. This man was no giant, just a fat Roman!

'Ave, amicus,' he shouted above the rattle of wheels. 'Quo vadis?'

'That's none of your business, cocksucker! And if you don't want to be gutted by this spear, I suggest you ride away and leave me alone.'

Sphax could see that it was going to be a ticklish problem. The man was not going to stop, and although he could easily ride alongside the two bays and force them to halt, doing so would offer his back as an easy target for the man's spear. He could also leap from Dido on to the carriage, but wrestling the man on a moving vehicle was, to say the least, uncertain and risky. He had no reason to kill the man, but the alternatives were growing rather thin. Corinna hadn't spoken highly of him, and he was Roman, after all.

'If you don't halt this carriage, I will have to kill you. This is your last chance!'

'Are you still here, shit-face? Shouldn't you be suckling on your mother's tit at your age?'

After this uncalled-for insult to both his mother and his youth, Sphax felt a little better about killing him. Urging Dido forward he galloped ahead until he'd gained enough ground to turn her around and run at the carriage. It was all over in a heartbeat. The man now slumped over the driving platform hadn't even had time to raise his spear.

Riding alongside one of the bays, he gently eased him to a halt, then turned both around and headed back to town. Corinna was waiting for him beyond the gateway with four young boys. In answer to his questioning look she said, 'Flavius' slaves. Poor boys!' And staring at the grisly sight on the carriage, added, 'I see you've returned Maximus. He was a nasty piece of work, that one.'

'He's now Maximus Mortuus, as I suspect is Lucanus Flavius,' he said. The lady simply gave him a wicked smile then stared at the carriage.

'Shall we take a look inside this thing?' An open arched doorway gave access to the inside, and Corinna hoisted herself up and through it. Moments later she called, 'Come and see this for yourself, Sphax.'

He climbed up and sat on a seat opposite her. On the floor between them were two chests strapped to the floor of the carriage. They both gasped when the straps were loosened and the lids opened. What they contained in gold, jewels and silver was not the wealth of a rich merchant, but that of a small kingdom. Corinna pointed out some of her own jewellery, given to her by Dasius.

'He must have sent Maximus to steal what he could from Dasius whilst you were negotiating at the gate. Dasius had also acquired considerable wealth from cheating his Roman masters. Flavius' greed was his downfall. If he hadn't delayed, he might have got clean away. How fitting for the bastard!' Ignoring the moral lessons, Sphax stated the obvious.

'Clastidium surrendered to Numidians, and these are Roman spoils. This is now the property of me and my men. But I will be generous.'

Corinna arched questioning eyebrows and flashed a smile. 'You better be, Numidian. You owe me much!'

Within the hour the ox carts and their precious cargo were rolling down the track towards the Padus, followed by the men from Brundisium on a motley collection of horses with an escort of twenty Numidians led by Hannon. Behind the last cart, Dasius lay trussed and gagged across his horse, guarded by Gulussa. 'Don't worry,' he'd told Corinna, 'Hannon will say they gave up the town willingly. Dasius' name will not be mentioned. He'll be held under an armed guard in my pavilion until I decide what to do with him.'

Clastidium's garrison now consisted of ten Numidians, two women and four slave boys. A fact that made him uneasy. As the evening drew in they began lighting fires at both gates and torches at intervals along the perimeter of the walls, anything to make the town look occupied and vigilant. Posting his men to guard the gates and patrol the walls, he made sure they were well supplied with food and furs for the long night ahead and prayed that Hannibal sent out a relief at first light.

It was late when he returned to Corinna. She was sitting at a banqueting table beside a roaring brazier, in what had been the audience room of the magistrate's house before Dasius had moved in and converted it to a dining room when the Romans left. Except for Flavius' villa, Corinna had told him this was the grandest house in Clastidium. Zwalia had packed the slave boys off to bed and retired herself, so they were alone.

'When the men of Brundisium reach your camp, will they be treated well, Sphax?'

His thoughts turned to Hannon. At that moment he didn't envy the poor man, guessing that by now he would be in audience with Hannibal. Delighted as his uncle would be that he'd suddenly acquired a Roman town and the prospects of feeding his army for a week or two, Sphax knew from bitter experience that Hannon would be questioned endlessly about how this had been

PART ONE: The Wounded Consul

accomplished. It was difficult to hide the truth from his uncle. But Hannon was an old hand, and he'd every faith in him.

'They will, I'm sure of it,' he answered at last.

'How can you be so certain?' Sphax poured himself a large cup of wine and wearily walked over to a comfortable sleeping couch beside the brazier. His wound was beginning to throb.

'The only way Hannibal can destroy Rome is to separate her from her allies, to force them to swear allegiance to Carthage and join his cause. Like the Hydra, he fears that however many times he cuts off her head, Rome will renew itself. But Rome can be made to bleed to death if she is deprived of the allies that surround her. Brundisium may become the first of these allies. From what you've told me it's a reluctant ally at best. If the sons of Brundisium are returned home unharmed, it sends a clear message.' She raised her cup and came to sit beside him on the couch.

'Then there is every hope,' she said. Sphax smiled and raised his cup before a sudden dart of pain made him wince. 'Are you in pain?' she asked, concerned.

'It's nothing,' he said unconvincingly, 'a scratch from our fight with Roman cavalry.'

'Let me see.' Despite the pain he managed a grin.

'It's nothing, Corinna, and the pain has passed.'

'Let me see!' This time it was a command. Reluctantly he put down his cup and raised his tunic to his ribs. Very gently she ran a forefinger over the linen binding around his waist. Even he could see that the cloth above the wound was moist.

'This is not a scratch, Sphax, and it has been weeping. Has it been stitched?'

'Yes, by a Greek physician.'

'Then it needs to be freshly bound. I will see to it. It's warm by the fire, take off your tunic and rest your head back on the pillows.' Even though the pain had eased considerably, he wasn't going to protest. The fire was indeed warm, and her every touch had sent a dart through his body more urgent than pain. As she bustled from the room he removed his tunic, recovered his cup from the floor and leaned back comfortably on the pillows.

Corinna returned carrying a bowl of water and fresh linen over her arm. Sitting beside him, she carefully unwound the binding from around his waist. To make it easier, he too sat upright, a finger's length from her lovely face. He could feel her soft breath on his shoulder. When the wound and the stitching were finally revealed, she gasped, staring at him in alarm.

'You should be in your sick-bed, not besieging Roman towns!'

'It's just a spear thrust. I'll live,' he protested with affected indifference, the pain now little more than a dull ache. Very delicately she ran the tips of her fingers along the length of the scar then raised them to her nose. Sphax leaned back and closed his eyes.

'There is nothing foul in the smell. But it should be cleansed and treated with yarrow root and honey

PART ONE: The Wounded Consul

before binding with fresh linen. Wait here.' Sphax had no intention of going anywhere, he was already in Elysium.

Returning with two bowls, she dabbed a strip of cloth into a bowl of water to clean the scar, then, after rubbing a fine powder into the stitches, began smearing sticky honey around the scar. 'Are you a healer?' he asked.

'I'm a woman. It amounts to the same thing,' she answered with a hollow laugh. 'A woman who cannot heal her own wounds.'

'Your son ... in Brundisium?' he suggested, tentatively.

Corinna nodded, but said nothing, and deftly began tearing the linen into a long strip. 'Sit up,' she said brusquely.

This time, as he did so he held both her shoulders and stared into those fathomless hazel eyes. 'I will help you rescue him and bring him to safety. Let me help you!'

Corinna smiled, and began fingering the ivory image of Artemis about his neck. 'You are a sweet boy, but I fear this task is beyond anyone, even your goddess.' It was only then that she noticed the *fugitus* sign, branded on his forearm. 'You were a slave!' she exclaimed, utterly horrified.

'Is your son alive?'

'I believe so.'

'Then thank the gods, woman. Your son still has a mother!' he said harshly.

In that instant the enchantment was broken. She picked up the strip of linen and began binding it around his waist, every movement heavy with the awkwardness that had now grown between them. When she had tied the linen neatly, Sphax drained his cup and slipped his tunic over his head.

'You should rest now,' she said firmly. He ignored her, swung his legs from the couch and strode over to the chair where he'd draped his beaverskin cloak. 'Where are you going?'

'Where do you think I'm going?' he answered coldly, avoiding her eyes. 'My men need me, and I need to be with my men.'

FOUR

Sphax was relieved that Hannibal had understood the urgency of the situation. By mid-morning his men were cheering from the northern gate at the sight of two hundred Iberian caetrae riding towards them trailing a fleet of empty wagons. And smirking, if the truth was known, for these fearsome warriors armed only with buckler, javelins and falcata were lethal on foot, but never looked comfortable on horseback. He rode out to greet them and was relieved to see Orison at their head. His uncle sometimes foisted the sons of high-born families from Carthage on Iberians, a practice that he, and often the men under them despised, but Orison was chief of the Oretani, a great bear of a man and a true warrior. Sphax dismounted and bowed low.

'Am I pleased to see you, Sir! Welcome to Clastidium.'

The chief roared with laughter and clasped hold of Sphax's shoulders. 'Thanks to you, lad, my men breakfasted better than they have in weeks. More renown for the son of Navaras, eh?'

'I don't know about that, Sir, but we've prepared bread, cold meats and fruit for your men, and there's wine by the flagon.'

'Spoken like a true host. Lead on!'

Within the hour, the garrison that had held Clastidium for a single night were ready to leave. That morning his men had looted Flavius' villa of anything of value, so besides the chests of jewels and silver, the four-wheeled carriage was piled high with everything from Apulian amphorae to the finest Samian tableware. Zwalia had three of the slave boys beside her on the driving platform whilst the fourth sat before Corinna on her stallion.

She rode beside him, but they exchanged few words, and despite them both stealing occasional looks at one another, the awkwardness from last night remained. It was as if they'd touched a place deep within each other that they were not yet ready to share.

It was almost dark when they arrived at the new camp, and to Corinna's alarm, there was no sign of Dasius or the men who were supposed to guard him. Sphax summoned his men. When they were all huddled inside his pavilion he asked Hannon what had happened.

'Hannibal is what happened, Sir. It was worse than being roasted slowly on a spit. Question after question, a good hour of it. Who did this? Who did that? Who said what?' Hannon sheepishly grinned. 'Me and three of the lads, Sir, we got so dizzy with the questions that in the end none of us knew right from wrong.' Sphax

PART ONE: The Wounded Consul

laughed at this, but glancing over at Corinna and Zwalia sitting stiffly on his sleeping couch, he could see they were not finding this amusing.

'Don't worry, Hannon, none of you has done anything wrong. It's difficult to hide the truth from our general,' and to his servants Cesti and Lulin, 'Bring wine and cups for my men.'

Jugurtha caught his eye and shrugged. 'Hannibal's been questioning Dasius and the men from Brundisium, I've seen them being led to his pavilion.'

When all their cups had been charged he raised his own. 'Then I give you a toast to my own spit-roasting ... due in an hour or so! In the meantime ...' he kicked open the lid of the chest where he'd placed all the silver, drained his cup then filled it to the brim with his share of the silver. 'The rest is to be shared amongst you.' After the stunned silence and gaping mouths, cheering erupted, then a table was cleared and the serious business of counting began. Sphax had no doubt that the real arguments would begin around campfires after rivers of wine had been drunk. But that was later; for now everything was sweetness and accord. Half way through the proceedings he kicked open the second chest, revealing its glittering contents in the lamplight.

'This was earned by the bravery of the lady Corinna. She has promised to be generous and reward you all. Are you content that this belongs to her?' There was resounding agreement, just as he'd intended, and they quickly turned their attention back to the silver. Sphax lifted the chest and placed it beside his sleeping couch at the back of the pavilion. For the first time that day, Corinna didn't avoid his eyes.

After his men left to begin their evenings carousing she turned to him. 'I don't know how you managed to accomplish that. But I thank you for it.'

'I know my men. They only have eyes for silver.' Removing two silver coins from his cup he handed one each to Cesti and Lulin. 'Buy food and wine for the lady and Zwalia, furs and bedding if you can find them.' Turning to the young boys huddled together in a corner he switched to Latin. 'I will not suffer slaves in my household. You are now free. Serve me and light my brazier, or stand before the lady as her servants. Do you understand?' They all nodded solemnly. 'Then do it now.' Three walked over to Corinna, whilst one trotted after Cesti and Lulin. At least they would all be warm soon.

'You trust your servants with silver?'

'Don't you trust Zwalia?'

'With my life,' she answered, shocked.

Sphax just shrugged. 'I lost all my wealth months ago. I owe them wages.' Sphax strode towards the vestibule entrance then turned to Corinna. 'I need to find out why Hannibal has taken Dasius. To do this I need to speak to my general, Maharbal. Cesti and Lulin will look after you. Wait here. I won't be long.'

But when he returned two hours later the only people sitting on his sleeping couch were Cesti and

PART ONE: The Wounded Consul

Lulin with the four boys between them. No one spoke; it was all too obvious what had happened. At least the brazier had been lit and the chest was where he'd left it. Sighing deeply, he sat beside the brazier and waited for the inevitable summons from his uncle. It was going to be a long night.

Maharbal had once advised him that on some days there were never enough hours in the day to accomplish all the schemes and projects Hannibal's fertile mind could conjure, yet on others, when the bane of Melqart descended and reduced him to black despair, it was unwise to enter his pavilion. As Sphax strode through his uncle's grand pavilion he prepared himself for the latter.

Before him was an all too familiar sight. In the soft light of Greek lamps he saw the three divans placed in a semi-circular position, so their occupants could recline and converse with each other at their ease. Before each was placed a low table with bowls of fruits and cheeses. Each outer divan was occupied by a reclining Greek, propped up on an elbow and swathed from head to sandal in a toga fashioned in the Greek style. Sosylos, a notable philosopher and historian lay to the right, whilst on the left reclined Silenos, Hannibal's private tutor and secretary. Only a fool or an exceptional mind would deem it necessary to take a philosopher and his tutor on campaign with him. And Hannibal was no fool. And this was no mere campaign; it was his destiny, and with it came the responsibility of recording it for all history.

'Why did you not hand Dasius over to me for questioning?' Hannibal was sitting bolt upright on his divan, his brooding expression magnified by the milky cast in his left eye. 'Hannon had instruction to put him under guard in *your* pavilion. Were you deliberately keeping him from me?' The ungrateful wretch, thought Sphax! What about the grain supplies? And the capture of Clastidium? He found it difficult to keep his indignation out of his voice.

'My actions have averted disaster! Without the supplies from Clastidium we would be starving, Sir. Not to mention the fact that a Roman town has been captured without the loss of a single man. I considered the fate of Dasius to be inconsequential, a matter of concern only for the woman he had power over.' Ever the diplomat, the silver-haired Sosylos intervened.

'Your uncle is remiss. He is indeed grateful for the supplies from Clastidium and congratulates you on its capture.' Hannibal shot him a look that would have silenced most men, but the venerable Greek continued. 'But there are other considerations—'

'What considerations?'

'Clastidium is of no strategic importance whatsoever, boy!' If anything his uncle's expression had grown darker and his tone icier.

'Or its grain, apparently!' Sphax responded, acidly. It was Silenos' turn to intervene.

PART ONE: The Wounded Consul

'Grain aside, Sphax, what you unwittingly uncovered in Clastidium goes beyond our immediate situation, or its outcomes. You touched upon a thread that may lead us to a wider realm in our war with Rome. These are the *considerations* that Sosylos is referring to. But without information and knowledge, we cannot hope to see how your thread is wound into the warp and weft of the fates.'

Incomprehension had finally dulled Sphax's anger. 'With great respect, Sir, you are speaking in riddles. What is this thread that I have uncovered?'

'It is not so much the thread itself, but how it may be woven into the greater picture. You know of the Fates. Even the might of Zeus must bow to the Moirai.'

'*Aisa, Clotho and Lachesis, hearken to our prayers, all-terrible goddesses of sky and earth*,' Sphax quoted from a lesson in his boyhood that now seemed a lifetime away. To his astonishment, his uncle was smiling at him.

He would never understand this man. His quicksilver mind could turn in a heartbeat from anger to amusement. Night became day and the stars in the heavens could be made to shine by the light of the sun. His genius was both incomprehensible and disturbing.

'Leave us now, my dear friends, and ask the woman to come forward. What we shall speak of will be painful. The fateful conjunction of two tragedies.'

Suddenly Corinna was standing beside him. His uncle gestured to the empty divans either side of him. 'Bring wine', he said to a servant. In something of a daze, Sphax sat where Silenos had been reclining moments earlier, drained his first cup and asked for it to be refilled. Corinna was staring at the ground, her cup untouched. His uncle cleared his throat.

'I want you to tell this young man your history, lady, as completely as you told it to me not an hour ago. Spare no details, especially Dasius' sordid part in this tale.' For the first time their eyes met, and suddenly Sphax realised how vulnerable and alone she must be feeling at that moment. Bravely, she held his gaze.

'I am the daughter of Queen Teuta,' she began. In that instant every nerve in Sphax's body jolted and he leapt to his feet, spilling wine. Corinna stared at him, suddenly bewildered and a little frightened by his reaction.

'Sit down, Sphax,' Hannibal commanded, 'and stay silent!' Slowly he obeyed, and sank back with his head in his hands. 'Continue, my dear.'

'When Illyria's war with Rome was lost some ten years ago, my mother was forced to abdicate in favour of her late husband's heir, Pinnes, though he was but a child of four at the time. By treaty, Rome banished my mother to the kingdom of Rhizon in the north of Illyria. As is my mother's way, within a year of being left alone by Rome her schemes turned to strengthening her power and influence. I was almost fourteen, at a marriageable age, and so she sought a match with Arsenios of Epidamnos, a Greek city grown rich on sea-trade with Corinth and Rome. We were married within months.

PART ONE: The Wounded Consul

'But when Rome received news of our union, it feared my mother was extending her power. An embassy was sent to her court in Rhizon demanding hostages, and my husband and I were to be amongst them. Threats were made. My mother was given no choice but to comply. So for the next two years my husband and I were held in Rome. We were never mistreated, and lived in some comfort. My husband had some influence with senators and a Praetor named Quintus Fulvius, who was later to become commissioner for the harbours in Brundisium. My husband had extensive knowledge of the sea-trade and commerce between Brundisium and Illyria. He persuaded Fulvius that he could make him rich on this trade. Fulvius managed to persuade the senate to allow us to continue our exile in Brundisium. And that's where my son, Cleon, was born, four years ago.

'That's when our troubles began. The Praetor Fulvius was replaced by another, a vicious and unprincipled man named Lucius Manlius.' Sphax's ears pricked up at this. If anything, Corinna's description was generous. 'In league with two other men, the Greek merchant Dasius, and a petty Roman official called Lucanus Flavius, Manlius began to take control of the merchant fleet and commerce that my husband had established. All the wealth we had accumulated in the hope that one day it would buy our freedom and passage to a distant land was stolen from us on the pretext of commissions and taxes. Silver was demanded for new vessels and warehouses, none of which, of course, were built. Then the three of them plotted the murder of my husband. Though I have no absolute proof of this, I am convinced of their guilt.

'If he took an oath to return within the month, my husband would be allowed to board a vessel bound for Epidamnos. Even in the time of our friendship with Quintus Fulvius, we were never permitted to set foot aboard a ship. I smelt a trap, begged and pleaded for him not to go. But Epidamnos was his home, his kingdom, and he hadn't seen his mother and father for years ...' Corinna trailed off, and stared at the floor for a moment before she regained her composure.

'His ship never returned. It was blamed on pirates, but his ship had an escort, which did return. By now I was in despair, my position hopeless. That is, until I discovered their new enterprise. Manlius had told them vast fortunes were being made in Liguria, where Rome's recent conquests of the Gauls had opened up new territories ripe for trade in slaves, wine and grain. Allies were needed to garrison these new settlements and supply the legions. Taxes could be gathered with impunity, trade in wine and grain from the south would fill their coffers, and Manlius promised slaves by the hundred. All Dasius had to do was raise a contingent from Brundisium to garrison one of these settlements. Greed did the rest. When Manlius was summoned north to command against the uprising of the Boii, he arranged for Dasius' contingent to garrison Clastidium.

PART ONE: The Wounded Consul

'It was then that I decided this was the best means of escape for myself and my son. In Brundisium every ship's captain and crew knew me by sight, none could be bribed or would take the risk of stowing me on board, and besides, I was constantly watched. But from Clastidium I could easily enter Gaul, or travel to Genua, where a ship would take me to Massilia, a Greek colony where I would be safe.

'I used my charms on Dasius, which wasn't difficult: from the moment he first saw me I could see the desire and lust in his eyes. I'm certain he was the instigator of the plan to murder my husband. The rest was easy. But I underestimated how scheming and malicious he could be. His character is the type that must have power over those around him so as to control and manipulate them. Just before we were due to sail for Ariminum, his men forced their way on board and forcibly took Cleon from me. Dasius told me he would be held by one of his stewards in Brundisium until our return. And if ever I disobeyed him, I would never see my child alive again. The rest of my story you know.'

'Have you any reason to suppose that Dasius' steward would harm your son in any way?' Hannibal asked.

'No, I have not. As long as my son lives, Rome has Queen Teuta's grandson as hostage, and Dasius has a guarantee of my compliance.'

'Then we should assume that your son is alive and well.'

'I pray so, Sir.'

'Then it is now time for me to tell you a story, lady,' gazing meaningfully at Sphax, 'a story equally full of tragedy that I would not trust another to tell it. It concerns your mother's war with Rome some ten years ago.' There was now no doubt in Sphax's mind what that story was. But why was he telling Corinna this? What could possibly be gained from it, except knowledge of yet more grief? He'd never told Corinna that he was Hannibal's nephew. She had no idea that her interrogator was his uncle.

'When the war in Illyria went badly for your mother, she called for aid, sending out embassies to Macedon, Crete and Carthage, begging that all Rome's enemies unite behind her standard. Her pleas fell on deaf ears in Macedon and Crete, but in Carthage they were welcomed. Illyrian envoys were allowed to speak to the Council of Three Hundred and the people's senate.

'At the time my father was gravely wounded in battle, and my brothers and I were at his sickbed in Iberia. None from my family played any part in the fateful decisions that were taken by the Council. But in that great chamber, it was decided to send an embassy to Queen Teuta to negotiate Carthaginian aid in ships and men, and in view of the magnitude of this mission, the Council chose a representative of the highest standing in the land. That man was Prince Navaras, my brother-in-law, a man beloved by my father who regarded him as a son. Accompanying Navaras was his wife and young son. His wife was Similce, my dearest sister.

'With a recklessness bordering on madness, Carthage sent out its envoy on a merchant ship without escorts. Off the island of Corcyra the vessel was intercepted by a Roman fleet and boarded. When they discovered Navaras and my sister on board, it soon became clear what their mission to Illyria was. Rome was handed a great gift. By blaming what happened next on the work of Illyrian pirates, Rome blackened the name of Queen Teuta so that no ally would ever again come to her aid. As for Carthage? Your mother would be viewed as nothing less than a treacherous serpent. Either way, Rome profited, so on the orders of Flaminius Nepos, the noble Navaras and my dearest sister were brutally murdered. Their son, a boy of seven, was made to witness the death of his mother, then spared for the life of a miserable slave in Rome. Their ship was fired and cast adrift.' By now Corinna was staring wide-eyed at Hannibal.

'When news of this reached my father in Iberia, he died within the hour. I believe the shock killed him just as surely as the wound to his chest.' Even his uncle had to pause at that moment and collect his thoughts. Eventually he continued.

'But the story does not end there. Last year, that miserable slave in Rome managed to throw off his shackles and escape. By the will of Melqart he reached my camp beside the Rhodanus, and I rejoice to say that he's been my faithful companion since that day.

'That slave is sitting beside me. He is my nephew, Sphax.'

For what seemed an eternity of silence, Corinna just stared at him. He'd never seen such sadness on a face so noble and beautiful, and in that moment his heart went out to her, and also in that moment, his heart was lost.

'All this!' she cried, 'because of my mother's foolish war.'

'From all the wickedness that flowed from these events,' Sphax said gently, 'you are innocent and blameless, and you have suffered as much as any.'

Throughout this exchange Hannibal had remained silent and watchful. Now he closed his eyes and spoke of the thread that had been uppermost in his thoughts throughout the revelations he'd forced Corinna to listen to. That fatal thread woven by the Moirai, as Silenos had observed, into the warp and weft of a greater picture. As his uncle continued, Sphax slowly began to read his uncle's intentions, and they had nothing to do with personal grief and loss; such expressions were foreign to him. Subtly, the thread would be woven by obligation, hatred and revenge, and her reward would be the only thing she desired: the return of her son.

'War is always uncertain, even the gods cannot foresee its consequences. What *is* certain, is that all the evil that has flowed as a consequence of Illyria's war

PART ONE: The Wounded Consul

can be laid at the door of our mutual enemy. Queen Teuta did not butcher my sister and her husband, or abandon my nephew to slavery. Your mother did not offer hostages. Rome demanded them! Rome is the cesspit of all this iniquity, whilst its citizens are schooled and seasoned in its greed and depravity. No, lady, it was not Manlius or Flavius that murdered your husband in cold blood. It was Rome! And it is Rome that holds the knife at your son's throat.

'Carthage has at last answered Queen Teuta's call for allies. Here we stand ready to rally once more behind her standards. This is not the time for you or your mother to lament Illyria's war with Rome. Illyria must rise up again and avenge these injustices, and your son must be restored to his rightful place on the throne. Only the grandson of Queen Teuta is the rightful heir to Illyria, not this puppet that Rome parades before your people.'

'I'm grateful, Sir,' she began, 'for this broader view of our ill-fated war with Rome, and some of its tragic consequences. Ignorance should never become a shield to hide behind, however painful the truth is to bear. But you place me in an impossible position. My son and I are still hostages of Rome. If it became known that I was in the camp of Rome's greatest enemy, and there of my own free will, my son's life would be forfeit.'

'Quite so, my dear. At all times your true identity must remain unknown, a secret. That is why I'm placing you under the protection of my nephew. He will make sure that your true identity goes unnoticed. Tongues will wag that he's acquired a new woman, no more than that. The men from Brundisium will be treated well, but remain in camp. The creature Dasius remains a problem, but he may prove useful to us, so he will also remain my captive under guard. But this I swear, when the legions of Rome have been driven from Liguria, I will send men to recover your son and restore him to his rightful place at your side.'

'Then I will be in your debt, Sir.'

* * * *

'What do you think?' The question was rhetorical. Maharbal didn't need Adherbal, or Sphax for that matter, to point out the obvious. 'Well!' he insisted.

Adherbal, sitting astride his mare beside Sphax just grinned, inviting his fellow captain to be the first to receive their general's ridicule that morning. All three were gazing at the Roman encampment of Consul Scipio, not two miles distant on the plains beside the river. Sphax just wanted to get this over with. It was so cold that every breath was forming a white fog before his eyes.

'A battle here offers no advantage to either side, save that a flank could be protected by the Padus. But the other flank would be wide open and exposed. Otherwise, it's as flat and unremarkable as the desert, Sir.' As Sphax spoke another biting squall of sleet lashed their faces.

PART ONE: The Wounded Consul

'How I would welcome the heat of the desert this morning!' groaned Maharbal, tightening his cloak. 'It is agreed, then. We fight here today.'

Ignoring the chorus of 'why' from his two captains, the general merely eased his mare around and headed back to camp. Sphax threw a questioning look at Adherbal, but his friend just shrugged, so they meekly fell in behind Maharbal, no wiser from their two hour reconnaissance spent in the biting cold and drenching sleet.

There was a welcoming gathering waiting for them outside Hannibal's pavilion. Warming themselves around a brace of campfires were every general of importance in the army, including the giant Libyan, Hanno, whose phalanxes of pikemen were its bedrock. Something told him that Maharbal had not been joking.

The three of them dismounted and Maharbal approached Hannibal. Sphax couldn't hear what was said, but it must have been brief, for within moments his uncle strode to the centre of the gathering to address them all.

'Today we offer Consul Scipio battle. If he's any sense he will refuse, but by doing so he will be made to look weak and fearful, and this is my intention. We must show the Insubres and Boii that we are strong and eager for battle.

'My informants tell me that the two legions of Consul Sempronius Longus are still days away, but they are moving fast, so we must act now, before Scipio is reinforced. Your men should anoint themselves with what oil can be spared to keep out the cold. They may wear every stitch of clothing they possess, as long as it doesn't impede their ability to fight. I myself will direct our forces as they arrive on the battleground. We march within the hour, and may the gods favour us.'

When Sphax informed his eshrin, it met with a chorus of groans.

'Scipio might be a Roman, Sir, but he's not a complete arsewit,' grumbled Hannon, chief of the bellyachers. 'He'll never take the bait! Which means we'll be sitting our mares all day, freezing our bollocks off.'

'It's only since you came into silver and can afford whores, Hannon, that you've worried about your bollocks.' At least this drew half-hearted laughter from his men. But Hannon had been right. By the time they arrived back at camp eight hours later, every man felt dispirited, chilled to the bone and dripping wet from a day of driving sleet. From where they'd stood for hours in massed ranks, or astride horses on that windswept plain, they could see the smoke rising from Roman campfires. Scipio had no appetite for a pitched battle on an open plain that offered him no advantage. For the first time, the men of Carthage envied their enemies and praised their good sense.

For Sphax, the only excitement came when Maharbal ordered forward some of his eshrins to investigate four squadrons of Roman equites that had ridden from their camp to see what all the fuss was about. At least their Numidians had been able to relieve the boredom by jeering at them for a while. Other than lone horsemen, that was all Sphax saw of the enemy that day. The real warfare was taking place back in his pavilion, albeit at a subtler level.

'Let me take another look at that wound of yours, my little dove?' For the life of him, Sphax couldn't understand why Corinna had taken up the endearment, 'little dove,' to keep up the pretence that they were lovers. It grated on him. He'd wanted to retaliate with 'little princess,' but this might have hinted at her true status, so he'd settled on 'little mouse,' which didn't have the same ring to it in the Greek tongue, but still irritated her. They'd maintained this war of endearments since leaving his uncle's pavilion two nights ago. Both of them knew it was utterly childish, but it was easier to play this game than acknowledge any deeper feelings they might have for one another.

'The wound's fine, little mouse,' he countered whilst moving the chair draped with his beaverskin cloak nearer the brazier. 'I'm on guard with my men this evening, so until Jugurtha arrives to summon me I'm not moving from this fire.' His teeth hadn't stopped chattering since entering the pavilion.

'I gather that Rome didn't play Hannibal's little game today?' Corinna asked, without attempting to hide her broad grin.

'I wouldn't describe sitting on your arse whilst the heavens piss on you as a *game*.'

'Well, whatever you call it, Scipio won't play until he's been reinforced by the legions of Longus. Then Hannibal will be outnumbered. What game will your uncle play then?'

'The same, I dare say,' he answered, slipping on a dry pair of Gaulish leggings that Lulin had found for him.

'To fight when outnumbered on ground that offers no advantage is foolish.'

'But we will not be outnumbered, at least not in cavalry.'

'Cavalry alone don't win battles.'

'No,' he countered firmly, 'but they do *decide* them.'

'When Longus arrives, Rome's numbers in cavalry will double. They will still be outnumbered, but it may be enough to cancel out your advantage.' If there was one thing he'd learned about Corinna, it was that she didn't like to lose an argument. And there had been a good many since they'd shared his pavilion. She was clever, could read and write, and unpick an argument quicker than he could tie a throwing thong on a javelin. And her education was far more extensive than the secretive lessons he'd received from his Greek teacher Elpis, when a slave in Rome.

'They would need four times that number. Even then we would rout them.' He slipped a clean tunic over his head and turned to face her. 'My eshrin, alongside Astegal's, not only wounded Scipio but finished off most of his squadron with one charge. Just one charge, Corinna! We have over three thousand Numidians, and when they get into the rear of an army, any army, be it Roman, Macedonian or Illyrian, make no mistake that army will flee for their lives.' Sphax was pleased to see she'd fallen silent.

All too soon Jugurtha arrived to summon him. This wasn't a duty he was looking forward to, but the rainclouds had drifted north, and the later part of the night was quiet and uneventful. The job of a captain on sentry duty was mostly to ensure that his men stayed awake, but in such intense cold, sleep was impossible anyway. When they'd crossed the snowbound Alps, he'd been told that if you did go to sleep in such cold, it would be your last, for you would wake in Hades.

Most of his time was spent relieving men who were some distance from a campfire, giving them the opportunity to warm themselves for a few moments before resuming their positions. It must have been well after midnight when Jubal approached him.

'I think I can hear something, Sir,' he said anxiously, 'come and listen.' Sphax followed Jubal to the watchtower platform at the eastern gate and climbed the few steps to the top.

Nothing. Just leaden darkness and the occasional glimpse of the silvered waters of the Padus when the moon emerged from behind cloud.

'Listen, Sir!' pleaded Jubal. Yes, it was faint, but there was something. Sphax almost fell down the steps as he charged through the gate. After two hundred strides he'd left all the night-time sounds of the camp behind. He stopped, stock still, and listened. Yes, he could hear it clearly now. It was the pounding of marching feet and hoof beats. Thousands of them.

The perimeter of their camp was fortified with stakes driven into the ground and ditches protected the three gates, but a camp was a temporary settlement, never intended to be a fortress. He knew that attacks on them were rare, but not unknown. And usually under cover of darkness.

He sprinted back to the gate.

'Sound the alarm!' Sphax screamed. 'The enemy is coming. We are attacked!'

FIVE

Even as he ran back through the gate a fearful din had broken out all around him; bells and gongs were clanging, men yelled for weapons or charged around in confusion. Sphax climbed the platform and shouted above the racket, 'Send men to the pavilions. Summon Hannibal and the generals. My eshrin outside the gate. Now!' He saw an Iberian officer trying to assemble his men. 'Caetra to the gate. Defend the gate!'

Rushing down the steps he joined his men beyond the ditch. 'Step forward ten paces and form a line, javelins ready.' It was so dark they could hardly see one another, let alone an enemy. But they could hear them. And they were drawing closer.

'One javelin, then we run back through that gate!' he said, knowing this to be nothing more than a futile gesture of defiance. Someone laid a hand on his shoulder and he turned to see Idwal standing beside him.

'Something's wrong. Legionaries would have charged swiftly into the attack, not tramped through the night making this fearful racket.' Instantly, Sphax knew Idwal was right. If it was an attack, they had already thrown away their most potent weapon; that of surprise.

'Go back and bring torches. All of you. Go!' Judging from the noise of tramping feet, Sphax guessed they must only be three or four hundred paces away, but the darkness was so impenetrable there was no way of telling. His men began to return, holding aloft flaming brands. He and Idwal grabbed one each. 'Let's find out what's going on, Idwal,' and Sphax strode forward into the darkness.

'I'm not sure that's a good idea ...' sighed Idwal, but he still followed his friend.

By the dim light of their torches, within sixty paces they began to make out what faced them, and as more of his men joined him holding their torches aloft, at last they saw clearly. Ahead of them was a vast horde of Gauls. Hundreds, if not thousands of them. All carried great shields, many spears, but swords were sheathed in their scabbards. They carried something else in their other hand. Two men came forward to speak.

'I am Maguno of the Boii, and this is Artos of the Insubres. We have slaughtered our Roman paymasters this night and marched from Scipio's camp. We wish to swear allegiance to Hannibal. Take us to him.'

Idwal stepped forward and answered them in the Gaulish tongue. Whatever he said brought a rousing cheer from the Gauls. 'Come, Sphax, spread out your men in a line to light the way back to our camp for our new allies. Maguno and Artos have brought over a thousand warriors to our cause.'

Beyond the ditch, the gate and platform were now bathed in torchlight. Sphax saw his uncle standing beside Hanno, flanked by dense phalanxes of Libyans, pikes held erect. So the Gauls would understand, Sphax spoke grandly in Latin.

'Maguno of the Boii wishes to speak to you, Sir. Will you hear him?' Maguno didn't wait for an answer.

'Tonight we cast off our Roman paymasters. Rome is weak! From this day forth we swear allegiance to Hannibal and our people.' Hannibal raised his arms.

'Months ago, Carthage solemnly swore before our gods and your chieftains to fight shoulder-to-shoulder in your struggle against Rome. My army is here to honour that sacred pledge. Long have the Boii and Insubres been our brothers-in-arms. Welcome, my brothers!'

During the cheering that followed, scores of warriors stepped forward and tossed into the ditch what they'd carried from the Roman camp. Soon the ditch began to fill with the severed heads of Roman legionaries.

* * * *

The next day he woke to that rare event in this winter of winters: bright sunlight shining from a peerless blue sky. Maharbal had given his eshrin a day of rest following their sentry duty, so Sphax suggested to Corinna they ride together.

For the past few days he'd felt his pavilion had been taken over by women. It had been so wet and cold that he hadn't the heart to turn out Cesti and Lulin to their miserable little tent, and with the addition of the four servant boys, Corinna, and her maid Zwalia, he'd felt outnumbered and surrounded. To his astonishment, language didn't seem to present a problem for these women. Cesti and Lulin, raised in Iberian Numancia, spoke only their native Keltoi tongue and bad Punic, whilst Corinna and Zwalia spoke only Latin and Greek. Though Corinna stood somewhat aloof from all this, the pavilion resounded with laughter and shrill treble voices. How could this be, he'd wondered?

Cesti and Lulin were particularly fascinated by Corinna's toilet, which they watched every morning, spellbound and entranced. First Zwalia would dress her mistress in her stola and arrange a suitable belt. Next came the combs, brushes, mirrors, face creams and perfumes. Combing through Corinna's lustrous raven curls seemed to take longer than Sphax spent grooming Dido.

And usually, by that stage of the proceedings he'd already been asked several times if he hadn't got better things to do than gawp at a woman having her hair brushed. When Corinna thought Zwalia was not looking, she would pull faces at him, arch her eyebrows or stick out her tongue, none of which had the intention she desired — quite the opposite; it only made him *more* attentive. When all Zwalia's efforts of combing and brushing had achieved perfection, she draped her mistress's entire head and shoulders in a palla that hid every combed curl and most of her beautiful face.

That morning, Idwal had arrived early in the midst of this routine to tell him that Hannibal's pavilion was besieged by Gaulish envoys pledging loyalty, and that many of last night's converts had been sent back to their villages to enlist more support for their cause. 'It's beginning,' he'd said, 'in a week we'll have ten thousand more men, and nothing to fear when Longus arrives.' Corinna had suddenly risen from her toilet to point out that Rome still held Placentia and Cremona, and Boii lands lay far to the south of these strongholds. Idwal was adamant. 'They will come,' he'd told her confidently.

After the false alarm they'd provided the previous night and the sight of hundreds of bloodied heads being tossed into that ditch, Sphax was heartily sick of the Boii and Insubres. Gazing up at the clear blue sky and the first warmth he'd felt in weeks, the only thoughts in his head that morning were of a day of peace spent in the company of Corinna.

Gazing up at the sunlight, it seemed Corinna had the same thought. Unfolding her palla, she tossed it to Zwalia and called for her crimson riding cape. With the sunlight catching her raven curls and sparkling from those hazel eyes, he thought she looked radiant that morning. 'Shall we ride together today, Sphax?'

'I would enjoy that ... but where?' he asked.

'You choose. It's so lovely that all I need today is my stallion.' Sphax hoped not.

'In that case let's ride south. I find the country around Clastidium pleasant, and there's an Anamares settlement where we would be welcomed with refreshment. A remarkable elder lives there named Garos. You should meet him.'

Even the drear featureless landscape south of the Padus looked easier on the eye in the sunshine, and as the woodland increased they began to flush bustard and woodcock, and the air came alive with the cackling of jays. He plucked up the courage to ask questions that had been puzzling him. 'Why do you submit yourself every morning to Zwalia's toilet, when I know you're completely indifferent to any sort of fashion? Your eyebrow-raising and face- pulling testify to this.'

'No they don't!' she replied tartly. 'If I didn't have you gawping disapproval at me I would happily close my eyes and abandon myself to this innocent pleasure. Like me, sometimes Zwalia feels lost and cast adrift. She has dressed me and tended my hair since I was seven years old. It is a routine that is familiar and comforting to us both, and it makes Zwalia feel useful and valued. 'Besides,' she added, looking him up and down, 'what about you?'

'What about me?'

'Here we are on this glorious morning, riding for our leisure, and yet you still feel the need to strap a sword to your back and carry a clutch of javelins.'

PART ONE: The Wounded Consul

'It's still part of my training,' he confessed. 'My javelin teacher insists upon it.'

'You still have a javelin teacher?' she cried, laughing.

'Of course! He's called Dubal, but he only refers to me as his arsewit. His breath alone would fell a man at ten paces and he's the ugliest Numidian you'll ever meet.' Trying to keep a straight face he added, 'I'm very fond of old Dubal. Don't you have a javelin teacher? I thought everyone had one.' When she'd stopped laughing, Corinna pointed to a copse of birch trees in the distance.

'See those trees?'

'Yes,' he replied, puzzled.

'Race you!' And like an arrow she sped off. Sphax hadn't a hope of catching her stallion, and so it proved. By the time Dido arrived panting amidst the birches, Corinna had her arms folded beneath her bosom and was smirking. 'It's not just a javelin teacher you need, my little dove—'

'And it's not just a saddle, bit and reins that *you* need, but the advantage of a bigger horse!' He smiled. 'One day I will teach you to ride without inflicting such instruments of torture on that poor creature of yours.'

Corinna's expression changed, and she looked seriously at him. 'Do you think such a day will ever come?'

'I hope so,' he answered equally seriously, but then shaped a smile, adding, 'if only for the sake of your stallion.'

'I hope so too,' she said, without returning his smile.

When they came within sight of the Anamares settlement his reception could not have been more different from that of a few days before. This time arms were raised in greeting, beckoning them forward. Garos was summoned from his roundhouse, led forward by the young lad who'd wielded the hunting horn. Sphax embraced the grey-haired old man and helped to settle him in a chair that had been set for him.

'I have brought a friend to meet you, Sir.' And sticking to the story they'd agreed, 'May I present Corinna, she is journeying to her family in Massilia.'

'Let me see you, child.' Which struck Sphax as a strange thing for a blind man to say.

Corinna came forward, and for an instant there was a flicker of revulsion as she saw the terrible mutilation that had been inflicted on the elder's eyes. But it lasted for less than a heartbeat. Kneeling before his outstretched hands, she allowed herself to be *seen* through his sensitive fingers, beginning with the folds of her hair and continuing from her forehead to her generous lips and chin.

'If I was a young warrior, I believe I would risk the wrath of Morrigu herself to win your favour. Come sit beside me, my dear,' and a chair was found for her at his right hand.

Sphax turned to a handsome, fair-haired woman who he knew to be Garos' daughter. 'I have a small gift for your villagers in these hard times,' he said, untying

PART ONE: The Wounded Consul

the ropes that secured a sack of wheat to Dido's rump. 'It's not much,' he added, apologetically.

'For many in this village, this is a great gift, Sphax, and I thank you for it,' a broad smile lighting up her face. 'You do not know my name, do you?'

'I know you to be Garos' daughter, madam, but not your name.'

'I am Artula,' and in the Gaulish fashion of greeting, she warmly enfolded each of his forearms in hers, clasping him below his elbows so they faced each other eye to eye. 'You have already met my son, Meilyr. He plays the horn fit to wake the dead.' By now benches and chairs had been removed from roundhouses and placed in a semi-circle either side of Garos. Artula took a seat at her father's left hand and Sphax sat beside her. He almost dared not ask, but knew he must.

'And what of your husband, is he safe in these warlike times?'

'The Anamares know only warlike times, Sphax. As for my husband, you may meet him sooner than I, for he is gathering men for Hannibal. When he arrives at your camp, I will join him and take my son.'

'Then I hope it will be soon, for your sake, and ours. We need every Gaul who can fight, though last night a thousand Boii and Insubres deserted their Roman masters and swore to Hannibal.'

Artula's eyes lit up at this. 'More will follow, including my husband, but he will only bring fifty at most, not thousands.'

'They will be more than welcome.' Young women brought bread, wine and baskets of fruit, giggling and fussing over Sphax. Artula gave him a wry smile and shooed them away with a Gaulish word he didn't quite catch.

'It's lucky you brought a woman with you, young man; with all these young hinds in season I would fear for your safety.' He began to blush.

'It's only because they haven't seen anyone my age for a long time,' he said quickly to hide his embarrassment. Looking around, he was indeed the only eligible man in sight. This was a village of old men, women and children. Every man of an age to wield a weapon had long since drifted north, to lick his wounds and gather his strength. 'Your menfolk are biding their time and sharpening their swords, Artula. They will be back.'

Artula still had that teasing smile playing around her lips. 'She is very beautiful, Sphax. Is she your woman?'

'Yes, and no,' he said, avoiding her eyes.

Artula's smile broadened. 'You mean *yes*, you would like her to be, and *no*, not yet?'

'Exactly so, madam.' He could hear Corinna's laughter and easy conversation with Garos. Somehow he found it irritating. To avoid further questioning from Artula, he pointedly gazed out at the grassland beyond the village. The warmth of the sun had melted the hoarfrost that morning, giving the withered grass an almost spring-like appearance. Idly

PART ONE: The Wounded Consul

he watched a young boy or girl, it was impossible to distinguish at that distance, running towards the village. Moments passed before Sphax realised there was something urgent about the child's movements. He got to his feet and stared. The child wasn't running, it was fleeing. He could now make out horsemen on the horizon, bearing down on the child. Maharbal had not sent out patrols that morning. They could be only one thing.

'Roman cavalry are coming,' he shouted. 'Go back to your houses and stay there. They have no reason to harm you if we leave and stay out of sight.' Sphax glared at Corinna, who hadn't moved from her chair. 'Come, Corinna!' he yelled, running towards the track that led to the settlement. Summoning Dido with a shrill whistle he heard Corinna do the same for her stallion. Soon they were astride their horses and galloping at full stretch for a patch of woodland half a mile away. Plunging into the trees, Sphax eased the mare to a walk and only brought her to a halt when they entered a thicket, deep inside the wood. Dismounting, he glanced up at Corinna still astride her stallion. 'Wait here,' he said.

'Not a chance!' she said defiantly. All Sphax could do was shrug. This wasn't a time for argument. Cautiously they both crept back to the edge of the woodland and found a patch of dense undergrowth in which to hide. Their view of the settlement was partially obscured by isolated trees and folds in the land, but the top of each roundhouse was clearly visible, and short of climbing a tree, this was the best they could hope for.

'It could be a patrol searching for that shipment of grain from Clastidium,' he whispered.

'Possibly. How many did you see?'

'About ten. Which means there'll be a decurion in charge.'

'They have no reason to harm the villagers, have they?' she asked anxiously.

'They're Romans, they don't *need* a reason. Let's pray they take what they want and leave them alone.' The wind had dropped and a deathly quiet had descended. If anything went wrong at least they would hear it, even if they couldn't see it. He found himself fingering his ivory image of Artemis. Time passed. He crouched, listening intently, his senses as taut as a bowstring. He was beginning to hope, to think all would be well, that the cavalry would leave without incident.

'By the gods ... no!' groaned Corinna.' Sphax looked up to see the thatch of a roundhouse burst into flames. Then he could hear it clearly: even though the voices were over half a mile away, they rang through his head and sickened him. The screaming had begun.

'Savages!' he yelled, now beside himself and flushed with rage. He stood up and let out a shrill whistle. Corinna guessed what he was about to do, got to her feet and gripped his arm.

'No, Sphax, NO!' she pleaded. 'There are ten of them. They'll kill you.' Sphax ignored her and whistled again, louder this time. Corinna gripped his arm more fiercely.

'Let go of me, woman!' he yelled as Dido crashed through the undergrowth and stood beside him.

'You can't save them! I beg you Sphax, please ...' viciously wrenching his arm free he leapt onto his mare, slapping her on the rump so she set off at high speed back to the settlement.

He had no plan. He needed no plan. His long hatred of Rome and white-hot rage would be enough. He had but one thought in his head, which he repeated like a litany, over and over again; I have four javelins and one saunion, make them count ... make every one count!

By now Dido was thundering towards the open space in the settlement where they had gathered beside Garos. One of the benches had not been removed and lay directly across his path. Beyond it he saw several cavalrymen hauling villagers from their huts. His javelin was raised and poised. Tightening the throwing thong he let Dido choose her leaping stride over the bench and fixed his eye upon the chest and shoulder of his first enemy. Within a stride his javelin had flown. There was no knowing whether it had *counted* or not. Flashing past, he got fleeting glimpses of startled faces frozen in fear before he was on the grassland beyond the settlement, turning Dido for another pass.

His enemy were no better prepared for his second charge. None of them had time to gather shield or spear before Sphax was amongst them. Once again, he was riding at such speed that other than an exposed throat above a red cloak, his impressions were fleeting, but he did see something slumped on the ground, stained in blood. As the bench was at least some sort of obstacle between himself and his enemies, he deliberately chose to jump it for a second time, after which he leant back on Dido's rump to bring her to a trot and turn her round. At last his mind overcame his rage.

Halting his mare on the track as it entered the settlement he could now see four equites on foot barring his path with shields and raised spears. None of the others it seemed had mounted their horses. He guessed the rest of them were still inside houses. There were now two limp bodies on the ground. So far he hadn't wasted a javelin. Where were their horses, he wondered? He'd never examined the settlement closely before. Now he did, but all it consisted of was six wooden roundhouses set either side of an avenue along which he'd charged, and where the shield-wall of four now stood. Only the thatch on one of the houses was burning, set alight by a flaming torch. An eerie silence had descended on the place. He needed to remedy that, and let the Anamares know they hadn't been abandoned.

Making sure he had his next javelin tied and readied, Sphax nudged Dido forward to confront the Romans barring his path. When he was twenty paces away he glared contemptuously and shouted, 'I am Sphax, Prince of Numidia. I stuck a javelin in that cocksucker you call

PART ONE: The Wounded Consul

consul and would have slain his bastard son if he hadn't run like a rabbit!' He suddenly dug his knees into Dido's flanks, and as she reared up, enjoyed watching the four of them take a fearful step backwards.

'You are all dead men,' he yelled. 'Surrender, you pieces of weasel shit, you Roman arsewits, before I stick a javelin up your arse!'

This stirred things up considerably! But he was almost caught off guard. Without any warning two horsemen emerged from behind a roundhouse and bore down on him. Sphax had just enough time to turn Dido and head back up the avenue towards the bench. His heart was in his mouth as he urged the mare to jump again, but she had just enough momentum to clear it. But his Roman pursuers had no such luck; they had the speed and momentum, but none of his skill.

The first stallion caught a leading hoof on the way over and sprawled to the ground, throwing its rider some distance. Sphax winced at the sound of breaking bones. He would have to put both out of their misery when all this was over. If he lived that long. Close behind, the second stallion made it over, but its rider landed so badly that for the next few strides all he could do was cling to his saddle in a desperate attempt to stay upright, not the best position in which to fend off a scything stroke from Sphax's Gaulish blade. Four down, and he'd been spared two javelins. The odds were improving, and he'd collected two spears into the bargain.

Nudging Dido around, he halted her by the upturned bench and taunted his enemies in triumph, 'Come out and fight, you spineless bastards! Come to Sphax and die on his blade!'

An extraordinary thing happened next. Artula and her son Meilyr dashed out of Garos' roundhouse carrying another bench. Whilst the boy returned the first bench to its upright position, the mother dragged out two chairs and placed them between the benches.

'Run Artula!' Sphax yelled. 'Take your son and run for the woods.' Artula must have been watching the fight from her hut and having seen two equites defeated by a simple bench, realised the usefulness of such a barrier, any barrier that placed an object between himself and his enemies. Sphax was grateful. The Romans that were left would have to learn to jump, or die in the attempt.

At last he heard hoof-beats. They were coming from his left, behind the huts. Rather than ride out and face them in the open he had a better idea. Forcing Dido through the gap between the chairs he nudged her to the walk, halting in the middle of the avenue whilst tying his next javelin. Whichever direction the enemy came from, he would force them to face that wooden barrier. By focusing all their attention on him, he figured it might also buy enough time for Artula and her son to escape. And there they were. Four of them, facing him on horseback, where he'd sat astride Dido moments before on the other

PART ONE: The Wounded Consul

side of the barrier. He couldn't help smiling at their predicament.

'Jump it, you arsewits!' he taunted. But he had absolutely no control over what happened next. Only Morrigu could have foreseen it.

Out of the roundhouse where Artula and her son had emerged strode Garos, looking magnificent in his full armour. He was armed with a spear and carried a great Gaulish shield emblazoned with white circles and golden scrolls. His polished helmet glinted in the sunlight and reflected on his coat of mail that stretched to a skirt about his thighs. For an instant the equites froze and stared at this perfect vision of a warrior Gaul. Then they raised their spears.

By that time Sphax was racing for the wooden benches, pacing Dido's jump. Garos had taken away all his options and left him with no choice. Once her hooves were solidly grounded he let the javelin fly at the cavalryman nearest the old man. Again, Dido's momentum carried him well beyond Garos and his assailants, so he had no idea whether his javelin found its mark or not, but a glance over his shoulder told him that he now had three of them on his tail. He was happy to lead them as far away from Garos as possible. After ten more strides he eased Dido to a trot, slid lithely from her rump and waited for her to turn, his fourth and last javelin already tied and knotted around his fingers.

Then everything happened so suddenly he was barely able to take it in. As he leapt astride Dido to face

The Winter of Winters

his pursuers something shot past him at high speed. He was dimly aware of a white sinuous shape, the sound of thunderous hooves and a cloak billowing in the wind like a crimson sail. An arm flexed and flashed something through the air. Sphax watched as one of his pursuers slumped in the saddle as the crimson horsewoman thundered past the stunned equites in the direction of Garos.

For one more cavalryman, this proved to be his undoing, for when Sphax came within javelin range, both had been so startled by what had just happened they'd reined in their stallions to a walk, ensuring he couldn't miss. Now there was only his saunion left.

Galloping after Corinna he saw her rein in her stallion before she reached Garos. Two Romans had beaten her to it, and judging from his plumed helmet, one of them was their leader, the decurion. In despair Sphax watched helplessly as Garos' mighty shield rose and fell for the last time.

Once more rage coursed through his veins and consumed him. He hardly noticed Corinna beside him astride her stallion, pleading he give her his sword. His only thought now was his saunion. It had been a precious gift from Maharbal himself. A forearm longer than his wooden javelins, it was cast from Iberian iron and tipped with a square barb that was said to resemble the fabled Egyptian pyramids. It had already slain fearsome Allobroges warriors, now it would pierce the black heart of the Roman decurion that had needlessly taken the life of a blind old man, a great hero and warrior of Gaul, the last of his line.

'Sphax, give me your sword,' she yelled. 'I'm unarmed!' Without a sideways glance he frantically unstrapped the belt and handed the sheathed sword to her before threading his saunion. He was ready.

There were now three equites facing him in a ragged line, his third javelin had only wounded, not slain, and the man was making good his escape. But Sphax only had eyes for that scarlet tasselled helmet of the decurion. He nudged Dido forward and allowed her to pick up her own pace.

When the decurion realised what was coming, he levelled his spear and urged his stallion to charge. But it was too late, by that time Dido was galloping flat-out and Sphax had his saunion raised and poised to fly. The decurion's round shield covered most of his upper body, but there was a small area exposed below his right shoulder where a silver brooch pinned his scarlet cloak. Sphax held his breath and aimed for the brooch.

Garos, now in the arms of Morrigu, had been avenged. Sphax's saunion had been flung at such speed and with such force that it had gone clean through the decurion's chest and emerged through a shoulder blade, propelling him backwards from his mount. Quickly checking Dido's momentum he turned, horrified to see Corinna confronting two equites astride her grey stallion, her Gaulish blade flashing and parrying with such speed and skill he realised how deadly it could be in the hands of someone who could wield it so gracefully. After a spear was sliced in two it was over in moments with a simple thrust and a scything stroke to an unguarded throat. Mightily relieved, Sphax rode over to her.

'I've failed you and Garos,' she blurted out, 'I rode out to help you, then saw Artula and the boy running towards me. I had to get them to safety, and when I returned …' her voice trailed and faltered, 'it was too late …'

'There was nothing either of us could have done to save Garos. He chose his fate, Corinna, he chose Morrigu rather than a lingering death as an old man on his sickbed, a warrior's death … a noble death. He lived by the sword and wanted only to die by it.' Sphax caught sight of the wounded eques beyond the settlement, heading eastwards as best he could. He was about to nudge Dido around when Corinna placed a hand on his arm.

'Leave him,' she pleaded, 'there's been enough killing.' Looking directly into his eyes, still wild and feral from the savagery, she smiled gently, soothingly. 'Come, take back your magnificent sword and sheathe it. Let it sleep, for now.' At last he felt calm enough to return her smile.

'I will. But only in your hands does it deserve to be called a sword, in mine it's no better than a useless stick.'

'You do yourself an injustice, Sphax. I've never seen such courage and skill.' Then she spoiled it with

PART ONE: The Wounded Consul

her teasing grin, 'But you are *so* reckless, my little dove.' Both of them caught sight of Artula and her son walking back to the settlement, hand in hand. He wondered if Artula already knew what sight would be awaiting them outside her home. Sphax and Corinna exchanged a significant look and prepared themselves to share the grief of a fatherless daughter and her son.

PART TWO

THE WINTER OF WINTERS

SIX

Entering Maharbal's brightly lit pavilion he was met with the sight of an apple winging its way towards him. He caught it. 'Stick it in your food sack. I've breakfasted, but I'm afraid you're going to go hungry this morning.'

Not the best start to a day, Sphax reflected. Firstly, being rudely awakened by the ugly face of Dubal in what had seemed like the middle of the night, and secondly, being told he was to forgo breakfast. It must be serious.

'I've just received a report that Rome is on the move. Consul Scipio has struck camp and his legions are on the march.' Maharbal had his back to him, eyeing a rack of javelins before making his selection. 'My guess is that he feels insecure here, with that river between him and Placentia. So, he's upped sticks and decided to move camp to the other side of … what's the name of that accursed—'

'The Trebia, Sir.'

'Quite.' The general now had five javelins clutched in his left hand. 'As I've told you many times before, an army on the march, is an army in ...' he paused, awaiting an answer.

'Peril, Sir.' A wedge of cheese was tossed in his direction as reward.

'We have a golden opportunity to destroy them today, Sphax. Ba 'al Hamūn has offered up our enemies for sacrifice. I've summoned all our Numidian cavalry and asked Hasdrubal to join me, we may need his Iberians later. But first I must confirm this report. Ride swiftly to the Roman camp with your eshrin and tell me if it's empty. You'll find me south of their camp mustering our men. Go, lad! We haven't a moment to lose.'

Sphax didn't mind exchanging breakfast for a bit of excitement, but for his men, no amount of excitement could make up for missing their favourite meal of the day. Stuffing their mouths with whatever food came to hand, they stomped off to the horse lines amidst a chorus of bellyaching.

Fingers of grey light were only now beginning to spread from the east as they set out westwards on the frosted grassland plain beside the great river. Ahead of him he could just make out the outline of the Roman camp in the gathering dawn. As they drew closer he began to distinguish the individual stakes that made up the perimeter palisade, each one driven into the ground, yet still standing taller than a man on horseback. In front of this lay a continuous ditch, broken only by gates positioned at the four cardinal points and flanked by formidable watchtowers, parapets and guard posts.

PART TWO: The Winter of Winters

Until a few hours ago this bastion would have housed a city of tents. All he could now see over the palisade were a few larger pavilions, left to fool them it was still occupied. Altogether, the engineering was impressive and redolent of Roman thoroughness, but its sudden abandonment signalled only weakness.

They didn't try the western and southern gates. Sphax knew they would be barred. Instead, he led his men directly to the eastern gate, guessing the consul's legions had left from that gate, and the last man across its threshold would have had no choice but to leave it open. He was right.

It was eerily deserted. Campfires still smouldered on empty ground where orderly rows of tents had once stood. Horse lines of hemp stretched between stakes now flapped idly in the breeze, the stallions that had been tethered long gone. But when they started exploring the pavilions and storehouses they were in for a shock. So much had been left behind! The camp was a looter's paradise.

A mouse would have starved on the food they'd left behind, but everything else had been abandoned where it had stood. Clay amphorae by the score stood everywhere. Sphax guessed it would amount to a small lake of wine. And it would be good wine, from Umbria and Etruria. Wine his men had not tasted since leaving Iberia.

In the grandest pavilion they found the most sumptuous possessions still in place, untouched, as if a consul of Rome might return at any moment to take up his seat on a cushioned couch.

But Consul Publius Cornelius Scipio was not returning. He'd left in a hurry and was travelling light. What worried Sphax was the temptation on display for his men. He could see it in their eyes as they ran fingers along silver dishes or weighed a golden wine cup in the palm of a hand. Plunder such as this would make a score of men rich overnight. He had to get his men out of here, and fast.

'Follow me men. Now!' he bawled, leading them out of the consul's pavilion to an open parade area in the centre of the camp. After whistling for Dido he began yelling, 'To me, men. To me! At once!' Reluctantly, his men emerged sour-faced from storehouses and lesser pavilions in twos and threes, shambling over to where he sat astride Dido.

'Whistle for your mares and mount up, we're leaving.'

Hannon eyed him, resentfully. 'Couldn't we just—'

'No!' Sphax shouted firmly. Aware that he'd been thrown into a battle of wills, if he showed the slightest weakness or indecision, he was lost.

'It's just a deposit … insurance, captain, that's all,' bleated Hannon, unable to look him in the eye.

'Just a little trinket, Sir,' Gulussa joined in.

'But it wouldn't stop at a *trinket*, would it, Gulussa? Next it would a piece of silver, a gold cup, then that wine. We have a chance to destroy two legions today.

I'm not leading a drunken eshrin into battle!' The muttering continued.

Slowly and deliberately, Sphax begun threading his saunion. 'Any man who enters a pavilion will get this in his back,' he said coldly, levelling the weapon. They knew he meant it. 'Now whistle for your mares. We're leaving.'

When the whistling began he knew he'd won this particular battle.

When his eshrin reached the open plain south of the Roman camp he saw that Maharbal was surrounded by several officers, including the Carthaginian, Hasdrubal, who'd been foisted on the hapless Iberians.

His general greeted him with a grin spiced with his habitual sarcasm. 'Here comes Master Sphax to give me my orders.'

'The Roman camp is indeed empty, Sir. But I think you should put an armed guard—'

'What did I tell you, gentlemen?'

'There's enough loot and wine lying around,' Sphax persisted, 'to keep an army drunk for a week. Consul Scipio left in a hurry and took little with him.' Maharbal's grin evaporated.

'My men can be relied on to perform such a duty, General,' said Hasdrubal, cuttingly.

Whereas Numidians can't, Sphax almost said, managing to bite his tongue. Judging from Maharbal's sour look, he'd also recognised the slur.

'Very well, Hasdrubal. In this fight your Iberians would be of little use, so guard duty it is.' Trust the general to give as good as he got! Turning to Astegal he said, 'I have twenty eshrins still mustering in camp. Go back with Hasdrubal and bring them forward with all possible speed. I'm going to need them today.'

With undisguised pleasure, Sphax noted the thunderous expression on Hasdrubal's face as he rode off with Astegal. He also noted the mischievous glimmer in the general's grey eyes, but nothing more was said.

They set out in three vast lines that straddled across the plain, twenty eshrins to a line; an irresistible force of almost two thousand horsemen, the finest Rome had ever faced. Sphax's eshrin was placed in the centre of the second line, directly behind Adherbal who led the first line with Maharbal beside him. Maharbal set a blistering pace as they rode east across the empty plain into the gathering light. It was a magnificent sight, thought Sphax, a sight to swell the pride of any Numidian.

Four miles later they came at last within sight of the rearmost columns of Scipio's legions which seemed to stretch to the horizon. With growing frustration Sphax had to acknowledge the consul had made excellent progress, and might just get away with his desperate gamble if something wasn't done about it urgently.

When they were within half a mile of the rearguard Maharbal halted them and signalled Sphax,

PART TWO: The Winter of Winters

Adherbal and several others to join him to take a closer look. They rode swiftly to within sixty yards of a solid wall of Samnite spears that had rapidly deployed to face them.

Phalanx upon phalanx had been drawn up to bar their path. He guessed they were facing at least two thousand spears besides the four turmae of Campanian cavalry that had been positioned on each flank. Behind them Sphax could see more Samnite infantry forming up as a reserve. Maharbal led their little group south to take a closer look at the Campanians.

Sphax had never seen so much bronze and silver on display. So much vanity! He couldn't help but smile at the Campanians' ridiculously gaudy uniforms and plumed helmets. Even their stallions were arrayed with scarlet plumes, some with ornate bronze chamfrons to protect their heads, every belt and buckle polished and burnished. Beyond this little army of peacocks he could see the rest of the legions trudging wearily eastwards in three columns.

'When did they leave their camp?' Maharbal asked when he'd seen enough.

'My scouts saw them just before dawn, but they must have set out in the middle of the night,' answered Manissa, a grey-bearded old veteran with more gold in his plaits than an Insubres' torc. 'I'm afraid we've given them a head start, Sir.'

'No matter,' Maharbal said levelly. 'We have sixty eshrins with twenty more when Astegal arrives. I'm sure we can make things unpleasant for them.' This met with grunts of approval.

'How far is it to that river from here?' Adherbal asked Manissa, whose scouts had been on patrol last night.

'The Trebia?' Adherbal nodded.

'Maybe three miles at most. By the gods, they'll get a good soaking there!' growled Manissa. 'It's deep, and cold enough to freeze their bollocks off.'

'Well, gentlemen,' Maharbal asked at length, 'how do we drive them into the river that will unman them?' There were a few half-hearted suggestions before his captains fell silent. Sphax had been giving this some thought whilst absently playing with his Artemis figurine when he realised Maharbal was grinning at him. 'Has that goddess of yours got your tongue, lad?'

For an instant he felt a reluctance to voice suggestions in the presence of these old hands, but sensed the general's indecision. His inhibitions lasted for no more than a moment. It wasn't in Sphax's nature to withhold an opinion.

'If a few eshrins keep these peacocks occupied until Astegal arrives,' he said, nodding at the Campanians, 'it would allow the rest to circle around and concentrate at their weakest point: when they ford that river. If it's as deep and treacherous as Manissa suggests, that's where Consul Scipio's legions will be at their most vulnerable.'

The general's grin widened. 'I agree, lad,' adding with a theatrical wink, 'you've just described the very

PART TWO: The Winter of Winters

plan I had in mind.' Turning to Adherbal he began issuing a flurry of orders. 'Until Astegal arrives, Sphax and I will keep the Samnites occupied with ten eshrins. Take all the rest south, Adherbal, and once you're out of sight, circle around to the north east and find that ford. That's where your work will begin. May Ba 'al Hamūn go with you.'

Soon, fifteen hundred Numidians were thundering over the grasslands to the south, leaving Sphax to ponder how best to tackle Campanians armoured from helmet to foot in bronze and iron and carrying round wooden shields. Maharbal was no help — 'you'll work it out, lad.'

Why did he feel that whenever the general was around he was continually being tested and examined? In truth he knew he *was* being scrutinized at every turn, and somehow this was part of the general's peculiar training method. But sometimes ... just occasionally, he would have preferred simple instructions and advice.

In the end, he and Himilco, one of the younger eshrin commanders, did *work it out*. The secret was to attack the enemy's ranks from the front and rear simultaneously. The bronze cuirasses the Campanians wore offered no protection from an attack from the rear.

Instructing his own eshrin he'd warned, 'They may well charge us. Campanians have never fought Numidians before—'

'No they won't, captain,' interrupted Hanon, 'all those fancy bastards on their big stallions see is our little mares, and us not having swords or proper armour ... they think we're harmless, so they won't charge.'

He'd been right, but Sphax could hardly believe it. The only way to meet Numidians was to fight fire with fire. Charge, move, retreat ... anything to avoid that lethal blizzard of javelins. To stand still was to die, and simply raising a shield was no protection from the lethal accuracy of Numidian javelins. But the Campanians had just sat there, transfixed, waiting to be reaped. After the second charge they fled.

This forced the Samnites into retreat. To cover this he could see the Campanians on their right flank forming up to charge. Numidians had already given them full notice what would happen if they stayed put.

'Himilco,' Sphax yelled, 'my eshrin will be the bait — take five eshrins and fall on their flank and rear, and ask Aribal to do the same with the other four.' Addressing his own eshrin he simply said, 'We're the bait. When I yell *now*, we turn. Form a line and prepare to charge.'

It worked perfectly. But not for the Campanians. This time ninety of them were completely surrounded by ten eshrins of Numidians and few escaped the slaughter. Sphax left his men to recover javelins whilst he galloped back to where Maharbal and his standard bearer, Bartho, had been watching the fight.

'You're doing well, lad,' his general conceded.

'I would do much better with Astegal's twenty eshrins ...' and that's when Sphax noticed the smoke. It was coming from the Roman camp.

PART TWO: The Winter of Winters

Maharbal saw him straining to stare at something in the distance. 'What is it?' he asked, turning around and following the direction of Sphax's gaze.

'I don't know, Sir. Smoke … from Scipio's camp. It looks as if it's being fired.'

'Dog's twat,' cursed Maharbal. 'What's Hasdrubal up to? By Ba 'al Hamūn I'll have his bollocks for breakfast!' The general urgently gripped Sphax's shoulder. 'Get over there as fast as you can. Ride that mare into the ground if you have to. And find out what's happened to Astegal. I need those eshrins now!'

The Roman camp was at least four miles away and Dido was tired. He'd ridden her hard since dawn, so he let her find her own natural rhythm, without pushing her. He'd no intention of riding her into the ground, least of all to save Hasdrubal's miserable skin. What was the man thinking? Surely he couldn't wriggle out of this one. He'd been ordered to guard the place, not raze it to the ground. As Sphax counted down the miles, his speculations turned to Astegal. Where could he be? His orders had been plain enough. He'd heard them himself: to return to camp and bring on the remaining Numidians. What could be simpler, thought Sphax. That he'd not obeyed them didn't come as a complete surprise — Astegal was a hot-headed fool. His best guess was that the slackhead had gone in search of glory for himself.

Sphax wondered if this day could get any worse. They had had two Roman legions and their alae strung out over the empty plain in weary columns, trapped by a deep river with a narrow ford between them and safety. At dawn they'd held Rome in the palm of their hand, but now, by late-morning, Sphax was beginning to think that Scipio's risky gamble had paid off.

The reek of smoke was growing ever closer. Ahead of him he could see the eastern gate of the camp with its watchtowers and recessed gate. When Dido's hooves clattered over the bridge spanning the ditch and echoed from the wooden walls of the gate, he came in for a terrible shock. The sound of laughter and revelry should have warned him.

Inside the camp, all was a chaotic orgy of revelry and looting. And it wasn't Iberians that were sitting around campfires that had been re-lit and blazed away. It was Numidians! Hundreds of them; at a guess, all Astegal's twenty eshrins. They were seated on benches and chairs dragged from pavilions, and each group of revellers had surrounded themselves with amphorae of wine. Most were roaring drunk by now. Those not carousing were busily strapping sacks of loot to the backs of their mares. What was worse, there wasn't a single Numidian officer to be seen.

Sphax found the Iberians outside Scipio's sumptuous pavilion. Drink was not fuelling them, just pure greed. They were all stone cold sober, methodical and practical, bringing pack horses and wagons with them to empty a consul's pavilion of all its wealth.

Rome's bounty had caused a madness to descend on them all, an orgy of looting and drunkenness, fuelled by a lake of wine. They were like the celebrants at the downfall of some tyrant, but Sphax knew the *real* tyrants were escaping, four miles away to the east.

Sphax's anger knew no bounds that morning. For the first time in his life he felt ashamed of his own people. Four miles away Numidians were fighting and dying for these drunken wretches. Leaping from Dido he raised his saunion and strode to the middle of a group slumped around a campfire. Kicking over several jars of wine in the process he picked up one that was half full and started to douse the flames with its contents. Most were as drunk as Scythians and far too gone to object. The few that did received a vicious kick that sent them sprawling.

'Whose eshrin do you belong to?' he yelled. But all he got in reply was incoherent mutterings. Giving up, he drew his sword and began slicing through the ropes that held looted items to the backs of mares. If any objected he pointed the sword at their throats and glared. Even so, he soon had an angry mob gathered around him muttering and cursing under their breath.

Pointing his sword to the east he yelled, 'Four miles yonder, scores of your brothers already lie dead and wounded on the field of battle. Adherbal and Himilco have the courage to take on the legions of Rome!

Only the gods know their losses ...' emotion suddenly choking-off his words. 'Your brothers are fighting and dying for you today. You make me ashamed to call myself a Numidian!'

There was suddenly a shame-faced hush around him: eyes averted, heads lowered, some slunk away silently. None dared look him in the eye. Then someone muttered, 'We deserve this, Sphax ... we've fought hard all winter.'

Sphax rounded on him. 'And my eshrin *deserves* your help,' he screamed at the man, 'not a drunken orgy.' In that instant he caught a fleeting glimpse of Astegal and several Numidian officers heading for the southern gate. Even more shocking was the sight of the man riding beside them: none other than Hasdrubal, the insufferable noble from Carthage, lower than a snake's belly. What scheme had he been hatching? Then he saw it.

That silver-tongued snake had promised Astegal a share of the booty, then led his twenty eshrins of Numidians to that lake of wine and awaited the inevitable consequences. And the fool had fallen for it! Meanwhile, Hasdrubal's men were soberly emptying the richer pavilions and transporting the spoils back to camp. When they were through, he felt sure Hasdrubal had given orders to raze the camp to the ground to get rid of any evidence of what had been taken.

How could Astegal have been such an imbecile, such an idiot? Sphax knew with absolute certainty this calamity would be blamed on Numidians, not

PART TWO: The Winter of Winters

Iberians. What could I do, Hasdrubal would say? How could I have prevented six hundred Numidians from drinking and looting, he would argue, wringing his hands? Whatever happened, Hasdrubal would come out of this blameless.

Looking around at the hundreds of wild-eyed faces surrounding him, he realised this was a lost cause. Many of them were so drunk they were incapable of riding a horse, let alone raising a javelin. As for the rest, they had eyes only for plunder. Whistling for Dido, he dejectedly mounted and rode amongst them.

'Numidians, I appeal to your honour! Fulfil your oaths of duty and loyalty. I have nothing but contempt for those who put gold and silver above the lives of their countrymen. They bring nothing but shame and disgrace on our people.' He raised his blade, 'Any who still have courage and a shred of dignity, follow me. As for the rest … henceforth, I will no longer recognize you as Numidians. I despise you! I shun you!' With that he nudged his mare to a trot and headed back to the eastern gate. When he reached it he turned to see that no more than fifty were following him. So much for his powers of oratory.

After two miles they came at last on a rising fold of land where Sphax could see a couple of miles ahead. Through the sunless mid-day gloom all he could make out was a swirling mass of horsemen. At this distance it was impossible to see who was attacking who, but he guessed it must be Himilco's eshrins, still locked in their desperate struggle with the consul's rearguard. There was no sign of Adherbal, but he would be miles to the east, hard by the Trebia ford.

Then he caught sight of another body of horsemen, south-east of them. Pointing, he turned to the men. 'Can anyone with sharp eyes tell me who those horsemen are?'

'Why, it's our general, Sir,' replied one of them. 'It's Hannibal himself, with his standard-bearer and guards of the sacred band. There are others with him, but at this distance I can't tell you who they are.'

Now he had an impossible decision. Should he ride on, explain the situation to Maharbal and join Himilco in his fight with the rearguard, leaving someone else to tell his uncle about the drunken looting? Or tell him himself?

Bringers of bad news were never welcomed. Should he ride on, or do his duty? Though it pained him he would do his duty. Only Hannibal and his officers would have the authority to put a stop to it, and Maharbal had his hands full. He had no choice.

'Ride east with all speed,' he told the men. 'Join Maharbal's men and this time do your duty. I'm going to inform our general what's happening in the Roman camp.' He managed a reassuring smile. 'None of you lot had anything to do with that ... eh lads?' This was met with a variety of relieved grins before Sphax nudged Dido in the new direction and forced her to fly. Best get this over with.

PART TWO: The Winter of Winters

When he drew closer he began to feel uneasy. Something was wrong. A small, animated group of horsemen were gathered around his uncle, and he was sure Hasdrubal and Astegal were amongst them. What webs of deceit had they been spinning? Surely they couldn't wriggle out of this.

When he drew level with his uncle one look at his thunderous face told him that he was in serious trouble.

'Hasdrubal tells me that your eshrin discovered the plunder, and Astegal informs me you encouraged the drunkenness and looting.' His uncle could barely contain his rage.

'I was ordered by Maharbal to find—'

'Silence!' Hannibal exploded. 'How dare you excuse what you have done? You have cost me the day ... which should have been mine.' His eyes flashed and blazed accusingly. 'Yet again have you disgraced me and dishonoured our family. You are dismissed! Go back to camp and await my summons.' With that his uncle wrenched Arion's reins and the stallion headed off at speed, closely followed by a swarm of his accusers.

For a heartbeat Sphax considered following and pleading his case. But with the next he decided against it; it would be his word against theirs, and his uncle's mind seemed set against him. Utterly shocked and broken by this turn of events, he nudged Dido around and headed slowly back to camp, turning the events of the morning over and over in his head.

The more he thought about it, the more he realised that Hasdrubal and Astegal would never get away with their lying version of events. Hasdrubal had been ordered to set a guard on the camp by Maharbal himself, and it was the general who'd ordered him to the camp after they'd spotted smoke. No, they couldn't wriggle out of this. The truth was there for all to see. Lies and deceit would be condemned. Maharbal would set the matter straight. Maharbal would clear his name.

'Why such a downcast face, lad?'

He'd been so lost in his own misery that Sphax hadn't noticed the approach of the chieftain Orison and his men. Dodging the question, he asked, 'Have you been relieved from garrison duty at Clastidium, Sir?'

'Yes. But why the long face?' laughed the battle-scarred old warrior. 'You look as if you've just met Morrigu.'

'I'm in disgrace, Sir, with my uncle … again.'

'Then it's worse than Morrigu. What in the name of the Carnutes have you done this time, Sphax? Sworn yourself to Rome?'

'Hasdrubal and one of our Numidian captains has accused me of encouraging our men to loot the Roman camp and allow drunkenness and disorder. The accusation is false, Sir, they are lying.'

At the mention of Hasdrubal's name, Orison's grin disappeared and he began a brief, ill-tempered discussion with his men before turning back to Sphax.

'That bastard isn't worthy of the name serpent, lad. Sooner or later one of his men will sink a javelin between his weasel shoulders. Sooner, I suspect. I'll look into this matter myself.'

Now Sphax was really alarmed. Did this really happen? Men killing their own officers? Hasdrubal was a lying bastard, but he didn't deserve death. 'I beg you, Sir,' he pleaded, 'please do nothing on my behalf. Maharbal will clear my name. I have behaved honourably today.'

Orison placed a hand on his shoulder. 'I would expect nothing less from the son of Navaras,' adding grimly, 'but I'll still look into it.'

Returning to his pavilion he slumped down in a chair beside the brazier and poured his heart out to Corinna. After he'd told her the story he sunk into a dismal silence, awaiting the inevitable summons from his uncle, much as a condemned man awaits the executioner's blade.

It was late into the night when the summons finally came, but it didn't come from Hannibal. Maharbal wanted to see him.

Maharbal's pavilion was dimly lit that evening. The sleeping area had been screened off and he could hear Ayzabel snoring like a pig. The general was seated on his usual stool beside the brazier whilst beside him Adherbal was slumped in a couch. Both men looked utterly spent. Sphax found a chair and helped himself to a cup of wine from a low table, re-charging their cups at the same time.

'Hannibal regrets what happened today,' said Maharbal in a voice drained of its usual vitality. 'He was not aware of the facts. But don't expect an apology, lad. If he apologised he would have to admit to himself that he was wrong, and your uncle is never wrong.'

'What will happen to Hasdrubal, Sir?' asked Sphax.

'He will squirm his way out of it like the snake he is. He's too well connected with the powerful in Carthage for your uncle to do much about him.' Sphax told them what the chieftain Orison had said about Hasdrubal. Maharbal exchanged significant glances with Adherbal. 'Well lad, by the gods you've made a powerful friend there. Perhaps something might be done about Hasdrubal after all.' Sphax hoped not, at least not in the way Orison had hinted at.

'And Astegal, Sir?'

The general sighed audibly, reaching for his cup. 'He's disappeared, lad. I suspect he's fled and we'll never see him again, unless his corpse turns up tomorrow with its throat cut. I should have learned my lesson after his stupidity at the Ticinus. His actions have cost us the opportunity of destroying Scipio's army.'

A thought occurred to Sphax. 'The legions left so much wine behind, Sir. Do you think they might have done this deliberately in the hope that such a situation arose?'

'Well by the gods it worked!' the general exploded, then remembering to keep his voice down so as not to

PART TWO: The Winter of Winters

waken Ayzabel, continued in a more measured tone, 'I hadn't thought of that, lad, but you're probably right. Loot is a terrible curse at times. But that's why our men are loyal and fight for us … by Ba 'al Hamūn, they're certainly not here for the pisspot amount of silver we pay them! That's why we have officers. To lead and keep them in check when temptation arises. How many times have I told you to be generous with your eshrin and reward them with glory and plunder? That's why your eshrin is a credit to you. From what I hear you are more than generous with silver.' Why did it not surprise him that the general was always abreast of the latest camp gossip?

'But what of Scipio's army, Sir? Did we do it any damage today?' Maharbal glanced over at Adherbal, who'd remained resolutely silent so far.

'Some, Sphax,' Maharbal's most senior captain answered in a voice beyond weariness. 'But not enough that it can't be repaired when Consul Longus arrives with his fresh legions in a few days' time.' Adherbal shrugged, as if unburdening the day from his shoulders. 'I have a few hundred prisoners, mostly skirmishers and alae, and the General routed the Samnite rearguard and put it to flight. But what we were after were Scipio's two Roman legions, and they escaped, untouched. So now, instead of two legions, we face four, and twice the number of allies. In terms of military disasters, Sphax, this day ranks as one of the worst. Mark my words, we shall pay for it in the days and weeks ahead. It might make our position here untenable. In which case we'll have to retreat.'

It was Sphax's turn to groan inwardly. To him, retreat was unthinkable, it would spell disaster and signal weakness and failure to their allies, the Gauls, who would desert in their droves like rats from a sinking ship. They had to fight, whatever the odds, whatever the cost. And they had to fight soon. He poured himself another cup of wine, downing it in less time than it had taken to pour it.

'Our numbers grow daily. Gauls are flocking to our standard, at least enough to offset Longus' advantage. Even with his additional legions, we still outnumber their cavalry. We must attack. And soon!' Sphax raised his eyes from his empty cup. But all he saw were two elderly Numidians, indulgently gazing at him with weary smiles.

* * * *

Next morning Sphax woke to the news that during the night Hasdrubal's grand pavilion had been burned to the ground. Fortunately, depending on your point of view of course, Hasdrubal had been spared. He'd spent the night between the legs of the Nubian, Aaliyah, the most expensive whore in camp, way beyond the reach of most of her silver-poor clients. The news was brought to them by Idwal, whose only comment was that the treacherous Carthaginian had been saved by the skin of his prick, a jibe that soon did the rounds of the camp.

PART TWO: The Winter of Winters

For the rest of the day the Iberian chieftain Orison showered gifts on the Numidian eshrins that had fought well. Sphax received a magnificent silver tray he'd first spied in a consul's pavilion. Later, a set of silver cups turned up, followed by a grand banqueting table that was far too large for his modest pavilion. Retaining a silver cup as his fair share, Sphax handed everything over to his men to keep or auction around the campfires that night.

By mid-afternoon it was obvious to everyone that Orison had not only discovered where Hasdrubal had stashed the spoils of war, he was also re-distributing it by merit. Sphax more than approved!

Distractions were welcome, for there was a strange, unsettling atmosphere around camp, an unspoken thought on everyone's lips. The army seemed to be holding its breath, waiting for the inevitable arrival of the legions of Longus when their enemy's forces would almost double in size. Would the coming man risk battle? Would he fight or sit tight? Rome controlled the Padus river to the sea and held the road from Placentia to Ravenna. Either by river or by road, their supply lines were assured. Would Longus sit out the winter, drilling his men and waiting for even more reinforcements in the spring?

They didn't have this luxury. Even with the windfall of the grain stores of Clastidium, hunger would once again come knocking on their door. To stand still was to starve. They needed to force a battle, and soon.

In this disquieting interval he and Corinna were able to ride every day. The weather was bitterly cold, but dry, with clear-blue wintry skies stretching to the vast horizons on the plain beside the great river. On these excursions Corinna began to tell him something of her strange and lonely childhood in Scodra, Illyria's capital city.

Amongst the Ardiaei tribespeople, her fearsome mother was known as the pirate queen. Although Corinna herself was not heir to the throne — her stepbrother Pinnes had this dubious honour — her earliest memories were of being trained and educated in the arts of war. She was to be moulded in the image of her mother, where skill with lance, sword and bow were prized above all things. She was destined to become a warrior princess, who would conquer and bring territory and glory to Illyria.

Sphax got the impression that her mother had always been a cold and distant figure in Corinna's life. She told him her real education began at fourteen, when she was married to Arsenios of Epidamnos. Arsenios, Corinna told him, was a civilised, cultivated man, sixteen years her senior, who'd been appalled by the wild tempestuous barbarian he'd married. He engaged tutors on her behalf and even as a hostage in Rome and Brundisium, she continued with her studies. 'I would not recognise my fourteen year old self,' she'd told him.

It had seemed like a bleak and loveless childhood to Sphax, but he was curious to know more about

PART TWO: The Winter of Winters

Arsenios. Even though he was dead, Sphax couldn't help but see him, or at least his memory, as a rival. Had she loved him? Did she still mourn him? And the most important question of all: could anyone replace him?

Though he tried on several occasions, Corinna would not be drawn on the subject of her husband. Whilst she never spoke of love or tenderness between them, it was evident she held him in great regard. Sphax convinced himself that high regard was not love.

In any case his curiosity, like his love, would remain unrequited, for after four days of these intimate excursions he did finally receive a summons from his uncle. Hannibal requested his company on a dawn reconnaissance to take a look at the new Roman camp.

SEVEN

Maharbal had described this gesture as a peace offering from Hannibal. One look at his uncle's mirthless expression reflected in the firelight told him this was just wishful thinking. But there again, Sphax was often too quick to judge him. From the age of nine, when he'd begged his father Hamilcar to take him on campaign, his uncle had known only war. His nature and character, down to the last furrow etched on his brow had been forged not by childish pastimes and idle pleasures, but on the battlefield.

'You are timely, Nephew, and welcome. Are you prepared?'

'I am, Sir,' replied Sphax, casting his gaze over the small party that were to accompany them. Hannibal's gaunt standard bearer, Annaeus, was the only one already mounted. The other six, chosen from his sacred band of guards, were enjoying their last sensation of warmth from the semi-circle of campfires that blazed around the entrance to his pavilion. It was bitterly cold and dark still, the moon having long since traced her course through the heavens. This was the last watch of the night, and at this time of the year, they would not see the first fingers of dawn for another two hours.

For the first few miles they rode on through the gloom in silence. Then, as the first slivers of pre-dawn light appeared above the eastern horizon his uncle turned in his saddle. 'Has anyone asked awkward questions of you and the princess?' Sphax was taken aback by the question and the use of her status, rather than her name.

'Not that I am aware of, Sir. She rarely leaves my pavilion, and only then in my company to exercise our horses.'

His uncle nodded. 'Good. Keep it that way.' And after a lengthy pause, 'Tell me something of her character and education?' Now Sphax was at a complete loss: his uncle *never* asked personal questions.

'It would be impossible to give you a complete picture, Sir, because our acquaintance is so very recent, but my impressions are of a woman with great strength of character, but with many facets to her nature. A complex soul, one who's faced the many trials in her life with stoical endurance and remarkable resourcefulness. As to her upbringing and education, her mother would have her be a warrior princess, so from an early age she was trained in arms. She herself admits that her real education was undertaken by her husband and continued throughout their time in Rome and Brundisium. She reads and writes fluently in Greek and knows something of Aristotle and *episteme*, but little of Zeno or Socrates.'

Hannibal smiled. 'Then I fear you will have little in common, nephew, unless you convert her to the master from Citium. I don't suppose either of you have much interest in paradoxes.' Sphax laughed and couldn't believe what he was hearing. His uncle was teasing him about the two Zenos!

'Indeed not, Sir, they're just idle sophistry.' They were now approaching the river Trebia, and the light was growing steadily. Other than a few stands of willow and birch, there was little cover beside its shallow sandy banks. At this point in its course the river looked deceptively sluggish, its waters separating into several channels. But Sphax had been warned that the main channel was remarkably deep. Dido struggled in its numbingly icy waters as he felt the tug of a powerful current on his ankles. Arion, Hannibal's magnificent stallion had no such difficulty, the water barely reaching up his flanks. At the midway point his uncle stopped.

'Mark the deepest point with your standard, Annaeus, I need a measurement.'

When they reached dry land his uncle asked him to dismount and measure himself against the standard's shaft. With teeth chattering like door slaves, Sphax stood next to the shaft and noted Annaeus' mark. 'It's almost to my shoulders, Sir.'

'Then this is a considerable barrier, especially for infantry.'

'And icily cold, Sir! Unbearably so,' added Sphax, still shivering uncontrollably.

'Indeed, Sphax, and we have not had rain for days. Remount and gallop upstream for half a mile and return. Report what you see. You and your mare need to warm yourselves.' He was grateful for such thoughtfulness. Digging his knees into Dido's flanks, she leapt forward eagerly.

'Warmer?' his uncle asked on his return.

'Considerably, Sir.' Collecting his thoughts he added, 'The character of the river soon changes. The separate channels begin to merge and I suspect the river runs deeper and the current swifter. This may well be the only ford in this stretch of the Trebia.'

'Would your Numidians have difficulty crossing here?' Sphax knew they would struggle, but he would never admit that to his uncle.

'No, Sir,' he replied without hesitation.

'Good. Then we must press on.'

They were riding more cautiously now, on the lookout for outposts or sentries. Ahead of them the ground began to rise, framed by the growing light on the eastern horizon. Half a mile later the path they were following entered a copse of birch and rowan. Even though the trees were widely spaced, the near-darkness forced them to walk their horses warily. Approaching the woodland edge, with a jolt

Sphax suddenly caught sight of two sentries warming themselves beside a fire. They were no more than fifty paces away. Both had their backs to him, so they hadn't been spotted. But they soon would be, and Sphax wasn't taking any chances. Without a word or flicker of hesitation he switched his saunion to his right hand, fingered his throwing thong and dug his knees into Dido. By the time he'd turned Dido around and selected a fresh javelin it was all over. Hannibal's men had dealt with the other sentry, and both bodies lay still beside their now redundant campfire. Against the background of trees, death had stolen silently out of the near-darkness of the western sky.

Sphax dismounted and recovered his saunion, wiping it clean on the eques' scarlet cloak. 'Legionary cavalry,' he whispered to his uncle, 'but where are their horses?'

'This will be their outer cordon of sentries,' he answered in a similar whisper. 'Beyond this, the outposts will be more substantial. That's where their horses will be. We must be wary now.'

'Shall we scout around for more sentries, general?' one of his men asked, a little too loudly. Hannibal rounded on him.

'No!' he hissed, putting a finger to his lips and glaring at the wretch. 'We've already penetrated their cordon. Look for fires, and lower your standard, Annaeus.' Ahead of them they could see another copse. If anything its trees were even sparser than the one

PART TWO: The Winter of Winters

they'd just left, but it would have to do. It was growing lighter by the moment, and other than these occasional copses, the ground was as bare of cover as the desert. Pointing to the trees ahead of him Hannibal whispered, 'Dismount and lead your horses. No one is to speak.'

They reached the cover of the trees without any more alarms and made for the densest patch. Sphax prowled ahead on foot until he could see the edge of the woodland. It was then that he caught sight of the new Roman encampment, framed by a pale sun beginning to rise above its ramparts. Constructed on top of a slight rise overlooking the Padus, he knew it must command excellent views of the plain below. A goat couldn't swim the Trebia without being seen from the massive watchtowers beside its western gate. Far to the south he could see trails of smoke rising in the still air and guessed this must be the town of Placentia. But far more alarming was the sight of a turma of equites, no more than two hundred paces from where he was crouching, and even at this hour, they looked wide awake and alert.

The sound of a snapping twig made him turn in alarm. It was his uncle. Relieved, Sphax pressed a finger to his lips then pointed in the direction of the equites. Hannibal nodded and crouched down beside him. Following the direction of his uncle's darting gaze, he knew he was carefully observing everything Sphax had seen. Allowing his uncle a few moments to take it all in, he then pointed due south and whispered,

'Placentia?' His uncle stared intently for a moment, then nodded.

A small flock of crows noisily took to the air above them amidst a chorus of piercing calls and flapping wings. Some of the sentries stood motionless, staring their way, perhaps wondering what had disturbed the birds. Two equites began walking towards them. Sphax and his uncle froze. The cavalrymen stopped at the woodland edge, no more than ten paces from where they were crouching. Sphax could clearly see them looking around, listening. He was terrified that one of Hannibal's guards would choose this moment to blunder through the trees in search of them. After what seemed an eternity, the equites appeared satisfied and walked back to their comrades and the warmth of their campfires.

Sphax's pulse was racing, but to his astonishment his uncle was grinning at him. He was enjoying this, thought Sphax, but then he noticed his uncle's hand firmly gripping the hilt of his sword.

There was another shattering sound. But this time entirely man made, a sound almost to be expected, considering the time of day and their proximity to an armed camp of soldiers. A trumpet was blaring out the morning call to arms. Men would be rubbing sleep from their eyes, yawning, throwing back blankets and looking forward to breakfast. This is how all soldiers began the day, unless, like the equites nearby, they'd been given sentry duty. For the equites, the trumpet meant relief; their day was ending, not beginning. Hannibal squeezed his shoulder and whispered, 'Listen. Carefully!'

The trumpet was still blaring away its repetitive call when another instrument joined in, its tone more strident and insistent. It hardly created a melodious duet. Music was virtually a foreign language to him, but even he could recognise an unpleasant cacophony when he heard one. His uncle raised a finger and stared at him, as if to point out the significance of what they were hearing. Sphax was mystified. Thankfully the duet came to an abrupt end and Hannibal signalled they should return to their men.

Back in the safety of the trees, Hannibal whispered, 'What did you hear?'

'Two out of tune trumpets playing the call to arms, Sir,' he answered, as puzzled as ever.

'Why two, lad? Think!' Slowly, its significance dawned on him and a smile gathered around his lips.

'Sempronius Longus has arrived, Sir! That's why there were two different calls. One for each of the consul's legions,' he answered triumphantly, struggling to keep his voice to a whisper in his excitement.

'That one piece of information is worth a score of scouting missions.' His uncle looked pleased with himself. 'It is well we set out before dawn, otherwise this knowledge would have escaped us.'

Hannibal gathered everyone around him and whispered instructions for their return to the river.

Now they'd lost the cloak of darkness, he told them, there was little point in riding cautiously. They were to ride at speed and stop for nothing. If they encountered cavalry they were to outrun them.

Later, as he was steeling himself to nudge Dido into the icy waters of the Trebia once more, Sphax realised he hadn't enjoyed such an exhilarating gallop since chasing Corinna through the woods of Clastidium. By the time they passed the slain sentries they were galloping at full stretch, and at that speed swerving through the trees in the copse had been both hair-raising and thrilling. To add to the enjoyment they were surprised by a turma of Roman cavalry who eagerly gave chase, only to give up half a mile later after dropping hopelessly behind. It was a race that Rome was never going to win. They all arrived safely at the river, laughing and whooping with joy!

But there was little joy to be had from entering the river's icy waters. Sphax kept nudging the mare forward, hoping to get through the ordeal as quickly as possible. When they'd gathered on the other side, shivering and dripping wet, Hannibal headed south to scout the western bank of the river. Sphax was grateful the pace was kept at a warmth-giving trot. 'Come ride beside me, Nephew.' The horse race and the fact that he alone had discovered the arrival of Longus had put his uncle into an excellent humour. Sphax was continually surprised, and if he was honest, more often disconcerted by his uncle's mercurial character,

PART TWO: The Winter of Winters

but it was somehow reassuring to discover that he also enjoyed the same things as Sphax. It made him more human, without lessening his genius.

'Tell me what you know of our newly arrived consul, Tiberius Sempronius Longus? Gossip will do.'

'It will have to, Sir, for I was never introduced to the man.' His uncle chuckled. 'He's not from one of the noble families ... hardly a Claudii. He has a reputation for being a quick-tempered hothead. That worries me, Sir.'

'Why, Sphax? If he lives up to his reputation he is exactly what I require for my design.'

'He worries me because his time in office is about to come to an end, Sir. Consular elections will be held in a few weeks' time, and consuls like to leave their mark: a great victory, a new colony ... Longus will be out to prove himself before history forgets him.'

'Turn your thinking on its head. What is our army's worst fear regarding the arrival of Longus' legions?'

'That Longus will sit out the rest of the winter in camp and wait for more reinforcements in the spring.'

'Exactly! Scipio has grown cautious. He will surely urge caution on his fellow consul. What we need right now is an ill-tempered hothead, out to make a name for himself.'

'But how will we exploit his rashness, Sir?'

'By showing weakness, Sphax. By showing weakness.'

They'd ridden about two miles since crossing the Trebia when they came upon a shallow channel that emptied its stagnant waters into the main river. He'd come upon many such ditches near the Anamares village. The water they contained was generally unpleasant and their mares had refused to drink it. This ditch seemed deeper than most, with steep sunken banks, but otherwise it was just another insignificant feature in what to Sphax was a dull and monotonous landscape.

But this was not the case for his uncle, who had dismounted and examined the depths of the channel in several places, each time climbing back up its banks to stand and gaze into the distance. The men were growing restless. To stand around in these temperatures was to freeze.

Mounting Arion, his uncle rode over to where Sphax sat astride Dido with the rest of the men. 'Nephew, dismount and lead your mare down into that channel. Once you've descended the bank, I want you to stand still and count to fifty. When you reach that number you may climb out and return to us. Annaeus, I want you to do the same. Leave my standard with the guards.' After delivering these bewildering instructions, Hannibal turned Arion, and to the consternation of all, rode off at high speed in the opposite direction.

Totally bemused, he and Annaeus were left staring at one another. With a shrug, Sphax grinned at the standard bearer, dismounted and did exactly what his uncle had told him to do. The banks of the ditch were slippery, and Dido seemed reluctant to put her hooves in the watery slime at the bottom,

PART TWO: The Winter of Winters

but other than this, the two of them suffered little inconvenience from his uncle's incomprehensible madness. By the time he and Annaeus walked back to the men, Hannibal had returned.

'Thank you, gentlemen. An invaluable demonstration,' was all the explanation they got. 'We can now return to camp.' For a mile or so they rode on in silence, his uncle lost in thought, then suddenly snapping out of his reverie he raised a hand to halt them all, dismounted, and stood stock still, gazing back at the river. By now Sphax was so curious to discover what was behind his uncle's strange behaviour that he too slid from Dido and stood beside him, following his gaze.

They were standing in the middle of nowhere, if you could call nowhere a flat featureless grassland without a single distinguishing feature to mark it as somewhere. Yes, there was the odd tree and an occasional clump of stunted willows, but otherwise it was just grass, and one blade of grass is more or less the same as the next. What possible significance could this bit of nowhere be to his uncle? Sphax watched him staring steadily at the ribbon of water that marked the course of the Trebia, two miles away. At last his uncle spoke.

'Mark this place, Sphax, just as history will mark it down the ages. Within the week a great battle will be fought here. A battle that may decide the fate of Rome ... or Carthage.'

He knew that something was wrong the instant he stepped into the pavilion. Corinna looked distraught, pacing backwards and forwards whilst Zwalia sat beside the brazier, head in hands, a rapid fire-storm of Greek passing between them. Cesti and Lulin were seated on his sleeping couch, an expression of bewildered alarm on both their faces.

'Silence, both of you!' he yelled. Much too forcibly. Shocked, Corinna froze, and with tears streaming down her cheeks sank back into a couch. Zwalia raised her head and glared at him. Sphax took a deep breath. After the morning he'd just lived through, with his uncle's momentous pronouncements still ringing through his head, he found it difficult not to see anything beyond this as commonplace trivia. Summoning his dwindling reserves of patience he asked in a more reasonable manner what had happened. 'And for the love of the gods,' he added, 'speak calmly.'

To add to Sphax's burdens, what had happened during the night was far from trivial, and its consequences were serious and now beyond their control.

Three Brundisians who were not under guard by Hannibal had killed Dasius' guards and freed him. Dasius had escaped camp, and was now on the run.

EIGHT

'How many times do I have to tell you, Sphax? My son is in grave danger! If Dasius reaches Brundisium he will kill my son to avenge what I've done to him.'

It pained him to look at her, to see the anguish etched on her lovely face and the tears glistening in her eyes. When she'd told him what had happened he'd immediately set out for his uncle's pavilion to ascertain the facts.

Yes … Dasius had escaped. But no horses were missing, so the fugitives were on foot and wouldn't get far. Parties of horsemen were already out searching for him. When the four of them were recaptured they would be made an example of and crucified. Using his network of spies his uncle had already put out the rumour that Dasius had betrayed Clastidium to Carthage for silver. Dasius would never be able to turn to Rome for help or succour. He was now a friendless outlaw who'd betrayed both Rome and Carthage. His days were numbered.

When Sphax explained all this to Corinna it brought little comfort. She required certainty. Otherwise there would always be a shadow hanging over her, and over the life of her son. Dasius the Pig had become a creature of nightmares. He would have to be found, and eliminated.

'I know the three that freed him, Sphax. They're as vicious and cunning as he is.' Corinna was a little calmer now, sitting beside Zwalia on the couch with their hands comfortingly intertwined. 'They will try to reach Brundisium. They'll be safe there. But to do so they'll need to travel by boat down the Padus, reach a harbour and then take ship.' Sphax's thoughts were racing.

'I'm sure you're right,' he said. 'If my uncle's rumours have worked their mischief he'll be a wanted man, and the whole of Rome will be on the lookout for him. Besides, the overland journey would take weeks.'

'I must find him! And soon, before he reaches the sea.' She paused and stared at him, a pleading look in her eyes. 'Zwalia and I must go now, he's already got half a day's start on us.' He was horrified.

'No! I forbid it!' he shouted. Knowing perfectly well he possessed neither the power nor the authority to stop her, his fears came out as an incoherent rush of thoughts. 'There are four of them. If they're as vicious as you say you will be hurt. This is Insubres territory. You know this land less well than the men Hannibal's sent out to find them. And what if Romans catch you? What—'

PART TWO: The Winter of Winters

'Don't be such a slackhead! I can talk my way out of that … I'll say that Dasius handed me over to Hannibal … as a hostage … that I didn't go willingly.' Sphax raised his arms in exasperation.

'Corinna! Think about it! Talking your way out of it won't make a rat's tail of difference … you'll be back in their custody, a Roman prisoner, a hostage, back where you started. How could this possibly help your son?' Corinna had risen from the couch and was pacing. He could see the waves of anger and frustration consuming her.

Then Sphax had a moment of inspiration. For the first time during these heated exchanges he forced himself to calmly gather his thoughts and weigh carefully what he was to say next.

'You're probably right about his means of escape. Dasius has had a long time to think about it. He will have reached the same conclusions that you have: escape down the river is his best hope.' Sphax paused and tried to join up all the loose threads. 'Firstly, you need a force that can easily overpower the four of them. Then you will need a good scout to track them down, and lastly, you will be travelling through the territory of the Insubres, so you need someone who speaks their language and knows their villages and settlements.' It was Corinna's turn to throw up her arms in disdain.

'And how am I to acquire such an *army*,' she asked sourly. Sphax couldn't help but grin.

'I will provide it,' he said. Corinna snorted then glared at him.

'How—'

'Listen to him, Corinna!' shouted Zwalia, her tone so urgent that both of them turned to stare at her. 'For once in your headstrong life, listen to the advice that someone is giving you. It's sound advice.' Corinna was so shocked by her servant's outburst that for the moment she fell silent.

'My scout Jugurtha could track the flight of a bird through a forest by examining the leaves its wings had touched, and his friend Hannon could dispatch Dasius' party with four javelins. I can spare both of them for a few days. As for someone who's travelled and lived amongst the Insubres — I know of someone who owes both of us a favour.'

At last Corinna was listening, and Zwalia was smiling encouragement. Turning to Cesti he asked her to bring Jugurtha and Hannon to the pavilion. Lulin and the servant boys were to prepare food and wine for guests. He reached for his beaverskin cloak and strode towards the vestibule.

'Where are you going?' demanded Corinna.

'To ask a favour,' he replied, before wrapping the cloak about his shoulders and striding out into the bitter cold.

After searching the encampment for over an hour he was about to give up, guessing the Anamares hadn't

PART TWO: The Winter of Winters

as yet moved into the safety of the camp. But then he caught sight of Artula, standing and waving amongst a group warming themselves around a campfire. She greeted him joyously.

'Sphax, this is my husband, Meilyr,' said Artula, smiling. 'Come and sit. We'll raise a cup in your honour and you can tell me your news.' To Sphax's embarrassment her husband fell to his knees at the mention of his name.

'I swear by Morrigu and all the gods that I will forever be in your debt for what you did for my wife and son.'

Sphax reached out for the Gaul's shoulders and bid him rise. 'You can never be in my debt, Sir, I won't hear of it.' But it was exactly what he wanted to hear, although he did feel a twinge of guilt acknowledging it.

Like Idwal, Meilyr embodied everything Sphax admired about the Gauls. A head taller than Sphax, he sported luxuriant mustachios and keen blue eyes that seemed to miss nothing.

Once the pleasantries were over he wasted no time in asking for the favour he was seeking, and explained why it was so important to Corinna. Further twinges of guilt followed when he dramatised its importance by using Hannibal's arguments that for the possibility of future alliances, the heir to the throne of Illyria must be protected from all threats. Sphax had serious misgivings about these future alliances, but this was not the time to voice them.

Throughout his exposition he'd noticed that the two men sitting either side of Meilyr were paying close attention to every word that was being said, so it came as no surprise when the two of them stood beside Meilyr when he pledged his help. Everything was soon settled.

Darkness had fallen when he returned with his four guests. The instant Corinna recognised Artula the two of them flew into each other's arms. Sphax begun his introductions.

'May I present Meilyr, Anamares chieftain, and his companions Gáeth and Certán. All are welcome amongst the Insubres and know every village from here to where the Padus meets the Adria. My Numidians, Jugurtha and Hannon, are yours to command, as is Zwalia, Corinna's handmaiden.'

From the outset Corinna vehemently protested that she should lead the expedition; after all, it was her son's life at stake, therefore the responsibility should rest with her. Besides, she'd agued, only she would recognise Dasius' three accomplices. It was only when Sphax pointed out that Hannibal himself had given strict instructions that she was to be stopped at every gate in the camp — 'So I'm a prisoner now!' — and that Zwalia would also be able to recognise the four Brundisians, that she finally saw reason. Agreement was soon reached that Zwalia would represent Corinna. The party were to set out at first light. Before they

PART TWO: The Winter of Winters

left, Corinna generously pressed a jewel into the hands of all who were acting on behalf of her son.

For Sphax and Corinna the night became a long sleepless vigil, waiting for the dawn. For Sphax, hours passed listening to her restless tossing and turning before he padded over to her couch and whispered that they should find a campfire and talk. Anxious that she might be disturbing Zwalia's sleep, Corinna whispered her agreement, and they both began dressing in as many layers of clothing they could lay their hands on.

Outside the pavilion she surprised him by reaching out for his hand and clasping it firmly as they headed for the brightest campfire they could see.

'Thank you,' she said simply, smiling across at him.

'For what?' Sphax was taken aback by the passionate response his innocent reply provoked.

'For saving me from myself! For being kind to me ... for not slapping me across the face for my stupidity ... for not calling me an imbecile, a slackhead, a dolt.'

Sphax laughed. 'You're passionate, perhaps even impetuous at times ... but stupid would be the last thing I would call you.' Returning her smile he added, 'And I would never strike you. I believe to do such a thing to a woman is unmanly.'

'So you think I'm passionate, do you?' she said laughing. 'What other qualities do you imagine I possess?' Sphax put on a mock-serious expression.

'I would say you were resourceful, tenacious and intelligent, but undoubtedly your most noble virtues are your ... irritability, stubbornness, quick temper, complete inability to admit that you are ever wrong, and your desire to beat me at horse races!' This earned him a thump on the shoulder. 'I could go on, but I've praised you enough.' By now she was laughing, despite the cold.

Benches had been placed around the campfire, and they were grateful for the waves of heat that were beginning to reach them. Searching for his hand once more, Corinna looked into his eyes and asked, 'Tell me about Fionn?' Without withdrawing his hand from hers he turned away and stared into the firelight, lost in reflection.

Fionn had been his first love. The scene of her death on a precipitous mountainside in the Alps still haunted his dreams. He knew it would haunt them forever. There could be no escape from that last image of her. The image of her sudden, brutal death, amidst screaming mountain Gauls and the avalanche of boulders they'd set in motion. He'd let go of her hand. In the next moment she'd been struck by a rock that had bowled her down the mountainside like a bundle of rags.

'I'm sorry, Sphax. I should never have asked. The grief must still be raw. I know something of how it feels, though I never loved the husband I lost.'

For the past few days he'd been desperate to hear these words, but now, in that moment, it brought him little consolation. 'I would like to talk about her,' he said at last. 'I fear her memory is fading, like some

PART TWO: The Winter of Winters

dream barely recalled. Yet she deserves remembrance. Even now I feel her presence ... strange as this may sound. Yet there are days when I can no longer see her face in my mind's eye.' At last he met Corinna's eyes. 'But tell me, who told you about Fionn?'

'Cesti and Lulin to begin with, but then Ayzabel is such a gossip. Eventually I asked your friends Idwal and Drust.' Both were daily visitors to his pavilion. 'Idwal is so discreet and protective of your feelings he advised me to choose an auspicious moment to ask you about her. Drust was more forthcoming, he even said I was a little like her in temperament.' Sphax almost smiled at this.

'If she'd lived, Fionn might have shared something of your spirit. But her life was so brief, Corinna, just a winter's day. I shared but an hour of it. In appearance you are as different as night from day. She had the palest skin I've ever seen, golden hair and eyes of a hue more lustrous than Idwal's. She was a Gaul from the northern lands. Artula reminds me of her.'

'Then she must have been truly beautiful, Sphax.' He said nothing. 'How did you meet her?'

'She was a slave of a master as brutal as mine. I helped her escape. She wanted to go to the north, in search of her kin, so our paths lay in the same direction. After we reached Massilia, I suppose we just stayed together.' Sphax returned his gaze to the fire. 'When we saw the sea for the first time near Pisae, she vowed never to set foot in the accursed country again. Yet every step we took on that terrible journey through the Alps brought her nearer the place she'd vowed never to return to. I brought her nothing but war and death, Corinna, and in the end, she fulfilled her own prophecy.' There seemed nothing more to say, so he lapsed into silence and stared into the flames.

'She was prepared to break that vow because she loved you, Sphax. You brought her joy and happiness. Sometimes even a winter's day is enough, if it is bathed in love.'

No one had ever spoken to him in words that were so tender and touching, words that seemed to spring from a wellspring of compassion. He turned to look at her. She was gently smiling at him, her eyes flickering in the reflected firelight. In that moment he knew with certainty that he truly loved her, passionately and deeply, and the feeling overwhelmed him.

It was time to let Fionn sleep her eternal sleep, and leave memory where it would always remain; treasured, but locked away. It was time to return to the moment, to the living.

'There's one thing I don't miss about Fionn.'

'What's that?' she enquired, frowning.

'Her snoring.' Corinna had to put a hand to her mouth to stifle a laugh. Sphax had his wish. The spell was broken.

'Do I snore?' She asked in some alarm.

'Why do you think I had to get you out of the pavilion this evening? Last night its fabric was shaking under your onslaught. Even the Libyans feared assault from a fearsome army of pigs!' He received another blow to his shoulder for his trouble, but at least she was laughing.

He wondered whether this was the right time to ask the question that had been eating away at him since he'd first set eyes on her at Clastidium. 'May I ask you a question?' he began, tentatively. 'It is rather personal, so I would understand perfectly if you wished to remain silent on the matter.'

'You are free to ask, Sphax, just as I'm at liberty to refuse to answer. Try me.' Bracing himself, he tried to summon the right words.

'Well ... your relationship with Dasius, was it ... intimate?

'Go on,' Corinna encouraged.

'I mean, did you ... have to ... well ...' he could feel those hazel eyes bearing down on him. Why, oh why had he risked offending her with such an indelicate question?

'I take this to mean that as the official whore of Dasius the Pig, you wish to know if I had to submit to his pleasure?' Sphax stoically fixed his eyes on the firelight, managing a desultory nod in response. To his amazement, Corinna started chuckling. 'I think I can easily set your mind at rest if I tell you that no woman has ever had to submit to his pleasure. Dasius was impotent, virtually a eunuch. But even eunuchs sometimes become obsessed and infatuated with women. That's what happened to Dasius.'

'I'm so sorry, Corinna, I should—'

'I'm not! It spared me from a fate worse than death—'

'I mean, I'm sorry I ever asked you,' he said hurriedly. Corinna laughed, reassuringly reaching for his hand.

'I know, Sphax. I'm just teasing you. If it pleases you, I have been chaste and pure since the death of my husband. But then …' again, that devastatingly wicked smile.

'Then what?' asked Sphax, hoping for no more revelations.

'Dasius derived an unhealthy pleasure from looking upon the nakedness of women. It pleased him, yet sent him into paroxysms of impotence and frustration. I confess to indulging his obsession … occasionally. It proved to be the only power I exercised over him, so you can hardly blame me for tormenting him so.'

Sphax laughed. 'I suppose not. But what a strange, unhealthy creature he is.'

'Dasius's mind is labyrinthine, and at the centre of this labyrinth is a monster. A minotaur if you like, not quite human, nor wholly animal.'

Libyans were on watch that evening, so their conversation was frequently interrupted by pikemen returning to the fire to warm their bones and grumble about the cold. Neither of them minded much, but as the night wore on, Sphax became increasingly irritated by the men's backslapping and sly winking. Sphax was known to all, and so it seems were the rumours about his new woman. After one such incident, Corinna grinned at him, amused.

'They think this is a lovers' tryst, don't they?'

'What pair of lovers would choose a hard bench and the coldest night of the year?'

'I'm not cold!' she said, with that bewitching smile of hers.

As the first fingers of light appeared in the east, they wrapped their cloaks tighter and made their way through the slumbering camp to the western gate. The five horsemen and one horsewoman had only just arrived and were greeting one another. Standing beside the ramparts of the gate, Sphax and Corinna said their farewells to the little party and wished them good hunting. Sphax had grown increasingly anxious about this gathering. He'd even suggested they slip away quietly in ones and twos, but nobody seemed concerned.

His uncle usually missed nothing. How would he explain this little hunting party?

So Sphax was praying that Hannibal would not be informed about the Nubian horsewoman, accompanied by two Numidians and a trio of Anamares warriors, riding into the dawn from the western gate.

NINE

'With all respect, Sir, this will drive the Insubres into the arms of Scipio and Longus!' Sphax pointed out in exasperation.

'Exactly,' replied Maharbal coldly.

They were seated opposite the general's brazier in his pavilion, Maharbal on his favoured stool, Sphax on a couch. He'd just come from a council of war where his eshrin had been ordered to loot every Insubres settlement east of the Trebia up to the very gates of Placentia. Sphax had been horrified. This was a betrayal. They were allies, not enemies! War had already brought famine to the Insubres. Looting them of what little they still possessed would bring about starvation and death. It would surely tip them over the edge.

'This isn't a time for noble sentiments, lad. We are at war with Rome. We must prod and poke, use every means at our disposal to stir our enemy into action, otherwise Longus will be inclined to sit and wait. For

PART TWO: The Winter of Winters

us that would be fatal. So we must prod and poke.' Maharbal half-smiled and gave him a shifty look.

'Your *friend* Hasdrubal devised this plan—'

'Hasdrubal! That snake will be the death of us all.'

'It takes a serpent to know a serpent, so I believe his plan will work. The Insubres will appeal to Longus and Scipio. Rome will have to decide whether to defend the Insubres or abandon them—'

'What about the six thousand Insubres pledged to us in our camp? You are also asking them to decide between their people and us!'

'It's risky, I grant you.'

'It's madness, general ... madness!' With that he stormed out.

'Wait—' yelled Maharbal, but it was too late. Sphax had gone.

He'd been entrusted with six eshrins. The most he'd ever commanded. Adherbal had twenty this side of the river, watching his back. Under normal circumstances his spirits would be soaring with pride, but all he felt that morning was despair: forever remembered as the officer in command of this shameful act. What had Maharbal said about loot being a terrible curse? "That's why we have officers. To lead and keep men in check when temptation arises." Now he was letting them loose like a pack of wolves on a flock of sheep. He was being dragged down to the level of Hasdrubal!

He thought the day couldn't get much worse, but as they approached the Trebia it began to descend into a nightmare he wouldn't forget in a hurry.

Last night's rain had swollen the river and its icy waters seemed colder than ever. Three men were swept away in its deepest course. Assembling his men on the eastern bank he addressed them, riding backwards and forwards amongst their ranks. But the instant he opened his mouth to speak the heavens opened and a deluge of driving rain and sleet drowned his words.

Despite the rain lashing his face he persisted, yelling, 'The Insubres are our allies, not our enemy. Take only what they can spare. Do not chase any that try to escape. If any of you wound a single Insubres you will have me to answer to!' It was hopeless, he doubted if any of them had heard a word he'd said, all they wanted was to get this over and done with as swiftly as possible.

After three more miles of torrential rain and mud-soaked fields they came upon their first settlement; nothing more than a score of thatched roundhouses arranged in a circular pattern beside a swollen stream. At first sight it looked deserted, but judging from the smoke fogging every thatchtop, its inhabitants were simply sheltering from the downpour.

He was riding beside Dubal, captain of the leading eshrin. Dripping water in torrents, Sphax halted the eshrin in the middle of the settlement and bade the men raise their javelins and wait his command. Out

PART TWO: The Winter of Winters

of the corner of his eye he could see entrance cloths twitching and scores of terrified eyes upon him.

He had one significant advantage over his fellow Numidians that morning: none of them understood a word of Latin, whereas the Insubres had learnt that guttural language, mostly under duress. To avoid bloodshed at all costs he'd devised a plan. But it depended on the Insubres responding as he intended. He was about to put it to the test.

'Fly, Insubres!' he yelled. 'Fly for your lives to Placentia or the Roman camp. My orders from Hannibal are that we are to slay every man, woman and child, then burn every village from here to Placentia. We are to show no mercy. But I am giving you this last chance. Take it while you still live. Fly for your lives!'

With palpable relief he saw that it had an instant effect. It was working. From every doorway there was a sudden exodus: women clutching babes to their breasts, yanking the hands of infants, older children shrieking and old men making what headway they could, raising their sticks at the Numidians in rage and defiance, only frailty restraining them from offering resistance.

As the shrieking and wailing faded into the distance, Sphax kissed the ivory image he'd been clutching as the village emptied, and offered up a silent prayer to the goddess.

Dubal stared at him open mouthed. 'By Ba 'al Hamūn, Sphax, what in this life did you say to them?'

'I asked them to leave,' adding with a wink, 'politely.' Looking around at the astounded expressions on Dubal's men he realised they would now have to act fast. The fugitives would raise the alarm in every village this side of Placentia. They'd been extremely lucky. If they'd entered a village with young men or warriors the outcome would have been *very* different. Addressing the eshrin he said, 'Remember what I said. These people are starving. Take little, and nothing of any value. Work fast! Load up your mares and go straight back to camp with Dubal.'

He could see his other eshrins gathering beyond the stream at the edge of the settlement. They needed to move fast. Nudging Dido around he headed off at speed, making sure his men gave the fugitives a wide berth. Mercifully, the rain had eased to a steady drizzle, no longer lashing their faces. It made little difference. Every one of them was already soaked to the skin and frozen to the bone.

They caught sight of the next settlement within three miles, but this was less of a settlement, more a large village of sixty roundhouses at least, centring on what looked like communal buildings, including a feasting hall. He couldn't see any villagers, so guessed the rain was keeping them indoors. So far.

This might be home to as many as four hundred Insubres. Convincing this many folk to leave their homes and flee for their lives called for more than empty threats, he needed a real show of strength. Halting the men he gathered his captains around him.

PART TWO: The Winter of Winters

'Hiempsal and Himilco will circle around behind the village and charge into it from the east. Aribal will circle around and charge from the north whilst Juba does the same from the south. I will take my eshrin into the village from here, from the west. Your signal will be when you hear shouting and raised voices, you're not to make a move until then. Got it?' Everyone nodded. 'Your men must have a javelin in their hand at all times and look threatening. Once in the village, cover the doorways and openings to roundhouses.'

'How do you intend to get them to leave, Sphax?' asked Himilco, shaking his head.

'By scaring them to death!' he said with a doubtful grin. 'It worked in the last settlement, let's hope it works here. I really want to avoid bloodshed,' looking at them in turn. 'None of you would relish killing women and children.' There was a chorus of no's at this.

As the eshrins thundered off in different directions he was left alone with his own men, miserably sitting astride their mares and dripping from every sodden garment they wore.

'By the gods, at least *try* to look like fearsome Numidian horsemen and not like a bunch of youths turned away from a whorehouse!' It was one of Maharbal's favourites. At least it raised a few weary smiles. Judging the other eshrins would be in place by now he shouted, 'Javelins,' and nudged Dido forward.

He began yelling his ultimatum in the midst of a dense cluster of houses near the western edge of the village, at the same time signalling his men to cover doorways and entrances. Sphax couldn't believe his luck. It was working like a charm! Continuing down the street he repeated his blood-curdling threats, adding embellishments and dire warnings. To add to the general panic, the entire village was now being flooded with Numidians with raised javelins knotted and ready to kill. He rode from street to street, yelling his message. That's when the shrieking began as hundreds of villagers flew for their lives. Many were fleeing to stables dotted around the village and mounting horses to speed their escape.

Stoically, he closed his eyes and ears to it all. Better that than the agonised cries of the dead and dying, and the ground littered with the bodies of women, children and old men. He was gambling on the fact that in these warlike times the men would be away, either with Hannibal or Scipio, for this was the stark choice that had been forced on the Insubres. He'd calculated that nothing less than a chilling ultimatum would engender instant panic and a stampede. Taking roundhouses apart one by one would eventually incur wrath and resistance, and lead to inevitable bloodshed.

They had some trouble with groups of youths. These teenagers didn't appreciate being turfed out of their own village, but now mothers and grandmas came to Sphax's rescue by placing restraining hands on shoulders and prodding backs to shuffle their sons and grandsons out of the village, and out of harm's way.

PART TWO: The Winter of Winters

His fellow captains were from a younger generation, not much older than him, a generation that had seen less killing, less barbarity, and all of them shared his reservations about this mission.

'I think we've done as much prodding and poking as we need to do today, Sphax,' said Himilco, levelly. 'Don't you?' Sphax couldn't agree more. But had he fulfilled his duty?

'By now at least four hundred Insubres are fleeing into the arms of Scipio, begging for his protection. We have accomplished what we set out to do.' Hiempsal's logic was undeniable. 'Your subterfuge has worked, Sphax. Let's head back to camp.'

'Allow your men to take what they must, and make sure it's just a token. Let's get on with it — the sooner they load their mares the sooner we get out of this place.' For a while he rode Dido through the village, keeping a close eye on the men to make certain they obeyed his orders scrupulously. He needn't have worried, his eshrin captains were doing the same, examining every single item. Sphax was satisfied.

But his conscience was getting the better of him. His men were following orders, but was he? Looting a small settlement and one village hardly counted as raiding Insubres lands up to the gates of Placentia. Odious as this mission was, if he turned back now, could he look Maharbal in the eye and tell him he'd done his duty? Groaning inwardly, he nudged Dido around and went in search of Himilco.

'I'm going to take my eshrin south and at least empty another village. You're in command here. Get them back to camp with all speed. I'm sure they've taken enough now.' Himilco's shoulders slumped.

'You've done your duty, Sphax, why push your luck?'

'You won't have to face Maharbal on our return.' Himilco shrugged and began relaying orders to his men.

Sphax should have listened. And he should have paid far more attention to the direction some of the youths had galloped off in. The goddess's luck was about to desert him.

It was some time before they came upon another settlement. Sphax guessed they'd covered at least six miles. Mercifully, the showers of sleet had drifted off to the east, leaving a misty haze in their wake which blanketed the ten or so roundhouses in a shroud of wood-smoked fog.

Using the same tactics that had proved so successful that morning, he split his eshrin into four teams and ordered them to charge from each of the cardinal points. But this time there was no exodus as he began his proclamation. Instead, a warrior suddenly confronted him in a doorway, wielding a Gallic blade and clad in helmet, shield and mail. Beside him stood his woman, screaming defiance at him in some Gaulish tongue he would never understand.

Sphax had his saunion wound and levelled. Taking an enormous gamble he decided to bluff it out.

PART TWO: The Winter of Winters

'Drop your blade or your woman dies!' Sphax twitched his saunion so that it pointed at her breast. The Insubres paled, so Sphax pressed home his temporary advantage. 'I will count to three. One ... two ...' Events saved him from reaching three.

The warrior grabbed his woman's shoulders and dragged her back into the roundhouse. From somewhere behind him a woman screamed and at the same time he heard the unmistakable sound of spears thumping into Numidian hide shields.

Frantically nudging Dido around to see what was going on he saw that the settlement had become a battleground. Three young boys, barely able to heft the enormous shields they were carrying, were throwing spears harmlessly at his men. Two boys lay bleeding on the ground, felled by his men's javelins and wailed over by hysterical women. Another woman lay dead, still clutching the spear intended to exact vengeance. The only exodus was of warriors racing *towards* them, armed to the teeth and bent on retribution. In the space of a single breath his ill-considered plan had unravelled disastrously.

'Fly Numidians! *Fly!*' The irony of these words were not lost on him.

When they re-grouped a mile or so to the west of the settlement, Sphax was profoundly relieved to see that all of them had made it out alive and unscathed. But it was a minor miracle that had nothing to do with his leadership, in fact quite the reverse: if he hadn't pushed his luck, if he'd scouted the village before charging so recklessly and paid more attention to those boys in the last village, he wouldn't have the blood of women and children on his hands. He felt ashamed of himself.

'I'm sorry, men. I swear I'll never make that mistake again.' Great guffaws of laughter broke out all around him.

'Of course you will, Sir!' It was Gulussa, the gentle giant of the eshrin. 'You're the son of Navaras, and you haven't half livened up our lives since we got you as captain.'

Sphax would never understand Numidians.

It took them the best part of an hour to catch up with the rest of his eshrins. When Himilco and the other captains saw that Sphax's men had returned emptyhanded, they guessed what had happened.

'News travels fast, especially on horseback,' he said to Himilco. 'They were ready and waiting for us when we turned up. We were lucky to get out of there with our lives. The boys we threw out of that village must have warned them.'

Himilco placed a sympathetic hand on Sphax's shoulder. 'I warned you not to push your luck. But listen, Sphax,' he said anxiously, 'if they can warn a settlement they can also raise the alarm with Longus. It wasn't just boys who rode off in every direction, some of them may have been tribal elders. There must be Roman cavalry patrols in the vicinity.'

PART TWO: The Winter of Winters

Sphax had been thinking along the same lines. Except for his eshrin, more than half the men were now encumbered with bags and sacks strapped to their mares' withers, slowing progress and making it almost impossible to use their javelins. Looking around him it was obvious that in a fight they would come off worse.

'Gather together all the men not burdened with plunder, Himilco, and form a flank guard on our right. Keep the men in single file, so if you do have to face a threat from that direction you can quickly form them into line. My eshrin will act as rearguard.' Sphax despaired at their slow progress. They would only reach safety when they'd crossed the Trebia, and that was at least three miles away. 'Now, Himilco, what are you waiting for? Make it so!' he yelled, galloping off to find Hiempsal's men.

'You must speed this up, Hiempsal. If we're trapped in this open country with the river behind us, we'll be in trouble.' Aribal rode over to join them.

'I know, Sphax, but what can I do? Most of our mares can barely manage a trot,' grumbled Hiempsal. Aribal nodded in agreement. Sphax made a decision.

'I'm not risking our men's lives for a few sacks of wheat and rancid hams. If you see me raise my sword you will order your men to cast their loot aside and either flee, or join us in battle. Understood?' They were both grinning. He was frowning.

'Yes, general,' they chorused.

'Himilco is protecting your right flank. My eshrin is the rearguard. But if the enemy attack us from the left flank, we're lost.' That wiped the grins from their faces. 'Look for my signal,' he reminded them before nudging Dido around and heading back to his own eshrin.

Once back amongst his men he ordered young Agbal to ride like the wind and find Adherbal. Their only hope now was that Adherbal's eshrins could defend them as they attempted the hazardous crossing of the Trebia. To Sphax at that moment, it seemed that nothing short of Adherbal's intervention could stave off the catastrophe that was looming. Sooner or later, Longus would attack them: call it instinct, but he could feel it in his bones.

By the grace of the gods they almost got away with it. But *almost* was their undoing. For their enemies caught them at their most vulnerable, just as Aribal's eshrin, laden down with booty, was struggling across the river. There was no sign of Adherbal.

Himilco's men saw them first and began waving and shouting. Two squadrons of equites were thundering towards them from the higher ground to the north. But what was more alarming were the dense columns of skirmishes and allied cavalry lining up behind them. Sphax knew immediately he was not dealing with a few scattered cavalry patrols. The legions were coming out in force.

'Forward,' he yelled at his eshrin, and together they cantered over to where Himilco was forming his

PART TWO: The Winter of Winters

men into line. Remembering how effective Maharbal's triple line had been when they'd faced Roman cavalry in the fight beside the Rhodanus, Sphax divided their seventy men into two lines. 'This way we can keep up a continuous series of attacks, Himilco. One line charges whilst the other rests.' Himilco understood immediately.

'Like we did at the Rhodanus.'

'Yes. I'll lead the first charge.' Sphax looked anxiously over his shoulder. Aribal's men had already crossed and Juba's eshrin were plunging into the water. Hiempsal was marshalling his men to follow. If they could hold the equites off for a little while they might just make it. Sphax nudged Dido into the line, selected a javelin and tied the thong. The equites had halted and were forming a line three hundred paces ahead of them. He raised his javelin.

'Forward!' That thrill tinged with fear surged through his belly as he dug his knees into Dido and she flew into a gallop. Four more strides and his spinning javelin was winging its way towards its victim. Numidians rarely saw their javelins strike home, for in that heartbeat of a moment they were frantically slowing and turning their mares to the left. A feat only skilled horsemen could accomplish after years of training. The instant Sphax led his men to the rear of Himilco's line he heard the captain yell, 'Forward.'

Slowly nudging Dido around, he watched as Himilco's line thundered forward. Sphax was breathing hard and his mare was panting. They needed this respite. To his utter astonishment the equites' response was to launch a few haphazard spears. They seemed frozen, paralysed in the face of Numidian tactics, and a score of them paid for their indecision. He'd seen it all before in that running fight beside the Rhodanus, but he knew that sooner or later they would charge. And when they did it would be devastating.

When Himilco returned with his men and threaded his way to the rear of the line he hesitated before ordering another charge. Himilco joined him and they both stared gravely at the growing Roman ranks.

'I'm glad you're pausing for thought,' Himilco said, relieved. 'They've been joined by four more turmae, and it looks like the velites are making their way to the front. Remember what happened when the Roman cavalry charged in numbers at the Rhodanus.' Sphax shuddered.

'Your last charge was devastating. But four fresh turmae means one hundred and twenty equites are now lined up against us, as well as what's left of the other two squadrons. I don't like those odds. Even if we combined our lines and charged, we would be outflanked if they charged themselves. What's happening at the crossing?' They both turned around to look.

'Looks like Hiempsal's about to cross,' said Himilco.

'Then it's time to cut and run.'

'I agree,' he said, relieved. Turning around once more to stare at his enemies Himilco suddenly stiffened. 'Dog's twat, Sphax. Look!'

PART TWO: The Winter of Winters

The equites had finally made their minds up. They were rolling forward, gathering speed with every stride, scarlet cloaks and horsehair tassels billowing with the momentum.

'There's another crossing,' Sphax was yelling, 'further downstream. We'll lead them past where Hiempsal's crossing and try and lose them in the thickets beside the river.' He raised his javelin and screamed, 'All of you, follow me!'

'Have we lost them?' Sphax was peering into the mist that was swirling around above the swampy ground beside the river.

'I can't see them,' replied Himilco, uncertainly. 'Neither can I hear them blundering around as they were before.' They were both on foot, hiding behind thorn bushes in a tangled copse of hazel and willow.

'The ford's close by. I think we should make a run for it.'

Tired though their mares were, they had easily outrun the equites' bigger stallions, but the Roman cavalry had doggedly pursued them. Now they were at least three miles upriver beyond the ford across the Trebia. As they'd come abreast, Sphax had anxiously glanced over to see Hiempsal's men were almost across, and was relieved when the Romans continued their pursuit of them. But there could be no doubt that the legions' skirmishers and velites would cross the river in pursuit of Hiempsal's men.

Struggling through the dripping vegetation they made their way back to their men waiting patiently beside their mares. Cold, soaked to the skin and exhausted, he couldn't recall encountering such miserable expressions on the faces of his men.

'We're heading out. The equites have given up searching for us.' At least Sphax detected relief as they mounted up and rode at a walk out of the copse. All he had to do now was remember where the ford was, exactly. They'd discovered it on the morning of his uncle's reconnaissance mission to the Roman camp. One of Hannibal's companion guards had been brave enough to risk his own life wading across. It had turned out to be shallower, and therefore safer, than the crossing his eshrins had used that morning. He knew it was close to the ditch his uncle had made him stand in.

Eventually he found it and they braced themselves for another soaking in the Trebia's freezing waters. When they safely reached its western bank something made him stop and dismount. He drew his sword and began cutting thin branches from a nearby willow, then pushed them into the rain-soaked soil in a distinctive arrowhead pattern that could easily be recognised. He'd realised it might be very useful to mark this unknown ford from its western bank. It might come in handy one day.

'At the canter,' he shouted. 'Let's warm ourselves up.' He led them in a north westerly direction, hoping to intercept his three eshrins that had crossed the

Trebia earlier and provide some protection from their pursuers. But when they breasted a short rise and the entire plain came into view they all brought their mares to a halt and stared.

Two miles or so ahead of them a miniature battle was in progress involving cavalry, skirmishers and his Numidian looters. The battle lines were clearly drawn.

'Himilco, return your men to their rightful eshrins. Stay behind our lines,' he ordered. Then looking around, Sphax yelled, 'My eshrin. Forward!'

TEN

As he drew closer, Sphax became increasingly puzzled by this strange little battle that was taking place. He'd already dubbed it the Battle of the Booty before he'd reached his own lines.

On the Roman side, squadrons of Campanian cavalry and legionary equites sat idle, watching their skirmishers attempt to wrestle back the booty from his Numidians. On their side, Maharbal had positioned several eshrins either side of the booty column, who'd become, like the Romans, idle spectators. The only real fighting was taking place around the eshrins of Hiempsal, Aribal and Juba, who'd formed themselves into a dense column, six horses abreast. By now exhausted and overburdened with booty, the column was moving at a snail's pace.

But this was a battle Rome's skirmishers couldn't possibly hope to win, for surrounding the column were hundreds of Iberian caetrae. It was as if the Lucanian javelinmen, in their attempt to wrest control of the booty had stirred up a hornet's nest. Lightly

PART TWO: The Winter of Winters

armed with buckler, javelins and deadly falcata blades, caetrae were skilled swordsmen, dancing alongside the Numidians like jugglers, wielding bucklers to ward off missiles whilst returning javelins in kind. Occasionally they would launch a raid of their own into the Lucanian ranks, before darting back.

As for the opposing cavalry, this was a perfect, if faintly comical, stand-off. Both sides were so equally matched that they cancelled one another out. If a single squadron from either side went to the assistance of their skirmishes, it would alter the delicate balance of power and almost certainly trigger a charge from their opponents. No one had the upper hand, so everywhere was stalemate in this non-battle. The only change in these dispositions was that every now and again the Numidians would retreat to keep in step with the column of loot and its waspish escort.

As Sphax got to within a hundred paces of his own lines he was sorely tempted to launch his eshrin at the open flank of a Roman squadron. But he was bewildered by all this. First he needed to find out what was going on. So instead, he directed his eshrin to form up behind the Numidians on the right, and went in search of his general.

He was in for another surprise. His uncle was astride Arion at Maharbal's side. He'd known Hannibal long enough to recognise his genuine smile, and that's what he received as he approached. 'Praise be to Melqart, Nephew. We were concerned for your safety. Aribal has given me a complete report of your actions at the Trebia ford. Your prompt action saved the day, and almost certainly saved our little column. You crossed the Trebia by the ford we discovered, presumably.'

It was Sphax's turn to smile. 'How did you know, Sir?'

'It was your only logical course of action.'

'I've marked the ford on its western bank with branches in the shape of an arrow. I thought it might be of some use to us.' Hannibal's smile returned.

'Indeed it might, Nephew ... a wise precaution.'

'General, I think another retreat is called for,' observed Maharbal, at the same time giving Sphax a friendly wink.

For the life of him Sphax couldn't understand what was going on. Why were they retreating? Back in camp they had enough reserves in cavalry alone to surround and destroy the forces opposed to them. Why was his uncle holding back? As they rode at a walk back to a new position two hundred paces to the rear, he plucked up the courage to put forward his proposition.

'Sir,' he began tentatively, 'if you would give me but four eshrins I will circle to the south then launch them at the exposed flank of the Roman cavalry. I swear by all the gods this little battle will be settled within the hour.' To Sphax's consternation his uncle started laughing. Maharbal was no better, chuckling as if he'd heard the best jest in weeks.

PART TWO: The Winter of Winters

'I'm certain it would, Nephew. But that will not be necessary. But thank you for your offer,' his uncle responded with excessive politeness.

A still chuckling Maharbal put him out of his misery, explaining; 'We are allowing Consul Sempronius Longus a minor victory today, Sphax. That's all. What you are witnessing is a sham, a deception, a show of weakness. We are retreating in the face of the invincible legions of Rome, and will continue to retreat until we reach the safety of our camp.'

'But why, Sir,' demanded Sphax, dumbfounded. 'Will it not put us at a disadvantage? Make us appear weak? Incapable of defending ourselves?'

'It will, Nephew. And that is precisely why we are doing it.' Hannibal was being perfectly serious now. 'In war, nephew, always demonstrate weakness in front of your enemies before you reveal your true strength in the final, decisive moment. The decisive moment will be the great battle I promised you when we stood on this plain not a mile from here.'

Sphax remembered. Shaking his head he lamented, 'I see my studies of Xenophon have hardly prepared me for the realities of war. Henceforth, my education will begin anew, Sir.'

'Not at all, Sphax!' his uncle replied earnestly, 'your studies have given you an excellent grounding. But what you must understand is that the art of war is as much about *deception*, as action.'

Sphax was indeed beginning to understand, even if he didn't like it. Deception didn't come naturally to him. He lapsed into silence, brooding over what his uncle had said. When four fresh Roman turmae arrived on the field he emerged from his reverie sufficiently to inform Maharbal they were probably the squadrons that had chased him and Himilco from the Trebia ford. Maharbal simply nodded and turned to an aide to bring up four more eshrins of Numidians.

Later, a fresh horde of velites took to the field and Hannibal personally ordered forward a similar numbers of his slingers from the Balearics. These lightly armed shepherds, recruited from the islands off the Iberian coast, could cast their slingshot pebbles eighty paces with deadly accuracy. Soon they began to exact a terrible toll on their enemies. Rome grew wary.

Mile after ignominious mile the retreat continued. Undoubtedly acting on orders, occasionally a Numidian would cut the cords holding his booty and let it fall. A gesture akin to throwing a dog a bone. Whenever this happened, swarms of velites would pounce on it as if they'd received a great bounty.

And so the great game continued throughout that dreary winter afternoon. Theoretically, he understood perfectly what his uncle was trying to do, but every fibre of his being felt humiliated by it. Ahead of them were perhaps two thousand of Rome's legions, there for the taking — why not destroy them now and even up the odds when they *did* have to fight that great battle?

PART TWO: The Winter of Winters

As a final demonstration of weakness, Hannibal himself marshalled eight thousand Libyan pikemen into line on the plain beyond the perimeter of their own camp. The Libyans were their finest and bravest, they had no equal on this earth. As eshrin after eshrin filtered through the gaps they'd left, Sphax joined his own men and led them into position behind the Libyans' impenetrable wall of pikes.

When the last column of looters shambled through the gates into their camp, Rome drew up its cavalry three hundred paces from the Libyans and began its final humiliation.

At first it was just jeering. Decurions would ride out from their ranks, ride to within twenty paces of a phalanx and begin jeering at them for their cowardice and weakness. Few Libyans understood a word of Latin, so this had little effect. But the pikemen *did* know their enemies were goading them. They'd done it often enough themselves.

Sphax nudged Dido angrily into a gap between two phalanxes so he could hear clearly. As the stand-off continued the equites grew bolder and the insults more humiliating. One particularly brazen tribune astride a chestnut stallion began to ride the length of the Libyan line spewing forth the most obscene insults and issuing challenges along the way. When he came abreast of Sphax he stopped, looked him up and down and yelled, 'All Numidians are cocksuckers.'

The Winter of Winters

At these words, something in Sphax snapped. Whether it was the shame at his part in the death and wounding of innocent women and children, or the humiliation of retreating in the face of an enemy they should have destroyed, Sphax couldn't say. All he knew in that hot and sudden rush of blood, he could take no more.

The tribune was casually trotting back to his own ranks, crimson cloak flowing in the breeze when Sphax threaded his saunion and dug his knees into Dido's flank. In three strides she was racing at the gallop towards the lone horseman.

'I will meet your challenge, Roman,' Sphax shouted at the tribune's back. Slowly the man reined in his stallion, turned him slowly around and glared, an insufferable smile forming on his lips. They were now no more than ten paces from one another.

'I am Sphax, Prince of Numidia.' The flush of temper had left him. He was now icy cold. He raised his voice so the ranks of equites would hear every word. 'What is your name, Roman? I prefer to know the names of those I kill.' The arrogant leer remained fixed on his enemy's lips.

'I am Manius Quintus, tribune of the second legion.' Spitting out the word with venom, he added, 'Cocksucker!' This was his first mistake. Not only would Sphax kill him, he would give the second legion a lesson in horsemanship.

In that instant Sphax dug both knees into Dido and she leapt at the stallion as a leopard pounces on its prey. He trusted Dido completely, but even she came close this time. As she thundered past the startled tribune, Roman and Numidian thighs touched. Quintus hadn't even drawn his sword.

Allowing his mare a wide circuit he put some distance between himself and his opponent. He was quite safe from the two thousand Romans drawn up and watching the contest with relish. Ancient custom demanded that a personal challenge be answered by that man, and that man alone. Neither Roman nor Libyan could interfere now, only fate and destiny.

Be still, Sphax told himself, find that calm. Then the sheer thrill and elation of speed took over his senses and he abandoned himself to instinct, becoming one with Dido. In the midst of exhilarating movement there was always stillness.

Quintus had at last drawn his sword and was brandishing it menacingly. But his second mistake was that he'd decided to sit his stallion and await Sphax's next charge. This was to court death. Humiliation first, thought Sphax.

Appearing to charge directly at Quintus, again he nudged Dido to the left at the last possible instant and she swerved past him out of sword reach. In two strides she'd slowed to a trot, enabling him to slide from her rump and turn around. The tribune was struggling to turn his lumbering stallion. Whistling for Dido, Sphax aimed and levelled his saunion at the unarmoured back of his enemy. It would have been too easy.

Dido approached at a trot and without breaking stride he leapt onto her back and forced the pace. As Quintus wrestled with his reins, Sphax noticed with satisfaction the look of terror on the man's face and the inviting gap above his bronze cuirass that exposed a pale throat.

As he turned Dido to face Quintus once more a decurion broke ranks, and riding up to the tribune, flung him a spear. Much good that will do you, thought Sphax. But with the weapon firmly grasped in his fist, the tribune made up his mind; this time he would charge his opponent.

By now they were a hundred paces apart. Sphax allowed Dido to pick up her own natural rhythm. He knew exactly what he was going to do. When they were fifty paces apart, Sphax anchored his right sandal in Dido's neck rope, waited until Quintus was about to launch his spear then flung himself over on to her shoulder and reached for the ground with his left hand.

Thundering past, all Quintus saw of the Numidian was a sandal and a shin, his spear sailing harmlessly through empty air. In an instant Sphax had flexed his body back into his riding position. But now he wanted that spear! Sliding back on to Dido's croup he managed to turn her in a couple of strides and gallop back to where he guessed the spear had landed. Finally he saw it. Reversing his procedure, Sphax lodged his left foot in the rope and immediately flung his body over Dido's right shoulder, stretching out and arm and fingers to

PART TWO: The Winter of Winters

pick up the spear. He should have kept half an eye on Quintus. Two would've been better.

After missing his target, Manius Quintus had yanked his mount to a halt and turned the beast around. He didn't like being humiliated by a boy not much older than his own son. A boy who refused to fight with honour, and instead used tricks and contrivances. It was unmanly. But now he had the upper hand. He could clearly see what the boy intended: with one of those tricks of his, the Numidian was going recover his spear from where it had landed. Quintus had time to cut him off, and cut him down. He drew his sword.

Sphax had the spear within his grasp when he felt a shattering blow. By the grace of Artemis, as he'd jerked himself to an upright position something had sliced through the spear, missing his fingers by a hairs width. In that instant, if he hadn't been flexing his body into an upright position, it would have been his neck, rather than the spear that suffered the blow. Even so, the force was enough to dislodge his foot from Dido's neck rope, flinging him unceremoniously to the ground.

Badly winded, he struggled to his feet, cast what was left of the spear aside and fingered his saunion. What saved him was the tribune's poor horsemanship. The momentum of his charge had carried him a few strides beyond where Sphax had fallen. By the time he'd reined in his stallion and turned him around for another charge, Sphax was ready for him.

Gathering his wits, he reminded himself that he practised with his saunion every morning for an hour, and some of that practice was devoted to throwing from a standing position, just as he stood now. Tightening his throwing thong he levelled the lethal iron javelin, and waited.

Quintus approached cautiously, jerking his mount forward, sword raised for the kill. This was his undoing.

It seemed Sphax had all the time in the world to steady himself and take careful aim at the tribune's exposed throat. His javelin took flight, uncoiling from the throwing thong that sent it into a rapid spin and increased its accuracy. It struck Quintus above his bronze cuirass, and it struck him with such force that he was bowled backwards from the stallion.

Quintus's stallion strode towards him and stopped, confused and disoriented. Sphax reached out and stroked his rich mane to reassure him. It was only then he became aware of the eerie silence that had descended. His saunion had been a precious gift from Maharbal, he needed to retrieve it.

Gently slapping the stallion's rump, he watched for a moment as the creature trotted back to the Roman lines. Quintus lay dead some few paces away, spread-eagled on the ground, Sphax's saunion still upright in his gullet like a signpost marking a departure from this life. He yanked it out and mounted Dido.

The Libyans were jubilant and cheering him as he threaded his way through their ranks and found

PART TWO: The Winter of Winters

his eshrin. Sphax felt nothing. Just bruised, empty and numb, as if he'd used up another life. He'd been lucky. And if he didn't learn to control his temper and emotions, one day that luck would run out.

At last the Roman equites were retiring and the Libyans began shouldering their pikes. Sphax caught sight of Hannibal and his generals leaving the field, his uncle's face set like thunder.

* * * *

Corinna had gone.

Cesti began to explain in her broken Punic until the tears started to roll down her cheeks, at which point Lulin continued the tale until Cesti felt able to continue again. When they'd both fallen silent, they began searching his face for clues as to how he'd taken this bitter news. Sphax wearily rose from the couch and sat by the brazier, staring into its glowing embers. He'd never felt so bereft.

Piecing their story together, it seemed that Zwalia had arrived at their pavilion in the middle of the morning. She'd seemed worried and concerned. The two of them had sat huddled together by the brazier, babbling away in what Cesti had described as their strange Greek. Sphax took this to mean their native Illyrian. Zwalia had done most of the talking. Sometime later, the two of them had left the pavilion, but returned within the hour with a man.

He'd questioned them as to who this might be. The best that Cesti could come up with was that he might be one of the men from Brundisium. But she was not sure. Corinna and Zwalia had questioned the man at length, in Greek. But they were certain that at times the conversation became quite heated, as if they were trying to force the man to tell them something.

They'd offered Zwalia and Corinna food and drink, but each time Corinna had waved them away. Only the man had eaten the food they'd offered. Soon after he'd left, Corinna had begun gathering her clothes and possessions in her saddle bags and Zwalia had picked up the chest containing the jewellery and golden trinkets. Corinna had embraced and kissed them both before leaving. This was all they knew.

Sphax's mind was racing. Obviously something had gone wrong. But what? Had Zwalia returned to tell her that Dasius and his accomplices had got clean away? In which case they must have chartered some river boat to take them down the Padus to the coast, then taken ship to Brundisium. This had always been Corinna's theory about his likely escape route.

To stay hot on the heels of Dasius would require time and a great deal of silver. Bribing Insubres riverfolk to risk the Roman blockade and transport them down the Padus was one thing, paying captains to sail on the next tide for Brundisium was quite another. If this was the case, he would never see Corinna again. Even if she managed to stop Dasius, she would want to rescue her son from the clutches of his conspirators in Brundisium. No, she would never return, and the thought of never seeing her lovely face again filled him with despair.

He was spared an evening of brooding self-pity by the appearance of his friend, Idwal.

'You're the toast of the camp this evening,' he said jauntily, before examining Sphax's expression more closely. 'What's wrong?'

'Corinna's gone! Zwalia returned this morning and they left together this afternoon. I'm never going to see her again, Idwal. I've lost her.'

Idwal frowned. 'Tell me exactly what happened.' Sphax launched into the account Cesti and Lulin had told him. When he'd finished Idwal got to his feet. 'Put on something warm, Cesti, and come with me.'

'Where are you going?' Sphax asked, puzzled. Idwal was already waiting by the vestibule.

'To find this mysterious Brundisian they questioned.'

Draco was a mean, shifty character with brooding eyebrows and eyes that evaded others. Lulin had laid out food and wine and he greedily ate anything and everything within reach. His manners were not endearing.

At first he was reluctant to talk. But when Sphax drew his blade and rested its point on his chin, his reticence miraculously melted away, and the drink they plied him with further loosened his tongue.

'What information did Corinna want from you, Draco?' asked Idwal bluntly.

'The whore wanted—'

This earned him a vicious slap across the cheek from Sphax, who decided if they were to get any more information from this man he'd better put his blade aside before he was tempted. 'Never use that word again, Draco! That is, if you wish to live through this night. You were saying about the Lady Corinna …' and by now Draco was visibly shaking.

'She wanted to know if Dasius had friends amongst the Taurini.'

'The Taurini!' echoed Idwal, shocked. 'We sacked Taurasia two months ago. They were at war with our allies the Insubres. The traitors had even declared for Rome.'

'Hannibal was bad news for Dasius as he was for the Taurini.'

'Why?' asked Sphax.

'Because Dasius had a lucrative thing going with their chieftains,' slurred Draco. 'He supplied them with wine, whores … anything, in exchange for slaves. In Rome a whore fetches a few asses, whereas a slave costs silver. Dasius was on to a good thing. He called the Taurini his silver mine, but your Hannibal shut down this trade.'

'Give me some names, Draco. Which Taurini chieftains? Where?' demanded Idwal. Sphax fingered the ivory guards on the hilt of his sword. Draco got the message.

'I swear by all the gods I know of only one name. I only went with Nestor and the other two—'

'Isn't Nestor one of the three that freed Dasius?' interrupted Sphax.

'Yes. Nasty piece of work, that one. As are the other two. Nestor ran the trade in slaves for Dasius. I only went because it was a big shipment, and they needed an extra pair of hands. I only went once. I swear it!' Draco was growing more desperate, his eyes darting between his inquisitors.

'We believe you, Draco,' Idwal reassured him. 'For now.'

'Where did this trade take place?' asked Sphax. 'Which Taurini chieftain was supplying you with slaves?' Draco hesitated. Sphax raised his dragon sword.

'All right ... all right! The chief's name was Lugotorix ... the settlement was Vigevanius on the Ticinus.' Idwal glanced at Sphax.

'With a name like that the man has pretensions to kingship.'

'He'd the wealth of a king,' muttered Draco.

Sphax was beginning to understand. He needed to talk to Idwal, alone. 'You may go, Draco.' As the Brundisian staggered to his feet, Sphax quickly gripped his blade and held it against the man's throat. Draco froze. 'If I find you've been lying to me, Draco, or not telling me the *whole* truth, I will pay you another visit. For you it will be a last visit. Do you understand?'

Draco could hardly nod. The sword-point was already digging into his scrawny neck. Somehow he managed to gurgle acceptance. When Sphax removed his sword, the man couldn't get out of the pavilion fast enough.

For a while the two friends sipped from their cups in silence. At last Idwal said, 'I'm afraid I wasn't much help, my friend.'

Shaking his head, Sphax grinned. 'I hadn't even the wit to go and search for the man with Cesti.'

Idwal laughed. 'I think you were a little preoccupied, and had forgotten your Socratic first principles.'

'I've always had you to remind me of them, Idwal,' he answered, his mood already lightening. 'But thanks to you, I think I've worked out why Zwalia returned this morning and the two of them left so hurriedly this afternoon.'

'You mean that *hunting* party that no one is supposed to know about, especially your uncle.' Sphax was grinning now.

'It's impossible to keep secrets in this place—'

'Especially when the Anamares encampment is next door to my pavilion!'

'Have you met Artula?' Idwal nodded. 'Then you know everything.'

'Not everything ... but some. But tell me, why did Corinna leave this afternoon?' Sphax sighed, staring into the brazier.

'Because my little hunting party as you call it have been looking in the wrong place. They've been scouring the banks of the Padus and questioning the Insubres. Zwalia must have returned to tell her mistress they'd drawn a blank. Then Corinna or Zwalia must have made the connection between Dasius's trading links with the Taurini and Nestor's visits to settlements along the Ticinus. The only person who could have confirmed this for them, was Draco.'

'What are you going to do now?'

'I don't know, Idwal. I really don't know …'

ELEVEN

Sphax passed the next two days in an agony of indecision. All his reasoning was telling him to sit tight and wait for news of Corinna. But patience was a foreign language he'd never mastered. Setting out at dawn, he knew he could reach the Ticinus by mid-afternoon. When he and Jugurtha had shadowed Scipio's legions westwards, they'd scouted the western bank of the river north from Ticinum for several miles. Vigevanius could only have been a few miles beyond.

But then the doubts and obstacles would arise, casting uncertainty on the path he should take. In that vast empty tract north of Ticinum, where settlements were far and few between, would he be able to find them? After the sacking of their chief settlement, the Taurini had sued for peace. But the Taurini owed Carthage no favours. Quite the reverse. More likely, once he'd set foot in their territory he would meet with open hostility. And even if he found them, what could he do? Defend Corinna? Corinna was more than capable of looking after herself.

PART TWO: The Winter of Winters

So every hour he waited and fretted. And every hour the pain of separation became heavier to bear. And every hour that darkest thought of all, that he would never see her again, gripped his soul.

He took some comfort from visiting Artula. She had no more news than he had, but talking about Corinna and Meilyr seemed to lighten his mood. Artula bore separation with more fortitude than he was demonstrating, so in a sense, she became something of an inspiration for him.

The afternoon of the second day of her absence found him where he'd spent most of the first; absently fretting in his chair beside the brazier, lost in thought. Cesti and Lulin were in despair. In the dark days following Fionn's death they'd seen him withdraw into himself and feared it was happening again. Both of them knew him as well as anybody, and both knew that the only remedy for his malaise was activity and purpose, so when every available horn in the camp suddenly burst into a strident fanfare that afternoon, they felt relieved.

At last the strident call to arms awoke Sphax from his brooding reverie. It seemed highly unlikely they were about to be attacked, so why were they being summoned? One way or another he cared little that afternoon. Throwing his beaverskin cloak over his shoulders he almost collided with Idwal in the vestibule.

'What's going on?' he asked.

Idwal scowled, 'From the rumours I'm hearing we're about to witness a barbarous piece of theatre, stage-managed by your uncle.'

This was intriguing enough to rouse Sphax from his indifference as they joined the great throng that was making their way to the eastern gate. Whatever theatricals they were being summoned to, it looked as if the entire army had been invited. As they trudged on Sphax asked his grim-faced friend if he cared to elaborate.

'You'll know soon enough,' was all Idwal was prepared to say.

When they passed through the gate and over the ditch where hundreds of severed heads of legionary infantry still lay rotting and blackening, he saw that on the plain beyond the gate the entire army was being marshalled to line a vast empty square. Even with his limited knowledge of military custom, Sphax knew exactly what the square symbolised and its purpose. The only question now was who was being punished, and for what?

By the time he and Idwal elbowed their way to the front, he estimated they were amongst a crowd of thirty thousand, and because every man had answered the call regardless of whether they were at drill or leisure, there was no order or design to the ranks lining the empty square. Libyans stood shoulder to shoulder with Iberians or Numidians. All stood in grim silence or spoke in hushed tones with their neighbours. Sphax was struck by the solemnity of it all.

PART TWO: The Winter of Winters

Each side stretched for some three hundred paces enclosing a vast area in the middle. A single Libyan, wearing full armour and bearing a pike, stood guard in each corner and five great chairs had been placed at one end.

To his right the ranks suddenly parted and Sphax saw his uncle stride into the arena, flanked by his Greek scholars and followed by Maharbal and the Libyan general, Hanno. There was a brief wave of muttering around the square as they took up their chairs. But what followed next was completely unexpected and stirred up an even greater chorus of muttering which his uncle had to silence by raising an arm.

Ten Gauls, shackled together in chains at the neck and ankle were being herded into the arena by their Libyan guards. Sphax had never seen such expressions of misery and degradation. What was left of their tunics and leggings was in tatters and offered little protection from the bitter cold as they shuffled forwards, barefoot. Their guards forced them into a sorry line in front of the chairs where they stood with heads bowed, awaiting their fate.

'They're Tricorii,' whispered Idwal.

Sphax stiffened. 'I didn't know we took any of them prisoner.'

'Just these ten. Your Uncle has been keeping them up his sleeve for just such an occasion.'

That fateful day in the mountains would forever live in his darkest memories. As their columns had straggled over ten miles of terrain that encompassed everything from deep ravines to vertiginous mountainsides, the Tricorii had savagely attacked them at several points. By late afternoon their marching columns had been severed. That evening Hannibal himself had been cut off from the rest of his army and spent an anxious, sleepless night on a rocky pinnacle, surrounded by his men. Dawn brought them victory, but at a terrible cost.

Only a week before, Tricorii elders had held olive branches aloft and offered hostages and gifts, swearing peace and safe passage through the mountains. Such treachery would never be forgotten.

As Sphax stared with displeasure at the shackled warriors, he found it impossible to stop himself thinking that any one of them might have been responsible for hurling the boulder that struck Fionn and tossed her into the abyss like a rag doll.

'What are they being punished for?' he asked. 'Being Tricorii?'

'You'll see,' Idwal grunted, 'soon enough.'

Sphax could see the Libyans in the crowd eyeing the prisoners with open hostility. Hanno's Libyans had been surrounded and trapped in a narrow ravine, suffering grievous losses as they'd fought their way out. It was obvious why his uncle had assigned Libyans to guard the prisoners, and it came as no surprise to see they'd been half-starved and ill-treated.

Crowds parted once more as stallions were led into the arena followed by slaves carrying clothing, armour

PART TWO: The Winter of Winters

and weapons. This appeared to be a cue for Hannibal and the Greek scholar, Sosylos, to rise from their chairs and begin the address. The silver-haired Sosylos always appeared frail beyond his years, but he possessed a remarkable gift for languages and a voice that was firm and resonant.

Hannibal stood before the prisoners, steadily gazing at each in turn before turning his attention to the thousands lining the square. 'If I were to offer you the means to win your liberty this afternoon, would you take it?' His uncle had spoken in Punic, the common tongue of the army, and now he paused to allow Sosylos to translate his words into a dialect of Gallic the Tricorii would understand. When he'd finished, bowed heads were suddenly raised and there was a great commotion amongst them.

His uncle took this to mean affirmation, and so continued. 'For some I offer not only liberty, but also gifts to enable you to return to your homes and villages. As for the rest, I also offer a great gift; an end to your misery and torment.' Hannibal paused again to allow the Greek to translate before continuing, 'I'm sure you would all agree that the most precious gift the gods have bestowed on mankind is our liberty. Throughout all history men have been prepared to fight and die to uphold their liberty. Are you prepared to fight for yours this afternoon?' When Sosylos stopped speaking the chains rattled as the Tricorii solemnly nodded.

'Even if it means fighting your fellow prisoners in mortal combat?'

There was some consternation at this shocking twist. Prisoners turned to stare at one another, but it only lasted for a moment. Soon heads were once again nodding in affirmation.

'Then you will draw lots to decide the order of combat between the ten of you.' His uncle clapped his hands and slaves began parading horses, arms and armour before the Tricorii. 'For the victorious, you will be rewarded with a horse and gifts of weapons, armour and clothing. You will be free to return to your homeland immediately. No man in my army will stop you or bar your path. This I solemnly swear before you.' Returning his gaze to the prisoners, his uncle continued, 'As for those amongst you who will be vanquished, I offer you an honourable death and a swift release from your miserable condition. To all I offer death or glory. Is there a man amongst you who would refuse such an opportunity?' When Sosylos' voice fell silent everyone heard the clang of chains as every single prisoner shook his head.

'Then so be it,' proclaimed Hannibal, raising his voice so all the gathering would hear. 'Let Melqart and Morrígu decide the fates of these brave men who have chosen death or glory above chains and shackles. To regain their freedom they are willing to risk death itself. Is this not an admirable and noble sentiment in all men? Let this be a lesson to us all!' His uncle paused again to let this sink in. 'Release the Tricorii from their shackles and let them step forward to draw their lots.'

Up until now there had been a hushed silence all around him, but as the prisoners were released from their chains and stepped forward to thrust an arm into a clay amphora to draw the lot that would decide their fate, Sphax heard a renewed wave of excited muttering surge around the square.

Idwal's Punic was rudimentary, but he'd understood enough of Sosylos' Gallic to be clear about Hannibal's intentions. 'Your uncle is about to enact a spectacle that will serve as an allegory for our army.'

'I understand the symbolism,' whispered Sphax, 'but why must it be driven home so brutally?'

'In our present predicament, perhaps this is the only message our common soldiers will understand.'

'I refuse to believe that,' hissed Sphax. 'After all our men have been through they surely know what's at stake.' Their whispered conversation was brought to a halt by the sight of two of the Tricorii sizing one another up and being handed swords and shields. A tense and uneasy hush now descended on the thousands forced to witness this spectacle of death or glory.

It looked to Sphax as if Morrigu had dealt one of the warriors an ill-starred lot. With black unkempt hair streaked with grey, his frame was slight and his bearing ungainly, whereas his opponent had youth on his side, was a head taller and looked fast and agile on his feet. But looks can be deceptive. Only skill with shield and blade mattered in these desperate contests and the younger man, though stronger and faster, possessed little. Growing increasingly more desperate, the younger man began charging forward with flailing sword and raised shield, and it was one such reckless charge that sealed his fate as the veteran suddenly lowered a knee and thrust underneath the shield.

Standing next to him was a Libyan veteran about the same age as the older prisoner. Sphax had felt his body jerking and twitching in sympathy with every thrust and parry the Tricorii made, even sensing the Libyan's relief when experience triumphed over youth.

Examining the faces of the men lining the square he could see that many were indeed cheering or jeering a blow that was struck or received. But some were not looking on with such callous indifference to the inevitable outcome. Sphax recognised expressions of pity, even compassion for what they were being forced to witness. The sight of the second death turned his stomach.

'I can't bear to watch this anymore, Idwal. It's barbarous!' and with that he forced his way back through the crowd. Making his way behind the western side of the punishment square he walked to where the side had been breached to allow the victors to ride in triumph from the arena and the bodies to be hastily removed. Sphax wanted to see for himself the expression and demeanour of those that had triumphed, but the first sight that met his eyes was of two Libyans dragging feet first the bloodied corpse of one the victims.

PART TWO: The Winter of Winters

As each Tricorii warrior left the square armed and newly mounted, with a fine cape around his shoulders, Sphax saw for himself that written on their faces was neither triumph nor elation, but the look of guilty men who'd somehow cheated death. The last of them was openly weeping.

'Gather around and form a circle,' came the cry that suddenly echoed all around the arena. It was over, thought Sphax, fingering his ivory figurine of the goddess. A circle meant speeches, not killing. Sphax managed to spot Idwal in the crowd and once more stood beside him as his uncle began to speak, translating the Punic into Greek for his friend.

'What you have seen,' Hannibal began, 'was more than a spectacle for your entertainment; it was an allegory of our own predicament, and I believe that fate has laid upon us far heavier chains. Within days we too will have the same stark choices offered to us by our enemy; a choice between death or glory, triumph or defeat. And we are not so fortunate as the Tricorii, who can ride back in safety to their homes and villages. Even our enemy can flee the battlefield and reach the security of their city walls and gates. But for Libyans, Iberians, Numidians and Carthaginians, home is unattainable. We are hemmed in by sea at every turn and the Alpine barrier is now locked in the icy grip of winter.

'Flight and cowardice are for men who see safety at their backs, who can retreat on easy roads and find refuge in their native lands. But they are not for you!

For you there is no middle way between victory and death or slavery. Cast all hope of flight from your mind. We are alone in a foreign land, surrounded by our enemies. We either conquer by the sword or meet death honourably on the battlefield. Melqart has given to man no greater spur to victory than contempt of death. And for you the prize of victory will be more than horses and cloaks, but to be the most envied of mankind, masters of all the wealth of Rome.

'As we stood together on that last Alpine pass before we descended into Italia, I said to you that only the bravest of the brave and the strongest of the strong could have endured the trials and tribulations of such a momentous journey. These words are truer now than when I spoke them weeks ago. Since then we have routed Rome's cavalry, wounded a consul and forced him to retreat to an armed camp beyond the Trebia. Rome is fearful and in retreat. Whereas every day our numbers swell with our Insubres and Boii allies.

'Wherever I look I see men of courage and audacity, men who have never been defeated in battle, men drawn from nations of noble blood, united by our common purpose and hatred of Rome. We are the aggressors, we the invaders of Italia, and we have already struck the first blow. It will be the first of many as we begin our march on Rome. Let nothing stand in the way of our invincible armies as we drive all before us.'

Cheering erupted the instant Hannibal fell silent, and it was still continuing as he left in deep

PART TWO: The Winter of Winters

conversation with Hanno and Hasdrubal for the warmth of his pavilion. The crowds too drifted away in animated conversation leaving Sphax and Idwal wondering what to make of it all.

'My uncle's speech was clear and to the point,' argued Sphax. 'There was no need to force those wretched prisoners to fight each other to the death to illustrate his argument. When Sosylos writes the history of this war they will be remembered as an insignificant footnote. Men's lives should not be reduced to a footnote! I found the entire episode distasteful, barbaric and ... quite unnecessary.' They were sitting in their usual seats beside the brazier in his pavilion with cups of wine, nibbling at cold meats and cheeses Lulin had managed to scrounge.

'I too found it abhorrent, Sphax, but I also saw the profound effect it had on our men! You saw their faces ... heard the arguments and discussions they were having as they left. I'll wager that right now, around scores of campfires our men are talking about your uncle's speech. And I can assure you they will not be questioning the morality of what he did.'

'Then they should,' Sphax sighed, recharging their cups. The debate between them had already been going on for some time. 'I believe there is a line that must be drawn and never crossed, otherwise we descend into depravity and barbarism. I believe my uncle overstepped this mark.' He found himself absently shaking his head. 'Both of us have seen for ourselves that war is a calamity, Idwal, nothing short of a plague on humanity. Even when war is fought for causes that are just, it's still a calamity. So I believe the least we can do is steer a course through its evils that will allow us to maintain our honour and virtue. My teacher, Elpis, once told me the story of Socrates at the battle of Potidaea. It has long stayed in my memory and I think about it often. I hold it to be an exemplar of valour exercised through honour and compassion.'

Idwal smiled, 'I too know the story. When his friend Alcibiades is wounded, he rescues him, binds his wound and stands guard over him until help arrives. At last we agree, my friend, it is indeed a noble story.'

'Then you will recall,' Sphax added, 'that when Socrates was awarded the prize for valour he turned it down and recommended it be given to Alcibiades. So I can add selflessness and modesty to my list of qualities we must try to emulate in war.'

'What a list!' laughed Idwal. 'Such Olympian ideals, Sphax. I for one will certainly fall short.'

PART THREE

THE SCOURGE OF ROME

TWELVE

Next day Cesti and Lulin had been trying their best to avoid him whilst inventing jobs for the four boys that would keep them out from under his feet. When in the late afternoon Maharbal entered unannounced, it came as a welcome distraction.

'Still mooning over that lady of yours?' Sphax said nothing. 'Brighten up, lad! Your uncle has just invited you to your first council of war.'

'Me!' Sphax leapt to his feet and stared at the general, then he couldn't resist adding, 'Does that mean I've been given a promotion, Sir?'

'Of course, Sphax! You're now to command all the whores, jugglers and dancers in camp ... all I know is he's asked for you. So let's find out what devious plan he has in mind for you. I'll wager it's the best jest I've heard in months.'

Moments later he was standing amidst a select group of generals and chieftains gathered before Hannibal. Wherever he looked he saw polished

PART THREE: The Scourge Of Rome

cuirasses and helmets dripping with silver and horsehair plumes. In his simple tunic and beaverskin cloak, Sphax felt uncomfortably out-ranked and under-dressed. That is, until he saw Idwal standing beside Mago, and then caught sight of Hiempsal, Hannibal's Master of Elephants, wearing a tattered hooded tunic that looked as if it hadn't been washed this side of the Alps. Hannibal stood, and for a few moments cast his ill-matched eyes over them all.

'Tomorrow we fight our battle, on ground of my choosing. This is how it will be conducted, and how it will be decided.' There was nothing boastful or conceited in his tone. It was said in a cool, factual manner, as if he was giving a stranger directions to the nearest town.

Hannibal gestured to a low table that had been placed in the middle of his pavilion. Sphax could see that it was covered in oblong tiles of wood the width of a man's hand. Each piece had been painted either black or white, and at either end of the table sat two larger blocks in red ochre. Flowing blue lines had been painted directly on to the table, and it was these that gave Sphax a hint of what this might represent.

Tracing with his finger the broader blue line as it traversed the length of the table, his uncle observed, 'The Padus River.' With growing excitement, Sphax realised this was an eagle's view of the area between the Roman and Carthaginian camps, represented by the larger red blocks. It was a map, and as if to confirm this, Hannibal swept his hand over the thinner blue line that joined its elder brother at right angles. 'The river we have come to know as the Trebia,' and pointing to each red block, said in turn, 'Our camp, and here the Roman camp.' Deftly he gathered up all the white tiles and placed them beside the Carthaginian camp, placing the black ones by the Roman camp.

'For the last few days I've been pointing out to anyone who has ridden with me the usefulness of this feature,' tracing a faint blue line that entered the Trebia far to the south. 'It's no more than a ditch, yet its banks are deep enough to hide an army from view on the plain above. My nephew can testify to the truth of this observation.'

So that's what it had been about! He remembered being mystified when his uncle had asked him to descend into the ditch and then promptly ridden away. Sphax grinned and nodded acknowledgment.

'Tonight, under cover of darkness, I intend to plant an army in that ditch. It will remain hidden until the moment is ripe. Idwal, Lord of the Cavari, has already proved himself against the Allobroges. Together with a thousand Numidians, I'm certain his eight hundred Cavari will gain great honour and reputation for slaying Romans. This force will be commanded by my brother, Mago, who has long complained that all I ever trust him with is the baggage train. I believe that he will also prove himself tomorrow.' At that point the gathering erupted in cheers and thigh slapping as Mago looked

PART THREE: The Scourge Of Rome

on with a broad smirk. Raising a hand for silence, his uncle continued.

'At first light, before trumpets have awoken our enemy from their tents, six hundred of our Numidians will attack the Roman camp. Roman cavalry will surely be drawn out to meet this challenge. But I believe its legions will follow. Consul Longus is eager for battle, and I am confident he will seize this opportunity to attack.'

Sphax was beginning to find this alarming. At the mention of Numidians his uncle's eyes had been fixed on him, and him alone. 'Numidians are expert in herding cattle, and with their excellent tactics of attack and retreat, they will herd the legions of Rome to our slaughter pens.' Sweeping his hand towards the Trebia he deftly placed three rows of black tiles parallel with its eastern bank.

Pointing at each in turn he identified, 'Cavalry, velites, and finally, the legions and their allies. Observe that the legions will be in three columns. On the march, Rome separates her legions into hastati, principes and triarii, so they may easily get into formation on the battlefield.' Again, Sphax felt the intensity of his uncle's gaze as he continued.

'Our Numidian cattle-herders' next task is to tempt our enemies across the River Trebia. If employed intelligently, I'm sure a combination of brazen insult and calculated injury will lure them across. Bear in mind, gentlemen, the river is badly swollen from the recent rains. It will reach a legionary's chest as they wade across.

The Winter of Winters

'So ... we finally arrive at the battle of my choosing, on the ground that I have decided. Consul Longus will form his allies and legions thus.' Some few miles west of the Trebia, Hannibal began to arrange the tiles in three separate lines. Again, pointing to each line in turn, 'hastati, principes and triarii.' In front of all will be their velites and skirmishers.' Finally, placing one tile either side of the whole he looked up at his audience. 'Roman and allied cavalry.' Sphax knew then that his uncle had decided on the site of the battle days ago, when they had both stood on that flat plain in the middle of nowhere.

'Longus is not a military genius, nor is he an original thinker. He will do as he's been trained to do in the time-honoured fashion of Roman warfare. Longus will do as he's been told, and tomorrow this will be the formation you see before you.' For a few moments his uncle turned away from the table and paced backwards and forwards, lacing his fingers together, seemingly lost in thought. Finally he came to rest, and picked up the pile of white tiles from the table.

'So, how will we respond?' Here his uncle paused, and half smiling, savoured the hushed silence that had fallen. 'Firstly, we should not hurry. Our men should enjoy a leisurely breakfast and eat well. They should select their warmest clothing, anoint themselves with oils against the cold, light additional campfires to keep themselves warm and take their ease.

PART THREE: The Scourge Of Rome

'Once our enemies emerge dripping wet and numb with cold from the River Trebia, it will take them at least four hours to marshal their legions into the formation you see here. Placing forty thousand men in strict formation takes time. I have done my calculations carefully, you can be certain of this. Neither do I intend to stand idly by as they form up for battle. We will send forward all our slingers and Iberian caetrae to disrupt them. Believe me, our enemies will pay a heavy price for their neat little lines.

'So gentlemen, there will be no need to hasten our infantry from the warmth of their campfires tomorrow. Firstly, our cattle-herders will rejoin the rest of their brethren on the left of our line, commanded by Maharbal.' Hannibal placed two white tiles just south of the Padus river. 'Then, our Iberian cavalry alongside our new Gaulish allies will form up on the right of our line.' Hannibal paused to place two more pieces in position.

'Finally, our entire infantry line will move forward into position. Gauls in the centre, Iberians on the right wing and Libyans on the left.' Sphax watched as his uncle carefully placed nine tiles in the exact position he required. 'If our Numidian cattle-herders have done their work properly and roused Longus before dawn, the enemy we face tomorrow will be not only weary and cold, but half-starved from want of breakfast.'

'Do you neglect elephants, my general?' It was Hiempsal, completely unabashed by the moment, or occasion.

'I do not, Master of Elephants, but thank you for reminding me.' He'd never seen his uncle in this mood. He was smiling and evidently enjoying himself. It was so out of character! What had suddenly possessed him? It so confounded his doleful nature that Sphax found it almost disconcerting. 'For you, my carpenter has made a special signifier,' and Hannibal reached for two white circular disks which he placed on either wing of the cavalry. 'Just so!' Hiempsal was beaming.

'As to the conduct of the engagement. We will wait for our enemy to attack us. Once the legions have closed with our centre, our elephants will charge, followed by cavalry from both wings. As we have twice their number in cavalry, Longus will slowly be encircled, at which point, Mago will launch his forces directly into the rear of their centre.' With both hands he dramatically swept all the black tiles into a disordered heap. 'The day will be ours, and Longus destroyed.'

He noticed the edge had gone from his uncle's voice, as if he was suddenly disinterested in the proceedings. Sphax suddenly grasped something of his uncle's mind and seemingly impenetrable thought processes. Battles were merely an intellectual exercise. Like unpicking the logic underpinning a Zeno paradox. Once the flaws had been discovered and identified, the rest was commonplace, if not a little dull. Sitting down heavily on his divan he made a gesture with his hands that invited comment or questions. It was not long before

PART THREE: The Scourge Of Rome

the giant figure of Hanno, resplendent in silvered helmet and bonze cuirass, edged forward to speak.

'An excellent plan, my general, and I'm sure that if we could lure our enemy into such a position, on ground of your choosing, the outcome would be exactly as you've predicted. But how can we be certain of this? Why should Longus do our bidding and meet us on our terms?'

'These are not unreasonable questions, Hanno. And as usual, I'm indebted to you for raising them. I have based my reasoning purely on logic and the information that I've gathered. But there is another element in my thinking, and that is the Roman character, in particular, the character of Consul Longus.

'I have two Insubres informants in Placentia who visit the Roman camp daily. Their information and assessments have been invaluable. Also, I questioned carefully our Gaulish allies that deserted their former paymasters, gleaning much information. This is my assessment of the Roman position.

'Consul Scipio was badly wounded during the fight at the Ticinus. He has taken to his sickbed and is incapable of service in the field. When Longus' legions joined him, Scipio's council was to wait out the winter and await reinforcement from Rome in the spring.

'Longus thinks otherwise. He is eager to give battle. His petty victory over us three days ago when we deliberately retreated before him and refused battle has given him an inflated view of Rome's prowess. As

I intended it should. Longus' term of office ends soon, by early spring he will be replaced by fresh consul nominates, and his moment of glory may pass forever. This weighs heavily on him.

'He yearns for glory, but like all Romans of his class, he is blind, foolish and arrogant. These people are ruled by temperament and know nothing of reason and logic. It is important to remember that generalship is shared by the consuls: each commands on alternate days. Tomorrow Longus commands. And tomorrow Longus will do as *we* command!'

Beside him, Sphax sensed Maharbal's growing agitation. 'I grant you the course of events you describe is quite likely, given the nature of Longus and the Roman temperament. But I know you better than you know yourself, Hannibal … there's something you're not telling us?' There were only two men his uncle tolerated such forthright questioning from. One had already spoken, and the other was Maharbal. 'Who are these six hundred Numidians you speak of? What are you keeping from us?'

That oddly sinister half-smile formed at the corners of Hannibal's mouth. 'What I have in mind, Maharbal, is my nephew, Sphax. He's the only Numidian I need.'

Sphax suddenly felt the intensity of a score of eyes cast in his direction. But he was so astonished by what his uncle had just said that all he could do was gape and stare. He was also aware that his uncle was enjoying the drama and deliberately prolonging it.

PART THREE: The Scourge Of Rome

'Isn't it obvious?' Hannibal intoned, clasping his hands behind his head and leaning back on the luxurious cushions strewn about his divan. This was met by an incredulous silence.

'I must confess that three days ago, when he challenged the tribune to single combat, I was furious with him.' Dismissing the murmur of disapproval with a wave of the hand, Hannibal continued. 'I know you all feel that after a day of ignominious retreats, he restored some honour to our cause. But I didn't want our honour restored! I wanted us to appear broken and defeated, *without* honour. But by some quirk of the fates, my nephew's impetuous actions played right into our hands and helped me crystallize my plans.

'Only one Numidian is talked about in the Roman camp. The Numidian who led his eshrin forward and wounded Consul Scipio, then challenged his son to single combat before being seemingly slain by a spear of a humble eques. So imagine their shock when he turns up weeks later in an Anamares village and slays a decurion and eight of his men in combat.

'How could this be? What miracle had been performed? Only the gods can restore mortals back to life. Have the gods made him invulnerable, they ask? Romans are a superstitious people, a people who would rather turn to their sibyls and augurs than examine a mystery with intelligence and the rigours of the mind.' His uncle paused and smiled at him. 'This is the talk of the Roman camp, and I must say it has provided

The Winter of Winters

me with much amusement this week feeding these rumours. When our reborn hero turns up to challenge a Roman tribune and defeats him in single combat, the myth is naturally magnified.

'As you all know, my nephew was restored by our excellent physicians, and as the blood of the Barcas flows through his veins, he is already favoured by the gods.' His uncle clapped his hands and a Libyan entered carrying what looked like a battered Roman standard. Bowing, he handed it to Hannibal. 'Adherbal's eshrin won this on the Ticinus.' His uncle rose from the divan and raised the standard aloft.

'This is not just a standard, it's a consul's standard. When my nephew carries this to the gates of the Roman camp at dawn tomorrow and challenges Consul Scipio and his son to come and recover it, I believe they will rise to that challenge. What army could ignore such an insult to their honour? Certainly not Rome. Longus and Rome would forever be remembered for their cowardice.' It was then that Sphax realised he himself possessed knowledge that could increase the chances of Rome meeting this challenge.

'Especially, Uncle, when I also challenge Praetor Gaius Lucilus to face the killer of his son. Lucilus is perfectly aware of who I am. This will ensure his division of cavalry will be first out of their gate.'

Hannibal laughed. 'A touch of genius, Nephew!' But then his uncle frowned. 'Are you sure he will be in the Roman Camp? His name is not familiar to me.'

PART THREE: The Scourge Of Rome

'I'm certain of it, Sir. He is a client of Longus. He will be there!'

'Then it is certain that Rome will do our bidding tomorrow. Make it so.' With that the council of war seemed to be at an end. Maharbal gripped his shoulder.

'Walk with me. I need to talk to you. Urgently. But not here,' and with that he guided Sphax out of the pavilion. After twenty paces Maharbal continued, 'Swear to me that you will only reveal that you are the killer of Lucilus' son if everything else fails. As a last resort. I mean that ... a *last* resort!' Sphax was genuinely puzzled.

'Why, Sir? I'm not going to hide from that snake, Lucilus. He beat me for ten years. This will be part of my revenge until I get the chance to run the bastard through with my saunion.' Maharbal stopped and gravely eyed the young man he'd grown so fond of.

'You'll be making yourself the most wanted man in the whole of Rome. You would be putting a price on your head. It would be like signing your own death warrant.' The general resumed his pace, shaking his head. 'War is uncertain, Sphax. Only Ba 'al Hamūn knows our fate. You may be captured or forced to surrender. Once your identity is revealed Rome will exact a terrible revenge. I would not wish a slow and painful death on any soldier, but I fear if you reveal yourself as a murderer, Rome will inflict such a death on you. Your infamy will demand it. Please, I beg you, only reveal yourself to Lucilus if all else fails.'

Sphax recalled how he'd stood outside the gates of Clastidium and issued Dasius with every threat they'd managed to contrive, yet all had failed until he'd used Corinna as a last resort. How he needed her counsel at that moment. But she was long gone, and he'd resigned himself to never seeing her again. When he faced his enemies tomorrow, he knew full well that he might have to resort to a Corinna solution. A last resort.

'I swear I will only challenge Lucilus if all else fails ... but it may come to that, Sir.'

'Let's pray it won't. Let's hope that your uncle is right, and a few insults and that standard will suffice.' Maharbal gave him a sly grin. 'Consul Scipio's son is obviously telling a different tale to the sorry account you gave me.' Sphax laughed.

'I told you the truth. Believe me, there was nothing heroic about it! Obviously the young Scipio is fabricating a reputation.' They had arrived outside Maharbal's pavilion.

'Let's get out of this terrible cold,' he said, leading the way to a chair and his favourite stool planted beside the warmth of the brazier. Ayzabel was summoned and asked to find a jar of Malacca and cups. Sphax smiled at his host. This was a rare treat. The general tended to hoard his store of this deliciously sweet golden wine.

'Will you choose the eshrins for me, Sir?'

'No! You can choose, lad. But you'll need some old heads with you tomorrow, so choose wisely. Commanding twenty eshrins is quite a responsibility.' Sphax nodded.

PART THREE: The Scourge Of Rome

Ayzabel and a slave arrived carrying the precious jar and cups. Pouring a generous cup for herself first, she winked at Sphax and handed him a cup. 'You are being honoured, my lovesick Numidian. Is this to help drown your sorrows?' A flat of a hand landed on his lady's shapely rump. 'Off with you, woman!' Maharbal said, as a giggling, Ayzabel left them to it.

'Was my uncle really furious with me for challenging the tribune, Sir?' Sphax asked, curious.

'Not so much furious as *livid*. In fact,' the general continued, chuckling, 'I think he was secretly hoping you'd come off worst ... which you almost did, if I remember. You've got more fancy tricks than a Sicilian whore!'

'I wouldn't know, Sir,' he laughed.

'You're not likely to live long enough to find out if you continue to play such games.'

Sphax drifted into silence for a moment, sipping and savouring his wine. 'The last thing I need to ask, Sir, is, will it work? Will the legions be drawn out?'

'Oh yes, lad, it will work. Rome is spoiling for a fight.'

It was dark when he went in search of Idwal. It never ceased to surprise him how safe and carefree an armed camp was at night. In Rome, when darkness fell citizens locked and barred their doors. Even his ex-master Gaius Lucilus would never venture into the pitch-black darkness of narrow streets without slaves bearing torches and armed guards by his side. His teacher Elpis had once told him there was a saying in Rome that it was wise to write a will before going out to supper.

He found Idwal in his uncle Mago's pavilion with his Cavari lieutenants, Cáel and Drust. All four were in high spirits considering the cold and uncomfortable night that lay ahead of them. He'd known his Cavari friends for little more than half a year, but they had been through so much together it seemed as if they'd known each other for half a lifetime. Mago was a different proposition from his brother, and only a few years older than Sphax himself.

He was the image of his elder brother, yet there was nothing brooding or forbidding about his open, trusting face. Modelling himself on Hannibal, Mago had the same close-cropped hair and beard, and Sphax had occasionally caught him imitating his brother's forthright bearing and gestures. But whereas his elder brother's pavilion was spartan, Mago's was the height of luxury and ease, *much* warmer, and without a single Greek scholar on view. Several Seleucid carpets, rich in red and lapis dyes were scattered over the floor, and painted wall hangings and Grecian lanterns added to the sense of opulence. Sphax was greeted warmly.

'Hail, Rome's new standard bearer! Returned from the dead,' said Mago gleefully.

'A temporary promotion, I fear,' Sphax pointed out, grinning.

PART THREE: The Scourge Of Rome

Drust chimed in. 'I hope you've been practising your Latin curses and insults for tomorrow, Sphax. It has to be convincing!'

'All you need is "cocksuckers," quipped Cáel, 'nothing pricks a Roman like the truth.' Wine and a cup were found for him and the banter continued for some time, the barbs of good humour flying in all directions. Sphax berated his host for serving him Etruscan, when he'd just been drinking the finest Malacca at Maharbal's table. This was followed by the usual rejoinder that a cavalryman's horse was a much better judge of a fine wine than its rider.

Before he took his leave he embraced them all and wished them the luck of the gods. Sphax couldn't resist a parting shot. Pausing at the threshold he said, 'Just to let you know, Astegal's returned, truly contrite, so Maharbal's giving him command of your thousand Numidians.' Sphax grinned as the four of them chorused, *'Astegal!'*

Another eshrin commander was waiting for him when he arrived back at his own pavilion. But Sphax loved and admired Maharbal's most experienced and trusted lieutenant, Adherbal, who'd sustained him through some of the darkest days on their momentous journey through the mountains.

'All is done. I've collected the standard from your uncle,' he said, nodding at the banner affixed to a wooden staff he'd placed on his humble table. Sphax couldn't take his eyes off it. The banner itself was dyed in the deepest Tyrian purple, and had been embroidered with gold thread. At its centre the letters SPQR shone out boldly, below which three interlocking circles had been emblazoned. The wooden staff that bore the banner was tipped by a leaf-shaped barb and at the bottom by a lizard-killer spike, both, seemingly, wrought in pure silver.

'Equites carry these, it's called a vexillum, but this one was made for a consul of Rome.' Adherbal was smiling at Sphax's bemused expression. 'I think the circles might represent the Scipios' family emblem.'

'Your men captured this, Sir, not mine. I don't feel worthy of carrying it. You, or one of your eshrin should carry this into battle tomorrow. Not me.'

Adherbal burst out laughing. 'Don't be ridiculous, lad. You covered yourself in far more glory that day than the Numidian who snatched this from a dead Roman. You shall carry this into battle tomorrow, and you will do it proudly.'

Sphax remembered his manners. 'Cesti! Lulin!' he bawled, 'what are you thinking of, bring Adherbal food and wine.' His servants scuttled off, leaving the four little Roman boys at a loss what to do. In the event they took up station around the table hoping to be of use, but all they got for their trouble was a tousling of their hair and a broad grin from Adherbal.

'Our general tells me that you will only challenge your ex-master, Lucilus if all else fails. I also need this assurance from you, lad. Believe me, it would be

PART THREE: The Scourge Of Rome

a foolish thing to do.' Adherbal fixed him with a solemn glare. 'Do I have it?' Sphax was spared an immediate reply by the appearance of Cesti and Lulin with bread, olives and wine.

'You have it, Sir. But nothing will be certain until I face tomorrow's dawn.'

'True.' He raised his cup. 'Good luck, lad. May it all go as well as your uncle predicts. He's right about most things.'

'And to you, Sir,' Sphax said solemnly. Adherbal made a face.

'Dog's twat, Sphax. I don't relish the prospect of a night in a wet ditch! I'm getting too old for this game.'

THIRTEEN

He spent what was left of the evening carefully choosing his eshrins. Bearing in mind what Maharbal had said to him about wise heads, he chose Manissa and another seasoned veteran called Gala. Mentioning this to Maharbal later, the general heartily approved, especially of Manissa, 'You still have much to learn from him, Sphax. Make sure you do.'

He held his own council of war around the warmest campfire near the eastern gate. When he began to describe Hannibal's plan in great detail, he sensed tension and excitement growing in equal measure. Reflected in the flickering campfire were faces that fully understood the gravity of this moment, and the part they were to play in it.

Together they'd fought wild mountain Gauls in deep canyons and precipitous mountainsides, scaled the snowbound mountains through storm and flood. They'd seen their comrades perish in their thousands. Grief and mourning had been constant companions along the way. Yet they were the survivors, the bravest

PART THREE: The Scourge Of Rome

of the brave. Stirred by Hannibal's rousing speech, together they'd chanted 'Death to Rome' from the highest mountaintop. They'd ridden a thousand miles to challenge Rome. Now it was their time, their page of history. And it would be written by Numidians.

When Sphax fell silent, he gazed in turn at the grave, sombre faces circled around the campfire, and waited patiently for the inevitable questions.

'By Ba 'al Hamūn, lad, I'm not looking forward to crossing that freezing torrent in the pitch-black of the night. It will be the death of me and Gala.' It was Manissa's growling voice that had raised the objection. The same thought had already occurred to Sphax.

'You're quite right, Manissa, it would be too risky in the dark, so we'll cross upstream at a shallower ford Himilco and I used days ago. It's much safer. But remember, we will have to cross the Trebia later that morning. But at least it will light by then.' The old veteran seemed satisfied with this.

'You went with Hannibal on his scouting mission to the Roman camp, Sphax, can you recall the journey well enough to guide us?' asked Aribal.

'I've been going over it in my mind all evening, so I think so. My uncle also pointed out to me the legions' method of posting successive cordons of outposts. Some of the guards even light fires, which will make our job easier. I intend to overwhelm all the outposts quickly and drive them back. So once we attack, we keep moving swiftly towards their western gate.' Nods and murmurs of approval came from around the campfire.

Sphax desperately wanted Manissa and Gala on his side. Deferring to their knowledge and experience would help, he'd decided.

'I have a question for Manissa and Gala,' he said. 'After I've issued my challenge and ground their noses in the mud, what do you think they'll do?' Sphax was pleased to see they were both smiling.

'I'd gather a good force together, fling open those gates and ride like the hound of Hades straight for you,' Gala answered, but it was Manissa that was chuckling.

'Don't forget, lad. After what you've done to their reputation, you're their chief calamity. They'll want you run through and spit-roasted!' he said with disconcerting relish.

'So we need at least four eshrins lined up behind me, and I need to be watchful—'

'You could say that … if it was me, lad, I'd be shitting myself,' Manissa added, still chuckling.

'Then I'll bring a fresh loin cloth and stay downwind of you, Manissa,' he replied in all seriousness. By now there was a chorus of laughter around the campfire.

'Fear not, Sphax,' shouted Himilco above the racket, 'I'm sure we'll manage to keep you alive until the real battle starts. Then the gods will decide your fate.'

When the laughter had died down he said, 'Your men need to eat a big hearty meal late tonight, oil their

PART THREE: The Scourge Of Rome

bodies and wear every stitch of clothing they possess. Otherwise, by midday they'll be in the same state as our enemies; half-starved and frozen. We will form up one hour after midnight outside the eastern gate. Go and prepare your men.'

* * *

'It's got to be close, Himilco. My mare just blundered into a rowan tree I recognised.' Sphax was trying to keep the desperation out of his voice. Twenty of them had dismounted and were scouring the riverbank for the arrowhead he'd made out of withies to mark the ford.

The moon had waned to a sliver, on the rare occasions they'd glimpsed it, for overhead the sky was leaden and overcast. When he'd set out last week with Hannibal they'd had the pre-dawn grey to light their path. Sphax had thought it too risky setting out so close to dawn. Besides, to reach the Roman camp in time they would have had to cross the Trebia at that deep ford, something he'd already ruled out. But now he was beginning to regret that decision. He hadn't bargained on the impenetrable darkness that everyone was blundering around in. Neither had he wanted six hundred Numidians to sit idly on their mares for almost an hour whilst he and Himilco searched for the ford.

Himilco saw it before him. 'What's that?' Sphax turned around and stared into the darkness.

'It looks like two lights moving towards us,' answered Sphax, mystified. As the light grew stronger, he realised they were Greek lamps. Closer still, and he began to make out the form of two men striding towards them. It was Manissa and Gala, with a few of their men.

'You slackheads can't find it, can you?' growled Manissa, holding out his lamp so Sphax could examine it. 'Thank Ba 'al Hamūn me and Gala came prepared.'

'You're right, Manissa. But thanks to you two, we'll certainly find it now.' Sphax held up the lamp in wonder. It was ingenious. The oil lamp itself sat inside a bronze cylinder whose concentric sides could be slid open to reveal more light, or when almost closed, allow only the faintest sliver to escape. Even on a windy night the flame would be shielded by the cylinder, and the simple carrying handle meant that it could be taken anywhere. Polished bronze seemed to reflect and magnify the flame creating the beam of light.

Sphax immediately grasped the lamp's usefulness for night operations. North east of them lay the Roman camp. Using the sliding device it would be possible to shield any light from escaping in that direction whilst directing it to where they needed it most: finding that ford.

Opening the cylinders as wide as they dared, he walked directly behind Himilco so the power of their combined lamps would better illuminate the riverbank. Sphax had indeed miscalculated. The ford was at least half a mile further downstream than he'd reckoned. But at last they found it, thanks to the 'wise heads,' and their ingenious device.

PART THREE: The Scourge Of Rome

When Manissa and his men arrived he advised Sphax to use one of the lamps as a beacon to guide the eshrins directly to the crossing point. Reaching up, he threaded the carrying handle through a willow branch and carefully opened the cylinder so the light would be seen from the south west. Himilco was sent to summon the eshrins. One of Gala's men handed him a coil of rope.

'Do you remember how we crossed the Druentia, Sphax?' He recalled the courage of the two Iberian shepherds, stripped to the waist as they'd plunged into that icy torrent, uncoiling ropes behind them. They were brothers, and one of them had got into difficulties, he remembered, but the other had managed to wade across and tie his rope to the trunk of a tree on the far bank.

'I do Gala, I witnessed the Iberians that day, and over the next week crossed it several times myself.'

'Then take this rope across, and attach it similarly, to a tree. Then place the lamp in the tree to act as another beacon,' instructed Gala, handing him the lamp.

'Crossing a deep river at night is always a perilous undertaking,' growled Manissa. 'The rope will guide our men across safely.'

Sphax had never felt so foolish. He'd spent the entire afternoon thinking about how they would approach the Roman camp. Other than deciding on this ford as their safer option, he'd payed scant regard to either finding it or crossing it safely in the darkness. It was humiliating.

The Winter of Winters

He'd completely overlooked something Manissa and Gala had carefully prepared for. As he mounted Dido, Manissa must have caught something of his pained expression.

'Don't worry, lad. You do the fighting, we'll do the thinking.' Sphax managed a hollow laugh.

Holding the lamp and javelins firmly in his left hand, he kissed his ivory image of Artemis, gripped the rope and plunged down the bank into the river's icy waters. The sudden stab of cold was so intense it almost made him cry out. By midstream his legs were so numb he'd lost all sensation in them. The last twenty strides were unbearable. On reaching the far bank he leapt from Dido, jumping around to restore life to his legs and shake the excess water from his leggings. Soon he had the rope tied and the lamp set up on a branch of willow.

Later, Sphax reckoned it must have taken only two hours to get all their men across safely, but in his anxiety, it had seemed like a lifetime. On this side of the river they were only a few miles from Insubres settlements, and there was always the risk of running into a patrol of Roman equites. He cautioned every eshrin captain that from now on their men were to maintain a strict silence. At least the leaden skies had cleared, revealing a sliver of golden moonlight and a thousand stars.

Making his way to the front of the column, he determined this was not the time to reproach himself for his miscalculations or ill-preparedness. There must be no regrets, no doubts, only the task in hand, and what lay ahead. And the men were jumpy. Every bark of a fox or howl from a distant wolf set their nerves on edge. When he was fretting about finding the ford he thought that time was against them. Now they had all the time in the world, it was still against them. Interminable miles allowed brooding fears to rise out of the darkness. His men would need him before the night was out. He was determined not to fail them.

Sphax asked Agbal from his own eshrin to stay four hundred paces ahead of the lead column to act as scout. Like him, Agbal had a keen pair of ears, and on a night like this, that faculty was more useful than eyesight. Each eshrin rode six abreast with a single scout riding four hundred paces east of them to give warning of a threat from that direction. But even in this compact formation, the column stretched back for half a mile. The pace was set at a steady walk.

As they followed the eastern bank of the river, the occasional copse or area of scrubby woodland encountered meant frequent stops or holdups to allow the column to reform and resume its shape. Sphax took to riding up and down the column, patting backs and gripping shoulders, even smiling reassuringly at his captains. Though in that darkness, whether any of them could see his face, let alone his expression, was doubtful.

And so those long hard miles, passed in brooding silence and perpetual darkness, slowly wound down.

The Winter of Winters

Eventually, he halted the column beside the ford they'd toiled endless miles to avoid crossing in the darkness: the main ford of the Trebia, where they'd already lost several lives and all Numidians had come to fear it.

It suddenly occurred to Sphax as he began martialling his captains for a whispered conference, that the wheels of Hannibal's great plan were now being set in motion. Like the tiles on his table map, Idwal and Drust would be mustering the Cavari. Shields were being hefted and those deadly Gaulish slashing blades strapped to waist-belts. Adherbal would be summoning his hand-picked Numidians for their nightlong vigil in the depths of a waterlogged ditch. And here, beside the quietly flowing Trebia, six hundred half-frozen Numidians were gathering to assault an unassailable armed camp that held forty thousand Romans. Only Hannibal could dream such dreams.

In hushed whispers he asked Aribal to marshal their men on a front of two eshrins, widely spaced, so that their half-mile column would be reduced to just ten lines of horsemen. Sphax had seen for himself how Maharbal had used a similar flexible formation at the Rhodanus. He was praying that it would work for him this evening.

Satisfying himself that Gulussa from his own eshrin was still bearing the Roman vexillum, he nodded Himilco to follow him.

'We must search out the first cordon of their night watch outposts. It will tell us who's on duty tonight.

PART THREE: The Scourge Of Rome

Look out for fires,' he whispered. 'If we can, we'll penetrate this cordon and take a look at their second line. I remember seeing large campfires and lots of men manning the third line.'

From his recollections that afternoon, Sphax knew the nature of the ground ahead was mostly grassland, but there were those patches of woodland where they'd hidden during Hannibal's scouting mission. It would have been madness in this darkness to use those woods to penetrate the outposts: horses could see much better in the dark than their riders, but light would not penetrate thick woodland and he was not willing to risk breaking a leg. Instead, they used the edges of the woodland to provide a dark background.

What was really nagging away at him was the thought that after the Romans had realised an enemy scouting party had penetrated their night watches, they would completely reorganise them. That's what his uncle would have done, he was sure of it.

When the first flickering campfires came into view he couldn't believe his luck. They were exactly in the places he'd recalled. Sphax could even make out the woodland Hannibal had directed them towards. If ever he needed it — which he didn't — it was a perfect demonstration of Rome's arrogance and complacency. He signalled Himilco to dismount.

'We go on foot from here, my friend', he whispered. 'Do you see that darker patch over there?' Sphax pointed to a dark scar between the glow of campfires.

'Yes. Is that woodland?'

'That's the wood our scouting party made for. Beyond that we'll see the next cordon of outposts. Follow me.'

Keeping low, he moved swiftly to the edge of the woodland, all the while keeping an anxious eye on the campfire to his right. Crouching, he slid behind the solid trunk of an elm. Himilco joined him. They could hear voices now, gathering around the fire. Sphax stared, but couldn't make out their uniforms.

'Equites!' whispered a sharper-eyed Himilco. 'Roman cavalry have been given the honour of defending their camp this evening.' So, he thought, everything had come full circle. The last time he'd entered these woods he'd faced the same opponents.

Hugging the edge of the wood, they followed its course for almost a mile, halting as the trees gave way to open grassland. And there they were: four more campfires arranged in a semi-circle, half a mile apart, just as he remembered. It was too dark to make it out, but Sphax knew there was another stretch of woodland opposite them. He'd seen enough.

'The imbeciles haven't altered the position of a single campfire,' he whispered. 'It's just as Hannibal and I found it, days ago. I know where the rest of the outposts will be. Let's get back.'

By the light of the two lamp cylinders pointed carefully away from prying Roman eyes, he began scraping on the bare earth with a javelin point.

PART THREE: The Scourge Of Rome

Crouching around him were five of his most trusted captains. They were over three miles away from the campfires, so there was no need for whispering.

Scratching the position of the first of the fires and the areas of woodland between them, he said, 'Ahead of us the ground is mostly flat, open grassland, broken only by occasional patches of woodland. It's broad enough to allow us to change formation. Instead of two eshrins ahead and two behind, each of you will now command four eshrins in line. This will reduce our column to just five lines. It is a formation I favour, and whilst I command, we will maintain it in the coming battle.'

'When we attack, we will split up. As each of you splits off from the main column it will be as a series of doors swing open.' Sphax used his forearm to demonstrate the movement over the ground.

'I will lead the first four eshrins against this outpost,' pointing to it with his javelin. 'To the north of this is a large wood.' Again, he pointed to it. 'Beyond this, Himilco will lead his eshrins against this outpost. Next, it's the turn of Manissa, and finally Aribal. Juba will remain in reserve behind Manissa's eshrins to deal with any contingencies.' Sphax looked in turn at the faces illuminated in the lamplight, then scratched the next four outposts on the ground.

'There will only be two or three of them manning each outpost. Once you've overcome the sentries, if you look ahead of you to the east, you'll see the next

The Winter of Winters

cordon of campfires. Do not hesitate, each of you must immediately attack the outpost due east of you.' Using his hand he swept it over the ground. 'Once this ring has been subdued, you must stop, regroup, and wait for my eshrins to join you before we attack their last line. Because of the woods that shield my outposts from Himilco's, I will be out of sight. That's why I'll lead the charges on this outpost. I know the way.

'We will form up before we charge the last outposts. That's where most of the equites will be.' He eyed them all again. 'Any questions?' There was a grave silence. 'Then all we can do now is wait for dawn.' Sphax carefully slid the cylinders shut and handed them back to Manissa.

It took some time to rearrange the column of five lines in its correct order with each captain leading the right hand eshrin, before explaining to his men the plan Sphax had devised. Gala rode over to him and asked if he could detach a man to stay behind and guard the lamp cylinders.

'What's got into you, Gala? Your politeness is beginning to worry me.' Gala laughed.

'Me and Manissa said we'd follow you. That's what we're doing, lad.'

'Well, those lamps of yours have saved the day, and they're much too valuable to risk in battle. Will you leave the man by the ford?' Gala nodded. 'Then you have my permission, captain.' All they could do now was wait.

PART THREE: The Scourge Of Rome

He knew that the mystery of pre-dawn light was shrouded in antiquity. Reputed to be an emanation of Cronus, it existed before Zeus illuminated the heavens and brought true light into the world. But tonight it would be enough. And that's what Sphax was waiting for.

When he could see the last line of Numidians in the column, he raised his saunion and signalled his men forward into the greyness of that grim, December morning. The world held its breath. Hannibal's battle was about to begin.

Nudging Dido immediately into a trot he felt the men around him respond instinctively. He wanted to overcome the outposts as quickly as possible, even if it meant taking a calculated risk riding in this half-light. The greyness might hide them from sight, but there was no disguising the sound of six hundred thundering hoof-beats. Raising his saunion again, he tightened his knees around Dido's flanks and she leapt into her easy canter, her hooves gliding effortlessly over the sward. They were eating up the ground now, but it was so alarming, like riding through a grey fog. Sphax knew he had to trust to the sure-footedness of their mares, and pray. Then he saw it.

The campfire looked different in the greyness, its flames dimmed and indistinct, but it was still unmistakeable. Raising his saunion, this time he pointed it in the direction of the glow, dug his knees once more into Dido and coaxed her to change direction. For a moment she galloped ahead of the eshrin, but his men quickly adjusted and soon his four eshrins were back in line, thundering towards a campfire that was glowing brighter with every stride.

Both equites were tearing back to a line where they'd tethered their horses. Neither of them made it. They didn't stand a chance. Sphax heard the whirr of several javelins. The next moment two crimson-cloaked figures lay prone on the ground.

Without breaking stride he raised his saunion above his head and slowly lowered it. A clear signal to his men to ease the pace. He sat back on his mare and allowed her to canter. It was going to be a long day. The mares had to be spared.

At the next outpost the outcome was the same. But this time two equites managed to mount their stallions before the javelins flew. It made no difference. Soon two riderless stallions were sniffing their mares.

Greyness was at last beginning to give way to true light as Eos pushed the gates of heaven aside and mounted her chariot. Now they had to move fast.

When at last he saw Himilco, Manissa and Aribal drawn up in perfect formation, his relief was palpable. They'd got away with it. Only that inner circle of Roman outposts now stood between him and the Roman camp. Gratefully, he circled around an abandoned campfire to warm his frozen limbs. That's when he saw something that gave him an idea.

Scattered on the ground around the campfire were a score of torches. What if, he thought, they arrived at

PART THREE: The Scourge Of Rome

that last Roman outpost as a wall of flame? A terrifying vision of a flaming firebrand, bearing down on them out of the darkness. He knew the answer to his own question. They would panic, and then run.

'Himilco, Aribal, Juba. Take some of your men and race back to the campfires. Collect as many torches as you can. Now! We haven't a moment to lose.'

All three of them were shaking their heads in bewilderment, but they obeyed. Sliding from Dido he began gathering up the torches, ordering his four eshrins to take up position ahead of Himilco's line.

Once his captains returned with armfuls of torches Sphax shouted, 'Light them and hand them to men in the front rank. I want to create a wall of fire and flame.' At last everyone was beginning to understand what he had in mind. When it was done, a quarter of the leading rank were holding a flaming brand in one hand. Quickly he mounted Dido and within ten strides, six hundred galloping Numidians were descending on the Romans' last line of defence.

Sphax could only imagine how the equites would react to this vision of Hades. Surely it would strike terror in the hearts of their enemies as this wall of flame approached like a thunderbolt out of the darkness.

He was right. They froze. It was only when some of them began to fall from Numidian javelins that they awoke from their stupor and fled for their lives. But by then Sphax's attention had been drawn to a face that had been illuminated in the firelight. A face that would forever be etched on the darkest recesses of his memory. The face of a man he'd sworn a solemn oath to kill.

There was no mistaking his ex-master, Gaius Lucilus. Ten years of slavery and a thousand vicious beatings meant there could not be a shadow of doubt it was him. He'd wormed his way into a tribune's uniform, but when Sphax caught sight of him he was reaching for his helmet, revealing a bare head and that snarling arrogant expression he'd long remembered. For a heartbeat their eyes met and acknowledged their mutual hatred of one another.

Sphax had sunk a knife into his son's scrawny back, and now it was the father's turn to die. Along with some of the survivors, Gaius was racing back the fifty paces to a rope-line where their horses were tethered. Whilst many in that race fell to a Numidian javelin in the back, he couldn't bring himself to dispatch Gaius in the same manner. He would face him, man-to-man.

But now everywhere was chaos and confusion. His Numidians were locked into combat with scores of equites trying to escape on horseback, whilst others were still scrambling to mount their stallions. Screams and cries of agony or triumph echoed on the night air, whilst the flickering torchlight added to the panic and terror, illuminating everything in flame or stark shadow. Sphax knew his duty lay in commanding his eshrins, but at that moment there was only one thought in his head, and it had nothing to do with Numidians.

PART THREE: The Scourge Of Rome

Gaius Lucilus had managed to mount a magnificent grey stallion and was yanking at his reins, intent on flight. Javelin poised, for an instant Sphax had a clear sighting, but in the next moment he was gone, lost amidst a tumult of horses and writhing bodies. He gave chase.

Magnificent as Gaius' stallion was, he was no match for a lithe jennet like Dido. Within half a mile Dido had caught up and was now a few strides behind. Sphax could clearly see the campfires of the Roman camp looming ahead. A javelin in the back would settle his oath once and for all. But he couldn't do it!

Honour demanded he face him. There was an alternative, but it was unthinkable: wound the stallion and unhorse its rider. Sphax had never harmed a horse in his life. Numidians loved horses. How could he wound one? His stomach was churning with rage and frustration, and with every stride the camp grew nearer. Still he hesitated.

The western gate of the Roman camp was almost upon them when he finally let fly the javelin with a cry of desperation. It struck the stallion a glancing blow on his croup. Faltering with sudden pain, he rose up on his hind legs and Gaius Lucilus slithered unceremoniously into the mud. For an instant, his ex-master stared up at him, terror etched on his face.

'Get up, you bastard and face me!' screamed Sphax, reaching over his shoulder for the hilt of his blade.

In that moment several things happened at once, none of which he'd bargained for.

Spears began raining down on him from a fighting platform above the gate. All were falling short, but what was more alarming was the sight of several equites sprinting towards him bearing shields and swords.

What he would never forget was the sight of Gaius, crawling on his belly towards them. Despite the unbearable frustration that was raging through him, Sphax started to laugh.

Grabbing their tribune's shoulders, two equites began manhandling Gaius back to the gate whilst three more closed in on him. Sheathing his sword he threaded a javelin. He wasn't in the mood to retreat. One of them didn't live to take another step. Sphax threaded another javelin.

Suddenly he heard hoof-beats from behind him and the sound of javelins whirring through the air. Two more bodies soon lay slumped on the wooden bridge in front of the western gate. He turned to see young Agbal and several from his eshrin threading fresh javelins.

'What kept you?' he said, smiling at Agbal.

'When you get that look of glory in your eyes, Sir, there's no catching you. Who's the fat bastard they dragged through the gate?' Sphax sighed deeply, releasing some of his frustration.

'Someone I'm going to kill today, if I get half a chance.'

He could hear a cacophony of shouted orders from behind the log walls of the Roman camp. The

PART THREE: The Scourge Of Rome

two fighting platforms flanking the western gate were filling up with men bearing torches. Sphax watched as the first finger of dawn pierced the eastern horizon. And with it, the last vestige of his madness dissipated in its light. This was not the time for vengeance or sacred oaths. Now he must do his duty.

'Where did you get to?' It was Himilco.

'I'll explain later,' he said, by way of answer. 'First we need to get our men ranged on the open plain facing this western gate. Remember the wide spacing Maharbal used at the Rhodanus, we need to do the same.'

Because many of his eshrin captains were familiar with it, there were soon five ragged lines of Numidians with wide intervals between each horseman. By temperament, his people were incapable of forming what a surveyor would call a straight line. That's why he loved them, and that's why he would lay down his life to fight for them. Sphax rode over to Gulussa.

'Hand it over. Let's get this battle started,' he said.

'Only if I'm allowed to escort you, Sir,' the big man said defiantly.

'And me.' Agbal had joined them. 'We don't trust you not to do something *brave*, captain.'

Sphax could only grin at them both. 'Then find torches, you shall be my flame-bearers,' he said, gripping the shaft of the standard and pointing its glistening silver spike at the wooden ramparts of the camp growing ever clearer in the gathering light.

It was easy to gauge what would be a safe distance to deliver his challenge. Sphax made for the spear that had been thrown the farthest. Staring up at the men now crowded on the fighting platforms flanking their gate, he took a deep breath, and began.

'I am Sphax, Prince of Numidia, beloved of the goddess Artemis who brought me back to life after the battle on the Ticinus. I am the scourge of Rome. I am the slayer of tribune Manius Quintus. It was me that wounded Consul Scipio.'

Raising the standard high so all could see, he continued, 'This was once the proud vexillum of a consul of Rome. But to me it is no better than a rag on a pole. So, unless Rome has the courage to send out someone to meet my challenge, I will drag this rag through the mud and my men will piss on it.' Sphax nudged Dido forward a stride and stared up at the men crowded on to the fighting platforms. He expected jeering and defiance. But all was now stunned silence.

'I suggest you close the gates of Janus, for in war Rome has lost all honour. Rome has disavowed all dignity. Rome now cowers behind its walls, cringing and fearful. Even your gods have deserted you! Mars curses you.' He allowed Dido another stride forward and dragged the standard over the muddied ground. This time the gasp from the fighting platforms was audible.

'A short while ago Tribune Gaius Lucilus crawled on his belly through this western gate. Why not send

PART THREE: The Scourge Of Rome

him out to meet my challenge and avenge the death of his son?' Silence.

'Why not Consul Scipio's son? Or is he, like all Roman cowards, afraid of facing my javelin?' Silence.

Sphax stared up at the gallery before dramatically plunging the standard into the muddy waters of the ditch surrounding the Roman camp. That, at last, brought an angry reaction from the men on the fighting platforms before the entire camp erupted in a cacophony of blaring trumpets. It was as music to his ears! Sphax smiled to himself; it had been easier than he'd expected.

Rome was mustering its legions, who would go hungry this morning. Hannibal would have his battle.

Agbal and Gulussa were looking anxiously at him. All three of them knew exactly what would happen if those massive gates suddenly swung open: scores, if not hundreds would pour out of the Roman camp. Sphax guessed they would be equites, bent on restoring their shattered honour. It was time for the scourge of Rome to make himself scarce.

'Let's get out of here,' he said. Not wanting to be encumbered by the standard, he tossed it into the ditch. It had served its purpose.

As they approached their own lines he saw Himilco riding out to meet him, desperate for news. 'We heard the trumpets! It worked then ... they're mustering?'

Sphax grinned. 'We stirred up a pit of vipers, but we'll be feeling their fangs shortly. Are we ready?'

'Yes. And eager ... if only to put some warmth back into our limbs! But what do you think they'll do?'

Sphax turned around and stared at the Roman camp. The jagged lines of timbers that made up the ramparts of the camp were sharply silhouetted against the light now seeping into the world from the east. Returning his gaze to Himilco he couldn't help scowling.

'I don't know what they'll do. But I know what I would do! They can see we're here in force. If I were them, I would begin to muster equites opposite our Numidians, turma by turma, thereby fixing our attention on what was happening in front of our eyes. In the meantime, I would send out every horseman and veles from the northern and southern gates with orders to circle around us. We would quickly become surrounded. If this were to happen we would certainly be destroyed.' Sphax grasped the shoulder of his friend.

'If I fall, Himilco, you *must* bear this in mind. For you will command our Numidians and for our plan to succeed the legions must ford the Trebia. Once delivered across the Trebia I'm convinced my uncle will destroy them. But if our little force is annihilated, Longus may well declare a great victory over Hannibal, retire behind the walls of his camp and sit out the winter. It's not enough to goad and humiliate. We must deliver our enemies across that river.' Himilco nodded solemnly.

'Should we send out scouts to keep an eye on those gates?'

'Yes. Now!'

FOURTEEN

Sphax couldn't have been more wrong. His uncle had been right: Longus was not the most gifted of tacticians. Equites did not begin to muster outside the western gate, neither did they pour out of any other gate to begin a threatening encirclement. The consul, it seemed, preferred to do nothing.

'What's Longus playing at?' he asked Himilco, bemused. 'It doesn't make any sense!' Manissa joined them. 'What do you think, Manissa?'

'They're Romans, lad! They're not allowed to think for themselves. Even tribunes have to ask permission to wipe their own arses. Only consuls command, and Consul Longus is probably saying farewell to the whore they found for him last night. They'll be mustering and parading in front of him soon. They'll be out soon enough. Then we'll have a fight on our hands, make no mistake.'

Sphax stared at the ranks of his Numidians, shivering astride their mares, some still holding torches aloft. An idea occurred to him. 'Then let's stir them up a little and remind them there are six hundred Numidians outside their walls.' Sphax turned to Himilco. 'Round up any of our men who still carry torches that burn, and get them out front.'

Soon he'd collected thirty men carrying flaming torches. Himilco was staring at him, perplexed. 'What do you intend to do, Sphax?'

'Just follow me with your four eshrins. I need you to deal with those velites guarding that bridge over the ditch.'

With that he led his flame-bearers forward. Many of their torches were already spluttering, so he couldn't risk speed dousing what was left of their flames, but eventually they arrived fifty paces from a few nervous velites guarding the bridge. Himilco joined him.

'Take an eshrin forward and chase them off, Himilco.' Thirty Numidians galloping towards them were all the excuse the velites required. Before a single javelin had been raised they'd turned on their heels and fled back through the gates. Sphax followed closely behind with his flame-bearers. When they reached the bridge he couldn't believe his luck.

Instead of being crammed with men as he'd last seen it, the nearest fighting platform protecting the gate was now lightly defended. Sphax counted just eight men. The second platform was partially hidden, being set at right angles from the walls of the camp, with the gates between them. After crossing the bridge over the ditch beneath the nearest platform, the roadway veered

PART THREE: The Scourge Of Rome

sharply left. Although this was the western gate to the Roman camp, the gates themselves faced south.

The problem was the bridge itself. By the look of it only three horsemen would be able to cross it abreast of one another. Himilco had also been eying that platform, and with it, the possibilities.

'I think I know what you have in mind.'

Sphax grinned. 'Let's ruin the consul's parade by burning down his western gate.'

'Three at a time should be able to cross that bridge.'

'Then get a move on, before my flame-bearers become flameless.'

Himilco was as good as his word. It took half an eshrin to rid the fighting platforms of their guards, leaving the field clear for the flame-bearers to toss their thirty torches onto the base of each platform where ladders led to the fighting platforms above. When all was completed, Sphax and Himilco led their men back over the bridge to a position sixty paces beyond the camps ramparts. From here they had a perfect view to witness their handiwork.

Flames were already licking up the ladders and had even reached the poles supporting the pyramid roof. Men were charging around with rope buckets sealed with tar as he'd seen Vigiles use in Rome, but there were not enough of them to save what was left of the platform.

'That should warm them up a bit,' laughed Himilco.

'Yes, but will it be enough to goad them into attacking us? The slackheads have three more gates!

Why aren't they using them?' The answer to this came in the shape of two Numidians galloping headlong towards them.

'They're pouring out of the northern gate, Sir. Skirmishers. Hundreds of them!' one of them said breathlessly.

'And the southern gate,' said the other. 'Legionary infantry, marching in column, Captain.' Their attention was suddenly drawn to one of the fighting platforms, collapsing in a shower of sparks and flaming roof timbers.

'Well done, lads. But did you see cavalry?' Sphax asked, anxiously. Both shook their heads. He felt mightily relieved. 'Then Longus indeed commands. Scipio would have known what he was up against and sent out every turma of cavalry he possessed. To Numidians, lightly armed skirmishers are no better than the walking dead.'

'You're speaking in riddles, Sphax,' said Himilco. 'Explain?'

'We annihilated Scipio's cavalry on the Ticinus. Therefore he fears us. Consul Longus, on the other hand, has never met our cavalry and does not fear us. He's also under the illusion that Numidians will retreat in the face of lightly armed skirmishers, what they call velites. We will correct this misapprehension shortly. What I fear, as I said to you earlier, is Roman cavalry outflanking and surrounding us, but it appears he's keeping his cavalry in reserve. At least for the moment.'

PART THREE: The Scourge Of Rome

Himilco was nodding. 'So what do we do now?'

'Kill a few velites, and get them to waste their javelins. Collect their javelins if we can: if not, by mid-morning we'll have nothing left to fight with.' Sphax could see for himself the first groups of velites rounding the northern ramparts of the camp, but there was no sign of the legions' columns. 'Now we have to fight with new rules, Himilco. Let's get back to our lines and gather our captains together.'

By the time his eshrin commanders gathered around him, three disciplined columns of legionaries were rapidly bearing down on them, bristling with spears and shields. Thirty paces ahead of the columns, a ragged line of velites lead the way, with scores more racing to join them. Aribal gave him an anxious look.

'We'll soon run out of ground to manoeuvre, Sphax.'

He knew that one charge of his Numidians would scatter the velites and send them scampering back to the columns for protection, but the ground between them was shrinking, and at this rate his eshrins would barely reach a canter. With their ranks swollen by so many of their allies, the velites were striding out with newfound confidence and their line was lengthening. Sphax felt that nagging fear that had dogged him since crossing the river: Rome closing in on him from every direction.

'Turn all your eshrins around,' he shouted, and pointing his raised javelin to the rear he yelled,

'Retreat, men. Retreat!' Weaving Dido through the four lines he reached a rear that had now become the front line. At a brisk trot he led them a good mile back to the smouldering campfires where they'd overcome the equites' last outpost and he'd caught his first sight of Gaius Lucilus.

'Now we turn around and face our enemy once more,' he shouted, nudging Dido forward through the ranks to join Himilco at the front again.

At last he felt secure. From here to the ford across the Trebia he knew the position of every patch of woodland, every blind spot and ambush position. To know the ground gave him the ability to use it to his advantage. Rome couldn't spring surprises here. Even so, he wasn't taking any chances.

'Send two of your best men to scout due south of us, Himilco. There may be a more direct road to the Trebia ford I'm unaware of.' Himilco nodded. Soon, two men headed off at speed to the south.

'We attack the velites, not the columns. If we use up all our javelins we'll be defenceless within the hour. So tell your men to use them sparingly. Our aim is to get the velites to use up *their* javelins. Got it?'

'What if we all dismounted and picked up their javelins—'

'That's it!' cried Sphax. 'If we advance with two lines, the second could trot forward and defend them whilst they do it. I noticed the velites only carried two or three javelins, whilst our men probably have four or

PART THREE: The Scourge Of Rome

five left. Once their javelins are gone they're of no use to the legions, we'll have disarmed them.' Grinning, he added, 'You'll be a general one day, my friend.'

'Then put in a good word for me with your uncle?'

Sphax laughed. 'I would be honoured to. But first we must win the day.'

'Agreed,' nodded Himilco. 'I'll explain to my captains what we're about to do.' Sphax rode over to Aribal's second line and did the same.

All too soon the ragged lines of velites came into view. He could even hear the rhythmic pounding of hobnails from the legions' columns behind them. Judging from their extended front and the variety of uniforms on display, many more of their allies had joined them. Sphax guessed there were now more than five hundred of them striding confidently forward. He rode along Himilco's line of eshrins and beckoned Aribal's line to close up.

Raising his voice he cried, 'Our plan will succeed. Once you've collected all the javelins you can carry, don't wait for orders, get on your mares and ride back like the wind. I will continue the fight with Aribal's eshrins. I swear by ba 'al Hamūn that we will defend you with our last javelin. Now let me hear you ... death to Rome!' he yelled. 'Death to Rome!' It thrilled him to hear six hundred of his countrymen taking up the chant in full voice.

Over the last two months, Maharbal and his javelin teacher, Dubal, had drilled it into him that his tactics had to change when facing an opposing javelin thrower. Even using a throwing thong, on foot a javelin could only be hurled sixty paces at most. Using the speed of their mares, Numidians could hurl theirs at least ninety paces, and many in his own eshrin could throw further. So they had the upper hand. Even so, they had to be more cautious, throwing and turning their mares much earlier, fifty paces from the enemy. He'd practised this drill with his own eshrin countless times, often under the watchful eye of his mentor, Adherbal. The trick was judging those fifty paces.

Raising his javelin he yelled, 'Forward!'

Sphax put all thoughts out of his head but one: judge those fifty paces, judge them accurately, perfectly, to the last stride. As the line of Numidians thundered into a canter he could see the velites bracing themselves and readying their weapons. Pulling his throwing thong tight, he threaded two fingers through the loop and nudged Dido into a gallop. They were eating up the ground fast now. He saw his enemy raise throwing arms and thrust shields forward. One more stride ...

'Now!' he yelled, unleashing his javelin. But he knew that few would hear him above the din of hooves. Every Numidian had to judge this for himself, measuring the difference between life and death. As over a hundred spinning javelins winged their way towards their enemies, hundreds more were hurled in the opposite direction. When a javelin thumped into

PART THREE: The Scourge Of Rome

the sward a stride short of Dido's hooves, he knew it had been a close call.

Screams echoed down the length of the enemy's line that was so densely packed that every javelin had met its mark. Grimly the velites stood firm. Suddenly he found himself amongst Aribal's second line surging forward to deliver another volley. Sphax quickly threaded another javelin, dug his knees into Dido's flanks and as she leapt into the gallop, sought out another target.

Once more Aribal's men overtook him and poured yet another fire-storm of missiles into the skirmishers' reeling ranks. This time they broke. Amidst the wails of the wounded the survivors abandoned them to their fate, turned on their heels and fled back to the safety of the legionary columns.

Until now, Sphax hadn't dared to look behind him to see how Himilco's men were getting on with gathering spent javelins, but with the routing of the velites, he finally turned around. Himilco's men were already retreating with armfuls of javelins. His relief was palpable. The plan had worked.

The legionary columns were now approaching the hundreds of bodies of their comrades carpeting the ground, but not for an instant did they pause or break step. At the head of each column stood six men shoulder to shoulder, hefting those great crimson shields. Each citizen soldier was helmeted, swathed in mail and carried two pila besides stubby swords strapped to their waist. Hannibal had explained that these were the hastati, principes and triarii; which were which meant nothing to Sphax. What *did* matter, was the fact they stood like some unbreakable wall of iron, inviolate and untouchable. Everything he loathed about Rome was represented by those three columns.

It would never be enough to break skirmishing lines. They had to be able to break the legions, otherwise their war with Rome was doomed to failure. Rome's great machine of war was driven by its legions, not by its skirmishers or cavalry. Sphax was still glaring at them when Aribal rode over.

'Are you thinking what I'm thinking?' Sphax couldn't help smiling as he examined the animated face of his friend.

'Maybe,' he replied guardedly, 'but how far do you think they can throw those ugly pilum things?'

'My men reckon no more than twenty paces.'

'So, if we settled on throwing twenty five paces out, can our men judge that distance?'

'You know they can, Sphax. Stop prevaricating. What are we waiting for?'

'I'm hesitating because I don't want to waste our precious javelins on shields and mail coats.' Sphax could see centurions and other officers forcing their skirmishers back to the front again. If they were going to attempt this, it would have to be soon.

'If we aim high, Sphax, many will find their mark,' Aribal implored.

PART THREE: The Scourge Of Rome

'Then command your men to do so. We'll feign a retreat to give us enough ground to turn around and gallop at them.' Raising his javelin he pointed to the rear and urged Dido to trot. Twenty strides later he looked down the line and saw that all was ready.

'Now men,' he yelled, raising his javelin. 'Turn around and charge!' One hundred and twenty Numidians abruptly wheeled and digging knees into their mares, urged them to leap into a furious pace. Six strides later they were galloping and levelling barbs.

Sphax felt slightly cheated that no pila were thrown their way, which meant they could have ridden closer, but even so, the effect of their volley had been devastating. Numidians had aimed high and true, so not only the heads of each column had been butchered, many javelins had found their mark amongst the ranks immediately behind. Limp bodies and writhing wounded were strewn on the ground where they had stood resolute; it was as if they'd cut off the heads of three serpents. Without the loss of a single horseman, Numidians had taken on the invincible legions of Rome, ground them to a halt and taught them a deadly lesson they would long remember.

He and Aribal shepherded their men back a hundred paces and formed a new line. Reluctant velites were now being forced forward with blows, curses and the flat of centurions' swords. Sphax pitied them. By now it must have dawned on them they were nothing better than a human shield for the legions. Numidian javelins outranged them and had already slaughtered them by the hundreds.

Recruited from Rome's poor, many of the velites looked the same age as him. It was even possible that as a boy he'd fought some of them in crossroad gangs or chased them through the alleyways of the Subura, boys who'd blackened his eyes or joined him on thieving expeditions to market places with easy pickings. They owed Rome nothing. And in return they'd been given little. Few possessed helmets; some wore wolf's heads or leopard skin headgear, but the majority remained bareheaded. They carried an oval shield not much bigger than an Iberian buckler, two or three javelins they'd never been properly trained to use, and a sword of Roman iron that would shatter the instant it met a good Iberian blade. And what was worse, in this winter of winters, to keep out the cold they'd been given nothing better than a knee-length tunic made of the coarsest hemp.

Forced out of their tents before dawn, unfed and shivering from cold, they were no better than fodder, destined to feed Rome's battlefields with their blood. Sphax didn't want to kill any more of the wretches. It was time to leave. Nudging Dido around he yelled, 'Retreat, men, we've done enough.'

They arrived back in their lines to a thunderous welcome of javelins beaten against hide shields. For the first time since they'd set out an hour beyond midnight, he felt elated that Longus' legions had been

PART THREE: The Scourge Of Rome

drawn from their camp without food or warm clothing. Skirmish lines had been shattered and their enemies' missiles squandered. Even the invincible reputation of Rome's legions had been challenged by Numidians. All he had to do now was lead them by the nose to the Trebia ford, taunt them to cross, and leave the rest to the tactical genius of his uncle.

If only it had been that simple. The first thing to puncture his euphoria was the sudden appearance of hundreds of Roman equites, galloping into position on the right flank of the skirmishing line. But far more troubling was the sight of two Numidians galloping flat out from the south. Sphax recognised them as Himilco's scouts, sent south to look out for trouble.

'Allied cavalry, captain,' one of them said between gasps for breath, 'hundreds of them, heading for the Trebia.'

'There's a track that leads to the Trebia we've never seen before, captain. That's where they're headed.' Sphax gripped both their shoulders.

'You may well be our saviours!' His thoughts were already racing. If they re-traced the path they'd taken from the Trebia ford before dawn, it included a massive dog-leg of a right angle. He knew enough geometry to know that the shortest distance between two points was a straight line. Better to gamble and head in a south-westerly direction, aiming directly for the ford.

The Winter of Winters

But this would be a journey into the unknown. If they were to reach that ford before the enemy, he had no choice. The fear that had haunted him since dawn had finally come to pass. Strangely, he felt relieved, as if an unknown weight had been lifted from his shoulders. Once, when faced with a seemingly unsurmountable obstacle in the Alps, Hannibal had said to him, "Yet another challenge for you to overcome, Nephew." This was just another challenge.

Weaving Dido back through the lines of eshrins, he halted briefly and repeated the same message. 'Allied cavalry are heading for the Trebia ford. We must retreat and head them off immediately. Follow me.' By good fortune his own eshrin was in the rearmost line, so all he had to do was yell, 'Turn your mares and follow me!' Sphax didn't even break stride. They would have to catch him up.

To begin with he skirted the edge of the woodland where he and his uncle had hidden, listening to the blaring trumpeters waking up the Roman camp. But once they'd cleared the last of the trees at the wood's edge, he was able to head in a south westerly direction. Eventually, Sphax stopped looking anxiously over his shoulder. Every glimpse had told him that his eshrins were in good order and keeping pace.

And pace was crucial. He could have led them off at a gallop, in which case they might reach the ford first, but on blown horses incapable of either risking the perils of the Trebia, or fighting off allied cavalry. So

PART THREE: The Scourge Of Rome

he'd settled on a steady canter, something their African jennets and Egyptian mares could maintain effortlessly all day long.

Sphax soon discovered that the secret to navigating these grasslands was to make decisions early, half a mile before they reached the next obstacle, be it a copse of willow or a larger wood. Spread out as his Numidians were, even his four eshrins in the leading rank occupied a front of six hundred paces. At this relentless pace they were counting down the miles swiftly. Sphax guessed the river could only be a mile or so away.

Directly ahead of him was a more substantial patch of woodland. He decided to head due south and skirt its eastern fringes, hoping that when they emerged beyond its edge they would come upon the track the allied cavalry were using.

Sphax did indeed come upon the track. But it was no better than a muddied furrow, ploughed by hundreds of hooves, and facing them not half a mile ahead, were rank upon rank of allied cavalry.

They had lost the race.

FIFTEEN

Except for the woodland immediately to their right, the ground to the west and south was empty grassland. Perfect cavalry country. Half a mile from the Trebia, the woodland gave way to grassland, and that's where the allied ranks began, using the trees on their left to protect that vulnerable flank. Sphax had scanned the ground minutely, looking for any advantage, however slight. During the course of this he'd noticed something else. Close to the western bank a group of horsemen were gathered around a Carthaginian crescent standard. He guessed that Hannibal and Maharbal would be watching his every move.

Sphax was counting turmae and carefully weighing the odds when Himilco, Aribal and Manissa joined him. He couldn't help but smile at their grim expressions.

'Cheer up,' he said as jauntily as he could manage under the circumstances, 'at least the equites haven't arrived — yet!'

'That is indeed a blessing, Sphax,' joked Himilco, just as lightly. 'But we all know they won't be far behind.'

PART THREE: The Scourge Of Rome

'Dog's twat!' cried Manissa. 'There must be cavalry from every bastard province in Italia. I see Etruscans, Sabines, Campanians—'

'—the last time you and I fought Campanians, Manissa, I seem to remember we routed them. So the gods smile on us, don't you think?' Manissa raised his eyebrows to the heavens. Sphax noticed that Aribal had said nothing during these exchanges, but gazed studiously at the enemy.

'I reckon we outnumber them. I see no more than four hundred facing us,' he said at last. 'So, what's your plan, Sphax? I've never known you not to have a plan.'

So he told them. When he'd finished he warned, 'My plan does not assure us success, it simply puts our eshrins in positions where we can do the most damage; the rest is up to you. Use your own initiative and seize the moment when it arises. Be bold and decisive.'

Nudging Dido around he said, 'I must inform Juba's eshrins of their part in this battle. Once I've done that I'll raise my javelin, Himilco, as a signal for you to set your eshrins in motion. That's when I'll start counting.'

Somehow, they had to allow sufficient time for Himilco's eshrins to ride unseen around the woodland so as to reach the enemy's rear just as Sphax's eshrins delivered a frontal attack. Timing was crucial.

They'd both guessed the distance to be just over a mile, and settled on a count of three hundred to account for the time it would take for Himilco to reach his objective. Sphax had reached two hundred. Juba's eshrins were also going to use those woods to shield them from the enemy, but they had a much shorter distance to cover, so they would only make their move when the allies were distracted by the frontal charge.

He'd reached two hundred and sixty. Taking a deep breath he calmed his racing thoughts, settled comfortably into Dido's withers and prepared to raise his javelin. 'Three hundred,' he said out loud.

'Forward!' he cried, nudging the mare to walk. As he nudged her into a trot, he'd one question on his mind: would the allies charge, or stand passively in defence of the ford? Surely the Campanians had learned by now that to stand still against Numidians was to invite a storm of javelins and certain destruction. Sphax guessed they would charge.

As they reached a canter he raised his javelin to signal that Aribal's eshrins, then Manissa's, should swerve to their left so as to make use of the open space on the allies' right flank. His four eshrins were now the only Numidians charging directly at the enemy.

The trap was set. It was their enemies' turn to roll the dice, but their number was up. Defend or retreat, their fate was sealed.

They were close enough now to see amongst their glittering ranks the tribune that screamed the order to charge. Sphax screamed a different order, for which his men were well prepared.

'Retreat! At the gallop.' Out of the corner of his eye, as Dido's front legs struggled to find purchase

PART THREE: The Scourge Of Rome

in the churned up mud, he caught sight of Himilco's eshrins rounding the edge of the woodland and flying into the rear of the allied cavalry.

On this muddied ground his Numidians were having to take an extra stride to manage their mares, but now his entire line was retreating at the gallop, drawing away from their pursuers who'd barely reached a trot.

The first volley of javelins was delivered by Himilco's eshrins and took a fearsome toll of their rearmost ranks. The second was delivered by Aribal and the third by Manissa. By the time Sphax halted his men and turned them around to face their enemy once more, he saw that the Campanians had been decimated by a firestorm of over three hundred javelins, most of which had found their mark.

As his eshrins reached a canter, Rome's allied cavalry reached the end of the woodland and saw their opportunity to escape further slaughter. Reeling from the succession of hammer blows, they'd now lost all semblance of order and so it was as a rabble they turned tail and fled northwards. It proved to be another fatal mistake. They simply ran into Juba's eshrins who'd been posted there for this very contingency, and his eshrins exacted another terrible toll.

Sphax halted his men and stared at the dead and wounded strewn on the ground that marked the passage of their enemies' death-ride. It was a terrible sight, and he drew no comfort from it, save for the fact that his own men had been spared. Even his Numidians had an air of solemnity about them as they recovered javelins from the dead. There was no jubilation or shield thumping, and Sphax was proud that his men did not loot a single trophy from the wealthy citizens of Capua and Neapolis.

When he'd last faced Campanian cavalry, Sphax had noted they favoured breastplates and cuirasses. Combined with shields, this offered excellent protection from a frontal attack but left them utterly exposed to assaults on their rear. By positioning the eshrins where he had, each successive wave had been launched on the Campanians' rear. They hadn't stood a chance.

Sphax was staring into the depths of the Trebia's icy waters when he noticed the lone Numidian galloping towards him from the south. It was Gala's man, who'd been left to guard the precious lamp cylinders. He'd had the good sense to hide when the allied cavalry had taken up position by the ford. Gala looked relieved.

'We cross an eshrin at a time in close formation,' Sphax shouted down his line. 'Let's get a move on, Roman equites can't be far behind.' With that he nudged Dido down the shallow bank and braced himself for the shock of its waters.

It felt as if he was being pierced by a thousand blades slowly working up his legs from his ankles to the middle of his thighs. Only with a great effort of will did Sphax prevent himself from crying out in agony. Half way across, Dido's left front leg must have stepped into a deeper pool.

His heart was suddenly in his mouth as she swayed and water rose alarmingly to her neck. Somehow, she must have instinctively swum a few rapid strides before finding purchase once more in the riverbed. His heart was pounding by the time they emerged on the western bank. It was only then he realised how close he and Dido had come to being swept away, like so many over the last week.

Sliding from her he began leaping around to bring life back to his frozen limbs. Next he gently slapped her rump to encourage her to trot around. It must have looked slightly comical, for when his uncle and Maharbal approached on horseback they were both laughing at his antics.

'Our enemies insist that a cold bath is invigorating, nephew, and beneficial to health. I see it is not to your taste!' Scores of Numidians were now pouring out of the river and joining in the wild dance as if possessed by demons. Maharbal was beside himself with laughter.

With life finally returning to his limbs, Sphax said, 'It is not, Sir, but I would give all the wealth I possess to bathe in a tepidarium at this moment.'

'If you have delivered the legions to me, I promise you this luxury in Placentia in a week's time.'

'Then I am already looking forward to this pleasure, Uncle, because the legions have been on the march since dawn—'

'Excellent news. Excellent!' lavishing one of his rare smiles. 'I must also commend your tactical skill in routing the allied cavalry. We watched carefully, and took a particular interest in your initial dispositions. Even Maharbal was impressed, is that not so?' he added, turning to his general of cavalry. Maharbal grinned and nodded.

'Although your work is not done, your eshrins' work has been accomplished for now. They should return to camp immediately, dry their clothes, take refreshment and anoint their bodies with more oil. We will not need them again until midday.'

'But ... Sir, how will we tempt their cavalry across—'

'Maharbal is about to bring you ten fresh eshrins, well breakfasted and not chilled to the bone. I dare say to Roman eyes, one Numidian eshrin looks much the same as another. But you, Sphax. You are a different matter. Rome has come to recognise you. So you must stay. If only to improve the taunting.' His uncle signalled to his standard bearer, Annaeus, that they were about to move out. 'Good luck, and may Melqart be with you on this auspicious day.'

* * *

It *had* been an auspicious start to the day. By the grace of the gods that morning they hadn't lost a single Numidian to the treacherous waters of the Trebia. A minor miracle in itself, thought Sphax, considering

PART THREE: The Scourge Of Rome

his own close encounter. As each eshrin reached the safety of the western bank, Sphax rode over to tell the commander the good news that they could return to camp. Without exception, each captain greeted the news as if they'd been granted a holiday.

By the time Himilco's eshrins had crossed, ten well-breakfasted fresh eshrins had formed up behind him. In between times, Maharbal insisted on a full account of the events of the night and the running battles outside the Roman camp. When he described his pursuit of Gaius Lucilus up to the very gates of the camp, the general's eyes widened.

'Then your fates are indeed entwined, and may be decided this day. But now the matter rests with Ba 'al Hamūn, not with your search for vengeance. Have faith in his divine justice, lad, and don't let this cloud your own judgement.'

Nodding solemnly, he said, 'I had him crawling on his knees like a dog. Perhaps that's enough humiliation.' It was not, and Sphax knew it. Neither would divine justice be enough if he caught sight of the bastard. He required earthly justice.

At that precise moment his account was halted by the arrival of Rome on the eastern banks of the Trebia ford. Red-cloaked equites. Sphax counted ten turmae, forming a line opposite them.

'Time to do your worst, lad,' said Maharbal, before nudging his mare to the rear. Although Sphax only knew half the names of his captains, the general had ordered them to follow his every move. So when he drew his dragon blade and nudged Dido to walk towards the river, he knew they would follow his lead. It was time to resurrect the Scourge of Rome.

Allowing Dido to get no more than her hooves wet in the river, he brought her to a halt. Across the gulf of the Trebia's waters, it would be impossible for any Roman to hear a word of what he was about to say, so he spoke in Tassynt, the ancient language familiar to all Numidians. If he couldn't challenge his enemies, at least he could rouse his own people.

'Welcome Rome,' he shouted, 'welcome to Numidia! Feel free to cross this little brook and enter our lands. We welcome your tax collectors, settlers and wine merchants, and we're so heartily sick of our women and children that we would gladly sell them into slavery. Cross the brook and I will arrange a market!' By now the Numidians behind him were laughing and jeering in equal measure.

'As to the lands we have taken from you? My bollocks have not thawed out since I stepped foot in Liguria. Your climate is execrable and you are welcome to it. So come and take it back. We hear the weather in Rome will be much more to our liking. So that's where we intend to take up residence.'

Theatrically waving his sword through the air he pointed it at his enemies. He felt rather foolish, but it was having the desired effect on his Numidians, who were now baying and jeering the equites, inviting them across.

PART THREE: The Scourge Of Rome

Roman numbers were growing all the while as fresh turma arrived and lengthened their line. When an entire turma of allied cavalry arrived and took up a prominent position on the equites' left, he decided on prudence, backing Dido away from the river. The enemy now had almost three times their number massed on the far bank, and Maharbal was nowhere to be seen.

Sphax rode the length of his line, encouraging the jeering but all the while keeping a watchful eye on the eastern bank. By the time he reached his last eshrin, their predicament had taken an alarming turn. Three dense columns of velites were now marching swiftly towards the river. There must be thousands of them, thought Sphax; where was Maharbal when you needed him?

What he really needed was to snap out of his malaise. He'd been so numbed by fatigue and the intense cold that his mind had gone to sleep and stopped working. Maharbal was *not* going to rescue him. He was on his own. So, he had to fight with what he'd got; three hundred Numidians. Then it dawned on him what Maharbal had in mind.

They were the sacrificial lambs: the goat tethered to the tree to draw out the leopard. If Maharbal had matched their forces eshrin for turma, Rome would have little to gain and much to lose from crossing the river. But three hundred lightly armed Numidians riding nothing better than ponies? Surely Rome would see them as ripe for plucking!

At last he was seeing things clearly. Rome had the dice in the palm of her hand. What would she do? The ford was so narrow that equites could only cross turma by turma. Thirty horsemen at a time reaching the western bank would make a tempting target for their javelins, and Rome had already tasted Numidian javelins. No! The tribunes on the far bank would never risk their finest on such a rash course of action. Which left the velites.

From what he'd seen so far that morning, Rome regarded their skirmishers as nothing more than human shields. But the columns were marching six abreast, and three columns could easily ford the river at the same time, ensuring they'd reach the western bank in numbers. On the other hand, he knew from painful experience that emerging dripping wet from that river virtually incapacitated you. He'd felt the effects of its icy waters up to his thighs; for men wading in on foot, it would rise to their chests. Poor bastards! They would struggle up the bank half paralysed, incapable of doing anything for a while, including throwing a javelin. There was an opportunity here.

Riding down the length of his line he told his men, 'I think their skirmishers will cross the ford first so as to shield their cavalry. I crossed that river almost an hour ago and my arse still feels like a block of ice. Those poor bastards will be in it up to their necks! When they stagger up the bank, their limbs will be so paralysed with cold they'll be incapable of holding a javelin, let alone throwing it.

'So, we strike them as they emerge from the river. When they're most vulnerable. From where we now stand, eighty paces from the western bank will allow our mares to reach a gallop. Each eshrin will attack in turn, beginning with the eshrin on the right which I shall lead. Let every javelin find its mark, for today we teach Rome that it is unwise to challenge Numidians!'

It cheered him to hear shields being thumped. Now there was nothing left to do but take up position on the right, pray his predictions were correct, and wait.

They didn't have long to wait. Sphax watched as centurions and a tribune began herding the heads of the columns into the river as if they were cattle. He noticed something else: a profusion of different uniforms. Campanians stood shoulder to shoulder with Etruscan javelinmen, Sabine skirmishers or legionary velites. There seemed to be no order within their ranks. Guessing that the morning's running battles had caused this chaos, he knew this would further test their courage and discipline when battle began. Men always fight better amongst their comrades and countrymen.

When the skirmishers reached midstream, Sphax sensed through the stiffness of their limbs the agony they must be feeling. Most cried out in pain. For the shortest, the waters left them gasping for air. All held their arms aloft, desperate to keep them out of the Trebia's bitter waters. But packed together like a shoal of fish, stumbles were inevitable and many were taken by the river.

Sphax didn't need to issue a command. Before their enemies splashed out of the river and collapsed on to its muddy banks he'd nudged Dido forward and swiftly brought her to a canter. The volley delivered into their helpless ranks was nothing short of murderous. He allowed the next eshrin to charge, but sickened by the senseless butchery of it all, stopped the third charge. They had become nothing more than executioners. Even the most battle-hardened veterans amongst them drew the line at needless slaughter. Yet this lay at the crux of the dilemma he was being presented with.

Even with the ten eshrins Maharbal had given him, given an inexhaustible supply of javelins, Sphax knew he could hold off the entire Roman army for the rest of the morning. Putting aside his scruples, not to mention honour and conscience, his eshrins were more than capable of turning the Trebia red with blood. The ford was narrow; only thirty cavalry, or perhaps sixty on foot could cross at a time. After the Trebia's icy waters had exacted its toll, the survivors staggering up the western banks would be at the mercy of three hundred Numidian javelins. Even the big-limbed Roman stallions would not be immune from the river's terrors, and in the intervals between crossings, it might be possible to retrieve javelins, or take them from the dead.

But what if this tactic worked *too* well? What if the legions were not prepared to pay such a high price for crossing the river? What if they turned around and simply marched back to camp? Hannibal's orders had been to deliver them across the Trebia, not prevent them!

In Sphax's mind it came down to a simple question: how many dare he kill before he allowed them passage and retreated? Scowling at the hapless skirmishers still staggering out of the water, he hardened his heart and stifled all conscience. Rome could take more punishment, so Rome would suffer.

'Forward!' he yelled at the next eshrin in the line. 'Drive them back from where they came.'

It was a sickening sight to witness, nevertheless, when they returned he sent the fourth eshrin forward to continue the slaughter. Then the fifth.

Over the course of these charges, Sphax confirmed something he'd always suspected about the Roman character: an unyielding, iron inflexibility of both mind and purpose. The river barred their path, so the river must be forded, whatever the cost in lives. Rome would not be denied. Flesh and blood meant nothing, just a necessary sacrifice to achieve an end.

He stared, disbelieving, as centurions began herding yet more columns of terrified skirmishers into the river using the flat of their swords. It spoke of a brutality that a civilised people would not even inflict on their own cattle. Sphax cursed them, loathed them. They were less than human! Such barbarism had to be stopped.

Halting Dido at the head of his sixth eshrin, he threaded his last javelin. He was saving his iron saunion for the throat of Gaius Lucilus. 'Forward,' he screamed, digging his knees into the mare so she bolted forward. The sickening sight of his own javelin piercing the breast of a defenceless Campanian javelinman brought him to his senses. Killing yet more of them would not stop this barbarity. Conscience and pity *must* prevail. It was time to give Rome passage of the Trebia.

* * *

Maharbal was waiting for him on the plain beside the charred remains of the old Roman camp. Behind him, scores of eshrins were already lined up ready for battle. Sphax added his ten to their number, then rode over to join his general.

'It's going to snow,' said Maharbal gloomily. 'I can feel it in these old bones of mine.'

For the first time during a morning which had seemed to last an age, Sphax examined the sky. All he saw was unending greyness, as if the brooding clouds had sucked all the light from the world and the sun had given up on them. It wasn't the clouds that bothered him, but the icy northerly breeze that bore them, cutting through him like a knife.

'If it rains heavily,' he said at last, 'only their cavalry will be able to re-cross that ford. It's already up to a veles' armpits.'

'For Rome, lad, that river is the Styx; once across it, there will be no way back.' Grasping Sphax's shoulder he added, 'Now go back to your pavilion and take your ease. Sit by your brazier, find dry clothes and eat heartily. Make sure those servants of yours anoint you in oil before you re-join us. I've left some Malacca for you as a reward for your exploits this morning!'

Sphax stared at the general in alarm. 'But I'll miss the battle, Sir!' Maharbal laughed.

'No you won't, lad, because it's not going to start for hours. Off you go. That's an order!'

SIXTEEN

It was the most extraordinary sight he'd ever seen. On the featureless grassland stretching arrow-straight for some two and a half miles, the Roman legions and their allies were being martialled for battle. Sphax was beside Maharbal and the general's standard bearer, Bartho. The old Roman camp had been deliberately situated on a slight elevation above the plain, so it offered a perfect vantage point to watch the grand vista that was unfolding, eight hundred paces from where they sat their mares.

For the thousands of skirmishers on both sides, the battle had already been raging for some time, with Rome getting the worst of it. Cheering frequently broke out from the ranks of Numidians lined up on the plain below as they encouraged Iberian caetrae to even bolder raids on the Roman javelinmen. Armed with falcata swords and javelins, these lightning quick swordsmen were as deadly with javelins as any Numidian and possessed sword skills that even Gauls envied. Working in groups of four or five, they would

PART THREE: The Scourge Of Rome

send over a shower of javelins, then dash into the ranks of the enemy, flashing those superior blades. Few could stand against such onslaughts.

Then there were the slingers. Hardy shepherds from the Balearics who could slay a wolf at sixty paces. Because of the slingshot's great range, even legionary infantry in the front ranks were not immune from their lethal pebbles or iron balls.

After watching for some moments, it was clear the Roman skirmishers were being slowly driven back. Over the entire length of the Roman line their dead could be seen scattered on the grasslands and Sphax could see for himself groups of Campanians and Samnites already retreating behind legionary shields.

Just as his uncle had described days ago at the council of war, Rome's four legions were being arranged into three separate lines. Sphax recalled the names of each line: hastati, principes, and a rear rank of veteran triarii. Yet Sphax counted six lines before Maharbal explained that Consul Sempronius Longus had placed two legions in front and two behind, noting that he'd placed his own two legions in the place of honour, on the right. It was his day to command, and so he could deploy Scipio's two legions as he pleased.

On the right flank of Longus' favoured legions stood Samnite infantry in phalanxes, hefting their more rounded white shields and bearing spears instead of Roman pila. Behind these there seemed to be a similar number of Lucanian infantry, garbed predominantly in scarlet, their burnished breastplates and helmets gleaming dully in the wintry sunlight.

Beyond them, facing their old camp, file after file of red-cloaked equites stretched northwards to the very banks of the Padus river. To the south, on the left flank of the legions, the line seemed to be continued by Campanians and then more cavalry, but at such a great distance, Sphax was struggling to identify uniforms.

Magnificent as the sight was, what truly fascinated Sphax was the way the legions' lines were being laid out. Something reminded him of pieces placed amongst the grid pattern of a petteia board. As a boy, his Greek teacher Elpis had taught him to play the game, though Sphax had never been very good at it, and usually lost all his soldiers within an hour of beginning a game.

Maharbal explained that each phalanx of legionary infantry was called a maniple, consisting of about one hundred and forty men. If each maniple filled up a square on a petteia board, the next square was left empty, and so on down the line of ten. But in their second line, three squares back, the maniples had been so arranged to correspond exactly with the spaces left in the first line, whilst the third line mirrored the first line. He remembered Elpis using this strategy to beat him at the game.

Maharbal laughed at Sphax's explanation of the pattern, insisting it had nothing to do with a Greek board game. If the front rank needed strengthening, he'd explained, the second line could advance into the spaces, creating a single continuous line that would be difficult to break. By the same token, if the first rank got into difficulties, it could always retire into the spaces of the second line, gaining instant strength from its reinforcements. The same would also be true of the triarii in the last line. But Sphax was also puzzled by this. At a guess, the lines were at least eighty paces distant from each other, so if any line needed support, they wouldn't get it in a hurry.

Sphax recognised how ingenious and flexible the system was. But it didn't make a legion immune from Numidian javelins. He was thinking about how horsemen could exploit those spaces when Maharbal interrupted his thoughts.

'Now you've seen them, what do you think of Rome's legions?'

Sphax shrugged. 'Aribal and I took them on this morning with four eshrins. We aimed high, at necks and faces. From what I saw of our volley, we did a great deal of execution. Those pilum things are useless! Aribal reckons they can't throw them more than twenty paces, which puts them well within range of our javelins.'

The general was staring at him, aghast. 'You didn't tell me about this.'

Sphax grinned. 'You never asked, Sir. Besides, all this Roman precision is beginning to bore me to death. I'm surprised the centurions haven't called upon surveyors to measure distances with gromae. They look as if they're laying out a grid for a new settlement, not setting up for battle!'

'Stop talking in riddles, young man! What's a groma?'

'A groma is why I hate all Romans, general. It's a complicated device surveyors use to measure heights and distances. Rome is incapable of thinking beyond a straight line or a grid. Romans are bereft of imagination or the higher faculties of reasoning. They are *measurers*, Sir, nothing more.'

By now Maharbal was roaring with laughter. 'You really haven't a good word to say for them, have you, lad?'

'No, Sir. Not a single one!' For Sphax, the less said about Romans the better, so he was relieved when the general's gaze and thoughts turned to the deployment of their own men.

Sphax recalled the wooden tiles on his uncle's battle table. He remembered the Numidian cavalry were to take up position on the left wing and their heavier Gaulish and Iberian cavalry were to occupy the right wing. These were already in place, but only now were the vast ranks of infantry leaving the warmth of their campfires and marching out from camp. These would take up the centre ground between the two cavalry wings, with the Iberians on the right, Gauls in the centre and Libyan pikes on the left.

All around him the grasslands now echoed to the sound of twenty thousand tramping feet. Hannibal

PART THREE: The Scourge Of Rome

had seen to it that they'd breakfasted well, and were as warm as anyone could be in the face of that icy northerly breeze. Last of all, Sphax saw two lines of elephants leaving camp, one of them heading directly for the Numidians.

He'd heard horrifying stories of how the mahouts goaded their animals into fury. First, by getting them fighting drunk, then inflicting pain on the most sensitive parts of their hides to drive them into a frenzied rage. Once their blood was up, his Numidians would be well advised to give them a wide berth today.

The Roman dispositions seemed to have been completed. Only a few of their skirmishers were still resisting the onslaught from caetrae. Most had now scampered back through the spaces, seeking sanctuary behind shields. Soon, their enemies' front ranks would be feeling the full force of javelins and slingers' pebbles.

Sphax spared a thought for Adherbal, Idwal and his uncle Mago, crouching in the bottom of that waterlogged ditch, two miles behind Rome's battlelines. Fingering his ivory amulet of Artemis he offered up a silent prayer for their safety. One thing was certain. Their ordeal would soon be over.

'It's time, Sphax,' said Maharbal gravely. 'We must return to our commands.'

'What are my orders, Sir? Am I to assist you today?'

'No. You are to lead the twenty eshrins you commanded this morning. I've formed them into five lines, just as you deployed them so effectively this morning. They are well rested after their ordeal, more than you, I fear, but you are young and strong.

'Your orders are simple. Hiempsal will charge the enemy cavalry on their right wing with eighteen elephants. They will cut a swathe through the Roman ranks just as surely as scythes reap a field of corn. I'm the last person to warn you about elephants, but beware, today their blood will be up. Follow them at a safe distance.

'If I'm right, you will find yourself in the rear of the entire Roman army. Then it's up to you. Use what you say our enemy lacks: imagination and higher reasoning.

'The son of Navaras will come of age today. You've more than fulfilled everything I've hoped you would become.' Sphax was so moved he reached out to clasp his general's hands.

'If I have, Sir, it's entirely through your noble example. You once told me that honour can only spring from duty. I swear that this day, Numidians under my command will do their duty.'

'Then I can ask for no more. Farewell, and may your goddess favour you on this momentous day.' With that the general nudged his Egyptian mare south as Bartho proudly raised his crescent standard

* * *

PART THREE: The Scourge Of Rome

As he approached his Numidians he saw that his eshrin captains were engaged in that well known counterweight to fear: jest and idle banter. Sphax's own little knots of fear were already making themselves felt in the pit of his stomach. Young as he was, he'd already learned that without this palpable reminder of his own mortality, there would be no check to his joy of audacity and daredevil risk-taking. Whilst everyone admired Astegal's lack of fear, in Sphax's opinion, a hothead like that had no place leading men into battle.

'Hail the boy general,' laughed Manissa, yet beating his shield in pleasure at Sphax's approach.

'At your venerable age, Manissa, shouldn't you be resting on your couch at this hour?'

'An excellent counter-thrust, lad,' growled Manissa, 'but do tell us how you're going to get us all killed in this battle?'

'Maharbal has already told us, Manissa,' interjected Himilco, 'we're to be trampled to death by our own elephants!'

'Bah! Elephants,' cried Gala. 'I've never trusted the beasts.' At that moment Sphax heard the unmistakable sound of trumpeting elephants. Swivelling around, he caught sight of a long file of elephants stomping towards them. For him, it was always a welcome and stirring sight.

'Then you'd better learn to love them, Gala,' he said, 'for here they come.'

Hiempsal was seated on the giant Syrian, a mahout's hooked iron pole in one hand and a clutch of javelins in the other, his hooded tunic as unwashed and dishevelled as ever. He halted the beast beside Sphax, greeting him genially as six hundred Numidians nervously edged their mares away from the monsters. Sphax had no such fear and nudged Dido forward so he could stroke the beast's shoulder

'When Maharbal told me the son of Navaras was to follow behind our great charge this afternoon, my heart leapt with joy. Many times did I celebrate victory with your father. Tonight I shall toast his son!'

'And I shall toast you and the Syrian, Hiempsal,' he laughed, 'for once the enemy hear his bellow, they will look to the gods for salvation and flee for their lives.'

'I hope not, lad,' Hiempsal replied with mock severity, 'I want to kill some of the bastards first.'

'Then lead on, Sir, and may Ba 'al Hamūn bring you victory.'

Hiempsal was as exacting at lining up his elephants as any Roman tribune. Animals had to be spaced out correctly, gaps checked and measured before the great charge could begin. It seemed to take an age. Sphax grew impatient.

He'd only ridden beside Hiempsal out of a burning curiosity to see the Roman cavalry's reaction to being faced by eighteen elephants and he was not displeased with what he saw! But now the mahouts began prodding and poking their beasts and the creatures were beginning to grow restless and jittery. When the Syrian gave out a great trumpeting roar, he decided it was time to get out of there.

His own eshrin were leading out the first of his five lines of Numidians. Sphax halted them a safe fifty paces behind the beasts. With every passing moment he'd noticed the trumpeting increasing and growing in intensity. There was both anger and pain in those piercing cries. Suddenly all the beasts let out a menacing shriek and the ground shook as they stomped forward to trample underfoot anything that stood in their path.

Sphax had forgotten how fast they could charge. He had to nudge his eshrin into a trot just to keep up with them. Only horses could outrun them. Anyone on foot could not hope to escape those massive feet and fearsome tusks.

Glancing to his right, he could see the solid ranks of Samnite heavy infantry coming into view, and behind these he knew there would be three more ranks of Lucanians. When his Numidians came abreast of the Lucanians, Sphax guessed what had happened.

At the terrifying sight of eighteen trumpeting war elephants charging towards them, the entire right wing of Roman cavalry had turned their big stallions around and fled for their lives. He could hardly blame them … mere flesh and blood could never stand against rampaging elephants. In one simple charge, not only had half the Roman cavalry fled the field, but their actions had exposed the entire right flank of the allied infantry to attack from flank and rear.

Sphax's thoughts were racing with the possibilities. The opportunity to concentrate on the vulnerable Lucanians and Samnites would only be possible if Hiempsal continued his charge and drove the cavalry back across the Trebia. If he gave up the chase and turned his elephants around, his Numidians would be trapped between marauding beasts driven mad with drink and pain, and the disciplined ranks of Lucanians. What would Hiempsal do?

They came abreast of the last line of Lucanians. It was now or never! He made a lightning decision. It was an enormous gamble, but he was suddenly certain what the master of Hannibal's elephants would do. Raising a javelin high in the air, Sphax pointed towards the south east and nudged Dido into a canter. The Lucanians were there for the taking. He intended to destroy them.

Leading his Numidians in a complete semicircle, he halted them two hundred paces in the rear of the Lucanians' last line. Now he desperately needed to pass on a score of orders at the same time. Every moment of delay would give the Lucanians time to prepare for the storm that was heading their way. Speed meant the difference between life and death. His first conversation was with young Agbal from his own eshrin.

'Chase after Hiempsal's elephants. Implore him to drive the Roman cavalry into the Trebia. It's imperative

PART THREE: The Scourge Of Rome

their cavalry don't return to the field.' His next stop was Himilco.

'I hadn't seen it until now, but we can use those spaces between the phalanxes to attack them from the front and rear at the same time. Get all our eshrin commanders to the front to watch. I'll demonstrate with my four eshrins what I want you all to do. Every line should then target a phalanx with the same tactic.' Sphax was about to play a game of petteia, and by using the spaces in the grid rather than the pieces, this time he'd figured out how to win.

'What's the tactic?' asked Himilco, staring at the ten phalanxes of Lucanians who'd been thrown into utter confusion by the Numidians' sudden wheel into their rear. Sphax could see their rear ranks frantically turning about to face this unexpected threat, but there was no time for explanations. Ignoring Himilco, he rode over to his own flank eshrin on the far right.

'Amal,' he shouted, 'we're going to attack the Lucanian phalanx in front of us. I want you to lead your eshrin with all speed in a wheel so you circle around them and deliver your javelins into their rear. I'm going to wheel my eshrin into that space,' he added, pointing, 'and do the same. Only our middle two eshrins will deliver a frontal attack. Got it?'

'Yes, Sphax,' nodded Amal. It took him a little time to explain to his other captains they must slow their charge sufficiently to give the two flanking eshrins time to gain the enemy's rear, but soon all was made clear. Riding the length of his own eshrin he simply yelled, 'We're going to charge into that space on their left and attack them from the rear. Follow me closely.' With that he rode to the left of his line, checked all four eshrins were ready, and raised his javelin.

After reaching a trot he quickly picked up the speed of his own eshrin so as to draw ahead of the middle eshrins. All the rear ranks of Lucanians had now turned about to face this new peril, but he wanted to fool them into thinking they were going to deliver a frontal attack, which meant leaving their circular sweep as late as possible. This required good judgement so as to allow his men on the right enough space to clear the Lucanian line. After glancing to his right to check that Amal was forging ahead, Sphax raised his javelin and swerved Dido to the left, nudging her into a gallop. Speed was all that mattered now.

Sphax saw a flash of bronze helmets, breastplates and raised shields before his eshrin thundered into the gap. A few hopeful spears were thrown in their direction but none found their mark. Soon he was leading his men in a tight arc that would place them in the rear of the phalanx.

As he placed two fingers through his throwing thong he could see the Lucanian rear ranks were now in a state of panic and confusion, not knowing which way to face, a confusion still unresolved when his eshrin delivered its murderous volley. Some had raised shields to face this unexpected threat, others had not. Lucanians

PART THREE: The Scourge Of Rome

that hadn't faced about were now carpeting the ground. Judging from the shrieks and cries from the rear ranks, these were also suffering Numidian javelins.

There was a new alarm when he turned Dido away to begin another charge. Phalanxes in the Lucanian middle line had seen the danger and decided to reinforce their rear line. But instead of marching back as a disciplined body, a fool of an officer had lost his head and ordered them to run back.

Clutching a spear in one hand and a great oval shield in the other, weighed down by breastplates, helmets and greaves, a Lucanian heavy infantryman was not designed for running. Within a few strides all order had been lost. Once-disciplined ranks had become a rabble. Now it was a case of every man for himself. This was an opportunity too good to miss.

Threading a fresh javelin, Sphax raised it and pointed at the easy pickings heading their way. Caught in the open, at their most vulnerable, the Lucanians didn't stand a chance. His Numidians did terrible execution, further compounded when Amal's eshrin delivered another fatal storm of javelins into their rear. Two phalanxes had all but disintegrated.

Whilst his men recovered javelins, Sphax took stock of the situation. Events were moving at lightning speed. Amal rode over to join him and they both stared about them, trying to make sense of it all.

'The Lucanians are finished, Sphax,' was Amal's final verdict. 'Look!' he suddenly yelled, pointing to

The Winter of Winters

the front line of Lucanians, 'Maharbal's men have got between their lines and are slaughtering them.'

Sphax could see for himself. When the entire right wing of Roman cavalry had fled the field in the face of Hiempsal's elephants, it had ripped open a gaping hole on the right flank of the Samnite and Lucanian infantry. Spacing lines eighty paces apart might be effective against an opponent's infantry, but against nimble, quick-thinking Numidians, it was a catastrophe waiting to happen. For Numidians, it was simply an invitation to gallop into the gaps and spaces provided.

Maharbal had forty eshrins with him, more than enough to seal the fate of the Samnites. His twenty now surrounded five Lucanian phalanxes. Instead of rescuing their comrades, to his astonishment the remainder of the Lucanians' rear line seemed to be going in the opposite direction, towards the legions on their left. Had they abandoned them to their fate?

His lightly armed Numidians were now locked in a desperate struggle with a thousand heavily armed Lucanians. By all the rules of war the outcome ought to have been a foregone conclusion. But Numidians didn't fight by the rules of war, and it was evident that Rome's tactics were unravelling.

His eshrins were charging furiously, delivering a firestorm of missiles into their helpless ranks. The Lucanians were virtually defenceless, unable to retaliate, for his men were careful to stay out of spear range. All the enemy could do was stand there and take it.

PART THREE: The Scourge Of Rome

The sheer noise of it all assaulted his ears. Besides the deafening roars of triumph and wails of the defeated, the endless clash of iron on bronze and thud of javelin and spear, the air was alive with a cacophony of fanfares and counter calls on trumpet and horn. In the distance Sphax could even hear the unearthly wailing of the carnyx. And above it all, like the continuous beating of a thousand drums, the thunderous roar of horses' hooves.

In the distance he caught sight of a lone rider. As he drew nearer, Sphax recognised Agbal, returning at the gallop from his mission to Hiempsal. He turned to Amal.

'Take command of my eshrin and continue your attacks. Agbal is approaching and I need news of the Roman cavalry,' adding firmly, 'stay out of spear-shot!'

Agbal and his mare looked exhausted. 'Hiempsal's driven 'em across the river, captain,' he said between gasps for air. 'The slackheads tried to make a stand in the middle of the river but the elephants just tore into them. He's left six of the calmer beasts this side of the ford to guard it. The rest are going to chase the bastards all the way back to their camp if needs be. Either way, that lot aren't going to do us any more mischief today.' Sphax gripped the young man's shoulder.

'Good, Agbal. You've done well! That's the news I was praying for.' Agbal was still panting and his mare looked blown. 'Rest up and join us when you're ready.'

Joining Amal on the next charge, he sensed something in the anguished expressions of the diminishing ranks of their enemy. He could taste it, smell it at the back of his nostrils. It was almost palpable, something he'd experienced before.

Months ago, on the banks of the Rhodanus, in the space between two heartbeats, Sphax had witnessed five thousand Volcae warriors cast away their shields and inexplicably flee for their lives. It was such an extraordinary and curious phenomena that he and Idwal had debated it frequently and fervently. The ancients were of little help. Zeno, even Socrates, had nothing to say on the phenomenon. The nearest he and Idwal had come to defining it was as a collective collapse of will. How this collapse was communicated instantly to hundreds, let alone thousands, remained a mystery. This is what his instincts had sensed just now, emanating like some fetid miasma from the Lucanians. He knew it would only take a spark.

The spark turned out to be the sight of men from the phalanx to their left breaking and fleeing in terror. Suddenly the Lucanians' will to resist had been broken and the contagion spread like plague. Now only the dead and wounded marked the positions where the five phalanxes had once stood so resolutely. The rest scattered to the four winds.

Most flew north towards the Padus, but some fled west, aiming for the Trebia ford. He watched as shields were flung to the ground. Then, as terror gripped the exodus at the thought of a javelin in the back, came discarded helmets, spears and even breastplates. Anything to lighten the fugitives' load.

Numidians were trained to chase and harry. That's what they did best. But Sphax realised that if he didn't take control of the situation immediately, his eshrins would pursue the fugitives in every direction over the battlefield. His six hundred would cease to be a potent fighting force, its strength scattered and dissipated, fighting countless minor skirmishes that would have no bearing on the outcome of the battle.

The Lucanians were routed and going nowhere. Besides, they'd thrown away most of their weapons and Hiempsal's elephants were guarding the Trebia ford. Pursuit was pointless.

Urging Dido forward, he raced amongst eshrins already pursuing fugitives, ordering them to stop and return. By the time he reached the last few captains, Sphax was hoarse from all the yelling and shouting, but at least his men were concentrated again. All they lacked now were fresh orders.

Summoning his eshrin leaders to the front, it was time to take stock again. What was already painfully evident was that the battle had left them far behind. They were now half a mile behind the legions' rearguard and what remained of the Lucanians.

It was astonishing to Sphax how quickly battles ebbed and flowed; take your eyes off them for a moment and you were chasing events, not ahead of them. He'd fought in many desperate battles since joining his uncle's army. But nothing like this. Not with tens of thousands of men spread over such a vast plain. It was the sheer scale of it all that he found so daunting.

Sphax guessed they'd routed less than half the Lucanians. The five unmolested phalanxes from their rear line and the survivors from other lines had joined to form a long column protecting the right flank of Longus' legions. Sphax noticed the gaps between phalanxes had disappeared. They were learning, he thought wryly.

Fundamentally, he reasoned, nothing had changed. Without cavalry to defend them, that long column of Lucanians was just as vulnerable to a javelin as before. Surrounding them was no longer an option, but they were open to frontal attacks, and routing them would prise open those wide spaces in a legion's ranks.

One piece of foresight was incalculable. He knew Hannibal's battle plan. When the time was ripe, he knew that his uncle Mago would fling Adherbal's Numidians and Idwal's Cavari at the Roman rearguard. If his men could wear down the Lucanians guarding their flank, he might be able to break into the legions' flanks at the same time as Mago assailed their rear. It was a plan, he decided.

Borrowing his uncle's trick, in turn he momentarily locked eyes on his commanders, then said severely, 'Not a single eshrin will pursue fleeing enemies without a direct order from me. Understood?' Manissa glared at him and spat.

'It's too late for that,' he growled angrily, 'they've already fled. We could have slaughtered thousands of the bastards ... but you just slapped their arses and let them go!' Sphax wasn't going to rise to this, but he was alarmed by the laughter Manissa's insubordination had provoked. He eyed them steadily.

'Every eshrin will now move in single file until we're perfectly positioned on the flank of the Lucanians to—'

'Kiss their arses and wave them farewell!' Manissa interjected with a hollow laugh. 'No, boy, you need to explain why you let thousands of our enemies escape?'

Precious time was slipping away, but he knew that Manissa's challenge to his authority had to be confronted, if only to crush any lingering doubts about his leadership amongst the other commanders.

Rounding on Manissa he asked icily, 'Tell me, captain, how those Lucanians would escape?'

'Straight across that ford, boy. Where else?'

'You mean the ford that's now guarded by six of Hiempsal's elephants, their blood up, eager to trample anything that comes their way?' That stopped Manissa in his tracks. 'Even the slackheads in your or Gala's eshrins would not have the courage to attempt a crossing in the face of elephants. Take it from me, Manissa, our fugitives are going nowhere.' With a jolt, he saw that all eyes, and ears he hoped, were back on him again. Manissa had fallen silent.

'For the benefit of those who were not paying due attention, we ride fast, in single file until we draw parallel with the Lucanians. Then, we turn our mares to face them and charge as a body, all six hundred of us. And we keep charging until we break them.' Staring deliberately at Manissa, he continued, 'When they flee, we let them. There will be no pursuit.' He allowed his gaze to encompass the circle of earnest faces now staring at him.

'This battle will be decided by Rome's legions, not a few Lucanians or Samnites. We must find a way to break into their ranks. That's where we need to do the damage. That's where our actions will be decisive. And that's where victory lies!' He nudged Dido westwards. 'Follow me.'

Sphax quickly urged his mare to canter. Instantly, a long thin line of Numidians stretched across the grasslands as it snaked its way through small bands of Samnites who'd given up the struggle against Maharbal's eshrins. Easy kills were resolutely ignored as the line forged ahead until it reached the static lines of infantry that were now locked together in deadly combat. Raising a hand, he eased Dido to a trot and then a walk.

Roman discipline now faced the ferocity of Gaul. Insubres and Boii had much to avenge, and over the course of weeks their numbers had been swollen by tribes with even greater grievances, such as the Anamares. Sphax had faced Gauls in battle more times than he cared to remember. They knew of only one tactic: attack. So when the carnyx wailed and Morrigu had decided their fate, they would heft their huge shields and surge forward screaming curses at anyone who dared face them.

Recollecting his uncle's table-top dispositions, he knew Iberians lay to their right and Libyans to their left. To the best of his knowledge, Hannibal's Iberians and Libyans had yet to be defeated in battle. The outcome would be inevitable. Rome was about to be annihilated, swept from the board as easily as his uncle had scattered those black tiles.

Raising a javelin, he signalled his six hundred to turn and face their foe. Threading the javelin he'd just raised with his throwing thong, Sphax stared grim-faced at the Lucanians and pitied them. But he never gave the order to charge.

Suddenly a great roar erupted from the legions as they surged forward in triumph. Gaul had failed, their lines broken as the carnyx fell silent. The sky had fallen and the unthinkable had just happened.

SEVENTEEN

In despair he peered beyond the sea of helmets at where he imagined the front lines to be. He'd not been mistaken; the standards waving in the breeze were those of the legions of Sempronius Longus and they were storming forward, relentlessly, and once more the Lucanians were on the move to keep pace.

Sphax's thoughts were in turmoil, his heart pounding. Was it just a setback, or did it portend the unthinkable, a bitter defeat? That the Boii and Insubres were retreating was certain, but surely the Iberians and Libyans would stand firm. Surely all was not yet lost. But on this accursed flat plain there was no way of knowing or seeing. Their only hope now was Mago's planned attack on the rear. That might save them.

But where was Mago? Surely they must have left their watery lair by now? Had they been delayed or prevented? Or worse still, attacked and cut off? He had to know!

One thing was certain. Somebody had to strike a blow at the legions' rearguard. It might be their only

PART THREE: The Scourge Of Rome

hope. And if Mago had been prevented from doing so, then he must attack with his six hundred.

Now that he'd made up his mind, Sphax felt calmer, but there was no time to be lost. Nudging Dido around, he galloped back down the single file of Numidians until he reached Himilco's eshrin, the last of the line.

'Do you know of Mago's planned attack on the Roman rear?' he shouted over to Himilco.

'Of course! It was all around the camp after Adherbal called for volunteers last night.'

'It was supposed to be kept secret,' Sphax said, scowling. 'No matter. I need to find out what's delaying Mago. I need to find out now. Before it's too late! The Gauls are retreating and all will be lost if we don't do something.'

Himilco was staring at him in alarm. 'You're going to find Mago?' he asked, wide-eyed.

'Yes! *Somebody* has to make that attack, and if Mago can't it will have to be us. It may be our only hope. Keep our men in position until I return.' With that he dug his knees into Dido's flanks and she raced off to the south east. Ten strides later the entire rear of two Roman legions came into view and he gradually edged the mare due south. She'd taken no more than six strides in this new direction before he'd brought her to an unexpected halt.

Stretched out for a mile, as if on parade, was a single line of Numidians. Behind them he could see rank upon rank of Cavari, swords unsheathed and shields hefted. Ahead of Adherbal's thousand Numidians sat Mago astride his sleek black stallion, sword raised to the heavens. As Sphax watched, he saw him lower it and point it decisively at the enemy. Mago's army surged forward.

It was the finest sight he'd ever witnessed. He watched almost spellbound, as the Numidians delivered a storm of a thousand javelins into the rear ranks of the unprepared legions. It was as if Adherbal had his men at drill, so perfectly was each consecutive charge executed. After the fourth charge Adherbal had his men scatter to the flanks to allow the Cavari to deliver the death blow.

With a great roar, Idwal's men rushed the enemy. Sphax had never seen a charge so ferocious and savage. The Cavari simply leapt at the shaken ranks of triarii, using their iron shield bosses as battering rams before scything down with those lethal Gaulish blades. Soon he could see the yawning gaps that had been torn in the legions' ranks. Gauls would decide this battle today, but not those in the van.

'Adherbal has charged, men!' he yelled repeatedly as he galloped back to his own eshrin on the extreme right. 'Adherbal has charged and Rome has been shattered. Rome is finished, men. Finished!' Raising his javelin he pointed it at the Lucanians once more, nudged Dido to a walk and screamed, 'Forward!'

* * *

PART THREE: The Scourge Of Rome

That's when the great slaughter began. It took his twenty eshrins three charges to convince the Lucanians it was time to flee for their lives. But flee they did, revealing gaps and wide open spaces between each maniple and the legions' three lines. Removing them from the field was like opening Pandora's box, and that afternoon Pandora was about to unleash all the calamity and misfortune in the world on Rome.

His Numidians were the first to break into the legions' lines, but they were soon joined by the eshrins of Adherbal and Maharbal. Next it was the turn of Iberian cavalry to swarm onto the killing fields, and within the hour, Libyan pikes and Iberian infantry appeared on both flanks. Two Roman legions, along with all their allies, were surrounded and being slaughtered like cattle.

Later, he could recall little of the endless charges, of dismounting to hunt down their enemies like wild beasts, of ripping javelins from the dead so the killing could go on, of the pleas for mercy that were spurned, of the screams of the wounded and dying that seemed to fuse into one continuous cry of agony. The sheer madness and horror of it all felt like some nightmare vision of Hades, best purged from all remembrance. As the hours of butchery passed, there came a moment when Sphax could kill no more.

He remembered coming upon Maharbal, grim and silent, standing beside his standard bearer Bartho, a tiny island of the living in a sea of dead and moaning wounded. Dismounting, Sphax had joined them. For a while, the three of them just stared in horror at the carnage surrounding them before Maharbal had broken the silence.

'This is the terrible face of victory, lad,' he'd said. 'For the sake of your soul, remember this sight.'

By late afternoon the gods took pity on them. No one had noticed the darkening skies. So when the first bolt of lightning struck a tree on the edge of the battlefield and it burst into flames, friend and foe alike stared heavenwards. A heartbeat later there followed a deafening crash. It was as if night had suddenly descended to spare them the terrible sights of this field of slaughter. With the next flash the heavens opened and a deluge like no other began, flailing hands, faces and bare flesh with ice-laden sleet, instantly drenching those still standing.

The gods had not sent a rain, they'd sent a flood, a deluge to wash away the stains of this bloody field. The torrents falling from the heavens soon created shallow rivers and ponds on the half-frozen grasslands. Men and horses began slipping, sliding and falling, finding themselves caked in slime and gore as they struggled wearily to their feet.

Then the strangest thing happened. Something that seared itself into his memory of that dreadful afternoon. The gods had made war impossible, forced a truce, and the killing stopped. As if by some mysterious unspoken pact, the battle was over.

PART THREE: The Scourge Of Rome

* * *

Along with the hundreds making their way back to camp, Sphax trudged wearily beside Dido, water running in torrents from them both. Never in his life had he felt so tired and drained, his mind numb, emptied of all thought and feeling. Every bone in his body ached, but it was far too dangerous underfoot to risk riding his mare, who was just as exhausted as him.

As the eastern gate of the camp came within sight, the deluge stopped just as suddenly and miraculously as it had started. The sky lightened a little and Sphax sensed a change in the air as the wind shifted to the north west.

Drawing nearer the gate his heart leapt at the sight of his dear friend Idwal, waiting to greet him. For a moment they simply gazed at one another, unsmiling, before embracing in solemn relief that they'd both survived this day. For the first time that afternoon, Sphax managed a grin.

'I saw for myself that first charge of your Cavari. It was the most courageous thing I've seen all day.' His friend remained oddly silent, meeting his gaze steadily. Instantly Sphax knew that something was desperately wrong.

'What is it?' he asked, suddenly alarmed. 'Please, Idwal, tell me what's happened.'

'It's Adherbal,' Idwal replied gravely. 'He was slain.'

Sphax felt a stab of anguished pain in his breast as if he'd been pierced by a blade. Sinking to his knees he bowed his head and unashamedly allowed the tears to flow. In the darkest days and weeks following Fionn's death on the mountainside, Adherbal had been as a father to him. His wisdom, humanity, and above all his compassion had been like a rock for him. In return, Sphax had come to love him as a father. And now he was dead.

Death had touched so many that day. He'd seen the gentle giant Gulussa struck down with a spear, along with Balam, a young man from his eshrin not much older than himself. His friends Aribal, Dubal and Juba, who'd fought so nobly on the Ticinus, all gone ... and now Adherbal.

'His eshrin want to give him funeral rites, but they're much too exhausted to go back for his body. So I said that I would do this honour for them. We owe a great deal to Adherbal and his Numidians today.'

Sphax got to his feet. 'I shall come too. I can't bear the thought of leaving him out there ... abandoned.'

'How did I know you were going to say that? I've brought my stallion to bear his body.'

'Then I shall walk with you.' Gently he ran a hand down Dido's mane and told her to return home, knowing she would trot obediently back to his pavilion where Cesti and Lulin would see to her needs. Idwal reached for the stallion's reins and the two of them set out on the long walk back to a field neither of them ever wished to see again.

PART THREE: The Scourge Of Rome

'My uncles,' he remembered at last to ask, 'are they unharmed? And Drust, and Maharbal—'

'All well, Sphax, and in rude health. Especially Hannibal, who is particularly pleased with himself. But then he has won a great victory.'

'Have we won a great victory?' he asked, with a wearied indifference. 'The last time I saw the Boii and Insubres, they were being pushed back.'

'From what your uncle has told me, it was far worse than that, Sphax.' Idwal described how Longus, with two legions, had broken clean through the Gauls and shattered their line. This had been the moment of crisis. But somehow, Hannibal had rallied them, restored their lines and re-sealed the front, securing their flanks with Libyans and Iberians. Which meant the two remaining legions and their allies were completely surrounded by Numidians on one side and Iberian cavalry on the other. To make matters worse for Longus, Mago's attack had shattered the rear of these legions. The Roman army had been cut in half. Sempronius Longus, Idwal told him, had been stranded on the wrong side of the battlelines with just two legions, without the numbers to effect the outcome and being pelted with javelins and slingshots by thousands of our skirmishers. Longus had then done what all consuls did in such circumstances: saved his own skin. Idwal thought that Longus, along with what was left of his legions, would be in Placentia by now.

'What happened to their cavalry?' Sphax asked when Idwal had finished his description.

'Hiempsal's elephants charged on each flank and drove them into the river. They fled, and haven't been seen since.'

Sphax recalled the sight of Gaius Lucilus crawling through the mud on all fours, knowing full well the bastard would have saved his precious skin.

'There's a rumour that Hiempsal's razed the Roman camp to the ground,' Idwal added. 'But to answer your original question. Yes, Sphax, this is a great victory. Two legions have escaped, so it's not a complete victory, but two legions and all their allies have been destroyed. What's more, their cavalry have fled the field. Rome has lost Liguria. They no longer have the strength to hold it. When news of this reaches the senate, this battle will fan the flames of fear and consternation in Rome.'

They were now approaching the battlefield where the butchery had taken place. Both of them steeled themselves for what they were about to see. Sphax deliberately kept to the fringes of the killing grounds, re-tracing the path his Numidians had taken before those last few charges on the ill-starred Lucanians.

With every step he sensed the air growing colder. The grasslands had soaked up the deluge, but he could now feel it freezing underfoot. Above their heads and to the east, the sky loomed an impenetrable grey. Stopping momentarily, Sphax turned and gazed at the western sky. They only had an hour of light left in the day. But somehow, he knew that Adherbal's last journey on this earth would be towards a glorious, blood-red sunset.

As he turned to continue their journey, the first delicate snowflake floated down from the heavens. Perhaps Maharbal's old bones had been right after all and it was going to snow today. Sphax held out his hand and the next snowflake melted on his palm.

'It should be quite safe to ride your stallion now, the ground's freezing.'

Idwal laughed. 'If anyone rides, my friend, it must be you. My battle began only a few hours ago, yours started before dawn. Besides, we must be close now.'

'Where did Adherbal fall, Idwal?' he asked, feeling again that stab of pain to his breast.

'His men said he was struck by a spear shortly after my Cavari charged.'

Peering ahead through the thickening snowflakes, Sphax saw immediately where he lay. Two hundred paces to the south, Adherbal's golden-hued Egyptian mare stood like a faithful sentinel. She had not left her master's side since he'd fallen.

When Sphax looked into that noble face once more, the tears began to flow again. Gently he removed the spear point that had buried itself into Adherbal's chest and flung it aside. Kneeling before him he closed those bright grey eyes for the last time and stooped down to kiss his forehead. He heard the approach of distant hoof-beats, but Sphax couldn't take his eyes away from the cold and lifeless face of his dear friend.

The Winter of Winters

The sound of trotting hoof-beats grew closer, more insistent. Now curious, Sphax got to his feet and stared into a sunset miraculously transforming greys and pinks into a myriad of red and gold. The grey stallion and its rider drew ever closer. At last he caught a flash of a hooded crimson cloak. Could he dare to hope?

'You live!' came the cry. 'You live!' Corinna leapt from her stallion and ran towards him. 'Cesti and Lulin are weeping. Your mare returned alone. They thought you dead,' she said as they flew into each other's arms. Rapturously he felt her tears wash down his cheeks as she clung to him.

'Thank the gods you live,' she said breathlessly, her face buried in his neck. 'I had given up all hope.'

'I never thought you would return,' he said at last. 'It is I that had given up all hope of seeing you again.' Corinna withdrew her head from his shoulder and they looked into one another's eyes. He could feel her soft breath on his moistened cheeks as he gazed joyously into those lovely hazel eyes. Then she broke the spell with that familiar teasing smile.

'You may regret my return, Numidian, for I am now a free women, and I have many snares ...'

'Dasius is dead then?' he asked, suddenly serious. Corinna nodded.

Idwal coughed. 'May I remind you moonstruck lovebirds that we are here to perform a sacred duty.' With a gasp, for the first time Corinna recognized Adherbal's lifeless body on the ground.

'I'm so sorry, Idwal,' she cried, staring in concern at Sphax. 'Is this not your friend, Adherbal?' He nodded. 'And he was like a father to you. I'm so sorry, Sphax. I beg you both to forgive me. I did not see ...'

'There is nothing to forgive,' he answered, reassuringly.

'Then together, let us bear his noble body to our pavilion, my darling, so he can be mourned by those who loved him.'

As he and Idwal carefully placed Adherbal's body over his mare's back, Sphax knew the faithful creature would never allow him to fall again. Sitting snugly behind Corinna on her great stallion, he entwined his arms around her waist and gazed for the last time on the steadily whitening grassland. By morning, in this winter of winters, its horrors would be mercifully unseen, hidden under a carpet of the purest white.

HISTORICAL NOTES

Firstly, I must issue a word of caution to all readers and students of the Punic Wars, in particular the Hannibalic War (also known as the Second Punic War). Our two chief classical sources come from Livy's *History of Rome* and Polybius' *The Histories*.

Livy's (59 BC — AD 12/17) *History* was written 200 years after the events in question and from sources rarely disclosed. Often his writing displays a lack of military understanding. He was writing at the time of Augustus, so is keen to exalt Rome's greatness and dominance at the expense of accuracy. Personally, I view Livy as propaganda for the emerging Roman Imperium, and read him to find out how the enemy thinks, not what they actually did. Polybius (c. 200 BC — c. 118 BC) however, is not so easy to dismiss. He was a Greek, who was transported to Rome as a hostage in 167 BC, and spent the next

17 years of his life there. Polybius is regarded as a father of historical writing because of the methods he established: visiting places where battles or significant events took place; interviewing eyewitnesses (presumably all Roman), and sifting through all the available sources for accuracy. Add to this the fact that he was a distinguished cavalry officer with a wealth of knowledge of military affairs, and it would appear his account should be trusted. On the other hand, it's not difficult to spot the spin and gloss he puts on things, and why he does it.

Polybius became a teacher, close friend and later counsellor of Scipio Aemilianus, the adopted son of Scipio Africanus. In my fictional account, Scipio Africanus (Publius Scipio) is the very same young man Sphax fights on the Ticinus battlefield. Polybius is very much part of clan Scipio. The bias in favour of Rome is subtle and nuanced, but nevertheless it is always present.

As I mention in the novel, only a general as remarkable as Hannibal would take on campaign with him a Greek historian and a Greek philosopher and teacher. Sosylos and Silenos both wrote accounts of the Second Punic War. Both Livy and Polybius cite them, and must have based much of their histories on their work. Just as Carthage was razed to the ground and the land ploughed by oxen to remove all memory of the city and its people, these two accounts written by faithful followers of Hannibal, have also been lost to history. What I would give to read these histories! Victors usually get to write their version of history, and it's wise to cover one's tracks.

When Hannibal's exhausted army descended the Alps in the autumn/winter of 218 BC it was a shadow of the original force that had set out from the Rhone in late summer. It's been estimated that he lost more than half his numbers, mostly through desertion and straggling. As to their condition: Livy describes them as 'filthy and unkempt as savages.' Presumably, they were also starving. To begin with, operations would have been impossible until men were fed and the condition of their horses improved. But unfortunately, the Carthaginians were not allowed such a breathing space.

Whatever pass Hannibal took (the perennial question which to this day seems to fascinate historians and retired generals alike), it would have brought his army into the territory of the Taurini, who were not only suspicious of him, but had recently made enemies of their neighbours, the Insubres. As Hannibal's army had arrived in the Po (Padus) valley at the behest of their allies the Insubres and Boii, this put them in an extremely difficult position.

Hannibal made overtures of friendship towards the Taurini; on both occasions they were rejected. He now took matters into his own hands, besieging their capital (Turin) and storming it within three days, putting many to the sword. By the standards of the day this is by no means an exceptional act of barbarity, but it clearly illustrates that when necessary, Hannibal was prepared to be utterly ruthless. This single act sent out a clear signal to all the Gallic tribes in northern Italy (Liguria). This is the situation when The Winter of Winters opens.

The Numidian trick of getting their mares to lie down and lying on top of them to spy out the land is well documented. Numidians made superb scouts! Maharbal (Hannibal's general of cavalry) would almost certainly have had scouts shadowing Scipio's legions, for as my book opens, it was common knowledge that a Roman army was operating in the Po valley.

My description of the battle of the Ticinus is largely accurate, but I must confess there is no evidence for Maharbal inventing a new cavalry formation, though it must be noted that Hannibal himself did lead the ferocious charge that shattered the Roman cavalry, and Numidians were indeed placed on both wings. Also, there's mounting counter-intuitive evidence that in this period, cavalrymen often dismounted and fought on foot.

So why was Rome's vaunted cavalry, formed from the elite equestrian class (hence equites) routed that day, along with a similar number of their allies? Again, the answer is staring us in the face, clearly set out by our primary sources: Livy and Polybius. Rome was outnumbered by at least six to one, and shackled to their javelinmen (velites), Scipio could only deliver

Historical Notes

a charge at a pedestrian pace, whilst Hannibal led his men at the gallop. Inevitably, when the velites caught sight of Hannibal's six thousand, they took to their heels and fled through the ranks of their own cavalry, further disrupting the momentum and order of the equites' charge. Once the Numidian squadrons flowed on to the flanks and rear, the game was over.

Consul Publius Cornelius Scipio was severely wounded that day and only escaped because of the valour of his son, also called Publius. However, in the earliest recorded account of this incident, it is not his son, but a Ligurian slave who rescues the consul — so take your pick.

According to Livy, Hannibal did consider storming the Roman grain store at Clastidium (modern day Casteggio), but bribery proved more effective. For the insignificant sum of 400 gold pieces, the garrison commander, Dasius, surrendered the place to him. The garrison and its commander were from Brundisium, a Greek city on the Adriatic coast of southern Italy, so we must assume the garrison was largely Greek. Hannibal's policy was to treat potential allies leniently so he could win them over from Rome. I have woven a rather elaborate web around this dull episode that has significant consequences not just in this story, but also (spoiler alert) in future novels in the series.

Little is known of the Gallic Anamares tribe. They were thought to live in the territory south of the Po, bordering Insubres lands. If this was the case it would

Historical Notes

place them in the line of fire of Roman colonisation south of Placentia (modern day Piacenza) in Liguria.

Included in The Winter of Winters are several incidents which on the surface seem implausible, yet are historically documented. The first of these is that Hannibal does form up his entire army on the empty plain before the Roman camp and offers Scipio battle. Sensibly, Scipio refuses, but in my story I deliberately link this with the next event: the desertion of two thousand of Scipio's Gallic auxiliaries who behead the Romans on watch that night and go over to Hannibal. There is an obvious connection between Scipio's unwillingness to rise to Hannibal's challenge and the Gauls' desertion. Severed heads as trophies figure heavily in Gallic warfare.

Scipio does indeed abandon his forward camp and relocate to a new one safely beyond the river Trebia and nearer his base at Placentia. This was a very risky manoeuver, and Hannibal had a golden opportunity to destroy Scipio's entire army that day. Scipio only survived because the Numidian cavalry disgraced themselves, halting their pursuit to loot and burn the Roman camp, giving the consul time to escape with his army intact.

Hannibal's scouting mission (with Sphax in attendance) to determine whether the legions of Consul Longus had arrived in camp is largely unsupported in the historical sources. However, there is a source that suggests it was Hannibal himself who first heard the separate reveille trumpet calls of the consuls' legions. To hear this he must have crossed the Trebia and threaded his way through outposts and sentinels before dawn to get within earshot of the Roman camp. This sounds like a scouting mission to me. That Hannibal scouted the area thoroughly where he intended to lure Longus into battle is beyond dispute. Hannibal himself discovered the ditch where he placed Mago's forces that played such a decisive role in the battle to come.

Hannibal did indeed allow his Numidians to raid Insubres villagers to pillage and loot. Maybe his so-called allies were not coming over to him as quickly as he expected, or were, as he feared, appealing to Rome for protection. Either way, Hannibal saw an advantage that could be exploited. Longus claimed a minor victory by assailing a few Numidian columns that were forced to relinquish their loot and return to camp empty-handed. I suspect this was Hannibal's true intention. In my fictional account, Sphax feels very differently about this mission.

What I describe as the death or glory episode, where prisoners willingly fight each other to the death to gain their freedom, is well documented by both Polybius and Livy. But I must confess that in their accounts, this incident occurred some time before the battle of Ticinus. I use some of Livy's phrases in Hannibal's lengthy concluding speech.

Very little is said about the river Trebia in both the historical sources and subsequent accounts by historians

Historical Notes

and military writers. I think the river is a key factor. All the original sources describe the weather in the days and weeks before the battle as atrocious, with rain and sleet swelling the streams and rivers. Even the battle itself is brought to a standstill by a terrible storm. In the winter there's a cold easterly wind called the Bora that can deluge the western Po plain with rain or snow. My novel is called The Winter of Winters with good reason.

Both Livy and Polybius describe the Trebia's waters reaching to an infantryman's chest. By any standards this is a considerable obstacle. In December its waters would be icy cold. Coupled with the fact that infantry were inadequately clad against the cold, crossing the river would make them virtually incapable of combat for some time, not to mention the long-lasting effects of extreme cold reducing their overall effectiveness in battle. Livy makes this clear:

> *'for when in pursuit of the Numidians they actually entered the river — it had rained in the night and the water was up to their breasts — the cold so numbed them that after struggling across they could hardly hold their weapons. In fact, they were exhausted and, as the day wore on, hunger was added to fatigue.'*

Riding their small ponies, Numidian cavalry would also find crossing the Trebia something of an ordeal. Fords are not mentioned in either Polybius or Livy, so

Historical Notes

I've conjectured that this swollen river could only be forded in a few places unless you followed its course a considerable distance upstream where it might have been shallower. Added together, these factors make the river a formidable barrier, one which you crossed to its western bank at your peril.

Before we move on to the battle itself, I must first say something about Hannibal's intelligence networks. Over the years, as his campaign in Italia continued, he developed a highly sophisticated intelligence-gathering network of spies and informers. Hannibal always placed great store on intelligence and information. During the Ligurian campaign of 218-17 BC he had one distinct advantage: the Roman colonies of Placenta and Cremona were isolated settlements in territory inhabited by his potential allies, the Insubres and Boii. Gauls served in the Roman camp, so he was probably well informed of rumour, gossip and the morale of his enemies.

Polybius describes Hannibal's instructions about the Numidians' role in luring Consul Sempronius Longus' legions out of their camp with the words:

> *'to ride up to the enemy's camp, and crossing the river with all speed to draw out the Romans by shooting at them, his wish being to get the enemy to fight him before they had breakfasted or made any preparations.'*

In view of the brevity of this statement (Livy's account is hardly more forthcoming), I do hope you will forgive me for my fuller and more inventive account of what might have happened.

As for the actual course of the battle: it is, give or take a few colourful inventions, as I describe. With a large proportion of the Roman army completely surrounded, the winter of winters intervened. Livy again:

> *'The river barred the way back to camp, and it was raining so hard that they could not see at what point in the mêlée they could best help their friends ... on their return to camp the men (Carthaginians) were so benumbed with cold that they could hardly feel pleasure in their victory.'*

And Polybius:

> *'They suffered so severely, however, from the rain and snow that followed that all the elephants perished except one, and many men and horses also died of the cold.'*

To discover how Hannibal exploited his great victory in the following year, readers will have to wait for the next instalment of *The Histories of Sphax*.

Dear Reader!

Thank you for reading The Winter of Winters. If you have enjoyed the story, I would really appreciate it if you took the trouble to write a review on the site where you purchased the novel. If, like me, your favourite place to buy books is from a bookshop on the High Street, you can still write a review on goodreads or any site where you enjoy sharing your passion for books. Please contact me on my website if you have any questions about Sphax and his adventures. I'd love to hear from you!

www.robertmkidd.com

goodreads

I'm also on
Facebook & Twitter

If you would like to read more about Sphax's adventures, why not try the first book in The Histories of Sphax Series — *The Walls of Rome*.

… details overleaf

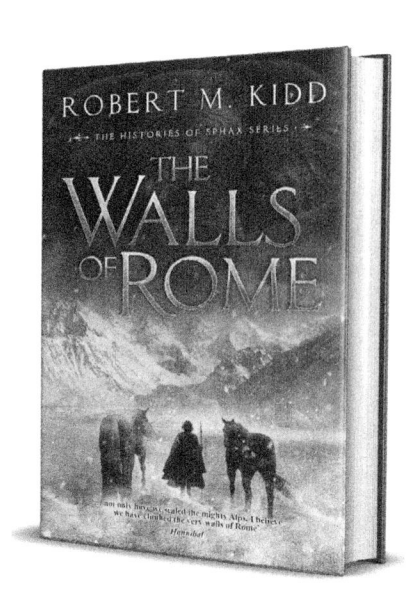

*'not only have we scaled the mighty Alps,
I believe we have climbed the very walls of Rome'*

— Hannibal

218 BC. Sphax is seventeen and haunted by the brutal murder of his parents at the hands of Rome. After ten years of miserable slavery he will make his last bid for freedom and go in search of Hannibal's army and his birthright. He will have his revenge on the stinking cesspit that is Rome!

Destiny will see him taken under the wing of Maharbal, Hannibal's brilliant general, and groomed to lead the finest horsemen in the world — the feared Numidian cavalry that would become the scourge of Rome.

From the crossing of the great Rhodanus River, Sphax's epic journey takes him through the lands of the Gaul to the highest pass in the Alps. This is the story of the most famous march in history. A march against impossible odds, against savage mountain Gauls, a brutal winter and Sphax's own demons.

This is more than a struggle for empire. This is the last great war to save the beauty of the old world, the civilized world of Carthage, Greece and Gaul. The world of art and philosophy — before it is ground into dust by the upstart barbarity of Rome.

PRAISE FROM READERS

"A fast-paced novel set in a period about which I have read little. The historical detail was really interesting and had obviously been well researched. Good plot, well-crafted characters, well thought through ending, unputabledownable! I look forward, with anticipation, to the next novel by this new author!"

"I am giving this book five stars because it is truly excellent. The author takes the reader with him on the legendary journey of Hannibal over the Alps, in a well researched, exciting and fascinating description of an amazing achievement. The description manages to cover the people, the horses, elephants, weapons, clothing and customs of all the different Celtic tribes and Carthaginian warriors in superb detail, but still manages to move at a fast and riveting pace. The characters are believable and engaging and draw you in. I can't wait for the next book."

"This book struck the perfect balance between entertainment and education — not unlike a Bernard Cornwell novel, by the end I had a really good understanding of the history of this period whilst being thoroughly entertained throughout. Highly recommended!"

"This is a real page-turner — right from page one! The research that has gone into this book serves up a roaring adventure through Roman Europe. Sphax himself is instantly likeable and I haven't stopped rooting for him. Well done Mr Kidd!"

"Most people know that Hannibal crossed the Alps with elephants, this exciting book takes us into the journey through the exploits of Sphax a runaway slave. A well researched book with colourful characters and a fast moving plot. A good and informative read."

"A great historical adventure to curl up with on the dark winter nights."

Printed in Great Britain
by Amazon